THE SOLOMON STONE

CHRISTINE SANDGREN

FAWKES PRESS

Edited by Twyla Beth Lambert

Cover design by Fresh Design

Cover illustrations by Lola Skjolsvik

Print ISBN 978-1-945419-49-2

Ebook ISNB 978-1-945419-50-8

LCCN 2020930167

To my mom, who made me 2,341 lunches.
And to my dad, who taught me that a shower
and a clean shirt is equal to six hours of sleep.

THE SOLOMON STONE

1

Ruby studied the horizon for a sign of the huge African cape buffalo she was expected to track today. Squinting, she focused on the web of invisible Lines that crisscrossed through her, connecting all the objects around her. Wherever the buffalo was on the island, one of the Lines would lead her to him. She mentally plucked at the three brightest ones, calibrating them with the information her other senses brought. One of the Lines flared red behind her and Ruby scowled. It was Kikoei—definitely not a buffalo.

"Ruby!" Kikoei yelled.

Ruby ignored him. She had to get the Lines ordered before the Big Man showed up and the hunt began.

"Did you clean the rifles before putting them on the rack?" Kikoei asked.

"Shhh," Ruby said. Kikoei was three years older than she was, and probably weighed twice what she did, but as a tracker she outranked him.

"Here." Kikoei stepped in front of her, obscuring the Lines, and pushed an official floral-print Hawaiian Hunting

Holidays shirt into her face. "My dad says you have to wear this today. We have to provide an 'authentically Hawaiian experience' for this Big Man."

Ruby rolled her eyes. There was nothing "authentically Hawaiian" about guiding rich tourists to hunt cape buffalo imported from Africa. "You realize none of us Hawaiians actually wear these, right?"

"*Us?*" Kikoei glared at Ruby's white-blonde hair, pulling an angry flush to her equally pale cheeks.

"Shut up."

"Also, you have to use your Hawaiian name today." He positioned the shirt so that the black lettering above the pocket spelling "Manakuke" filled her vision. "So, good morning, *Manakuke.*"

"That's not my name," Ruby said, knowing it wouldn't make a difference. They all called her "Manakuke," the Hawaiian word for "mongoose," no matter what she did.

"Isn't it?" Kikoei feigned confusion. "I thought mongooses were foreign pests, brought to Hawaii by igno-rant white farmers and left here to pester and annoy the native species." Kikoei cocked his large head at her in mock curiosity. "Isn't that exactly what you are?"

Ruby yanked the shirt from him. Her hands were greasy from cleaning the guns and she smeared her oil-blackened forefinger over the word "Manakuke," smudging it out and hopefully ruining the shirt. She wadded it into a ball and stuffed it behind a dirty ammo box in the pickup. "I wonder if there's a Hawaiian word for 'so-bad-at-tracking-that-my-daddy-had-to-hire-a-little-girl-to-do-my-job,'" she said, taking a bag of chips and a soda from the cooler. "'Cause that could be your nickname."

"Those are for the clients," Kikoei said, grabbing at the chips.

Ruby easily dodged and chomped another. "If my stomach growls while I'm tracking, it will scare the animals away. You'd know this if you'd ever actually been on a hunt." *Or if you'd ever actually been hungry.*

Another Line tightened and Ruby hid the chips as Tua, Kikoei's dad, strolled in, depositing thick coils of rope in the truck.

"Everything ready?" he asked. Kikoei straightened slightly at his father's presence.

"Yep," Ruby said.

"Where's your Hawaiian Hunting Holidays shirt?" Tua asked.

Ruby shrugged.

"She threw it in the back of the truck," Kikoei said.

Ruby scowled. "Seriously? You're tattling on me? You're, like, fifteen years old."

"You have to wear it." Tua fished the scrunched shirt out of the truck bed. He frowned at her hair. "And a hat."

"The hats are too big. They get in my way."

"This client is important," Tua said. "He's friends with Mr. Smit."

"So?" Ruby asked.

"Sooooo, since Mr. Smit, you know, *owns* the entire island," Kikoei said with mind-numbingly bad sarcasm, "keeping his friends happy is a big deal."

"You can't make me wear that shirt."

"He could fire you," Kikoei offered.

Tua frowned. He and Ruby both knew that he couldn't. She was the best tracker on the island. But he stared at her for so long that Ruby started to worry he actually would take her off the job. Friends of the Owner always tipped well, and she needed the money. One-way ferry tickets off of Pan'wei weren't cheap.

"Fine," Tua sighed. "You don't have to wear the shirt if you wear the hat. But you *will* be Manakuke today."

Ruby didn't answer, swinging herself into the passenger seat of the truck. In the mirror, she saw Tua and Kikoei heft the cooler into the truck bed.

"If you go now, you can make it to school before it starts," Tua said to Kikoei, glancing at his watch.

"But—" Kikoei huffed.

"School," his father said firmly.

Kikoei sighed and stomped off, glaring at Ruby as he left and ignoring his father, who was looking at him with such unearned affection that Ruby's nose twitched. She turned away. She might have the Lines, the job, and more brains than Kikoei, but at the end of each day, Kikoei slept in a house with his parents while Ruby had to scrounge a meal and a few feet of sofa from whichever one of Pan'wei's two hundred and six residents were the least annoyed with her at the time.

———

 Ruby lay still against the cool volcanic rock, matching her breath with the breeze. Not that it mattered. The cape buffalo would smell the Big Man long before it saw her. She crinkled her nose against his flowery, antiseptic scent.

"You stink," she said.

"Manakuke!" Tua hissed. "You can't talk to the Big Man like that."

"He reeks," she said.

"Say you're sorry."

Ruby stared ahead as if she hadn't heard.

Tua sighed and smiled apologetically at the Big Man. "So sorry, Dr. Callahan, sir," he said in an exaggerated accent. "Manakuke excellent tracker. But she no right in the head."

Ruby snorted. All day long she'd been fighting this ridiculous hat, chafing at that ridiculous name, and listening to Tua's ridiculous fake accent. All for the benefit of Dr. Miles Callahan, a Big Man so stupid he'd doused himself with aftershave before the hunt.

"What's wrong with how I smell?" Dr. Callahan asked Ruby.

"You smell like a Big Man with a gun. You'll scare the buffalo," she said.

He pulled a pristine handkerchief from his stiff breast pocket, doused it with water, and scrubbed at his neck and face.

"Better?" he asked.

Ruby sniffed him and shook her head. She grabbed a handful of moist antelope droppings, squashed them in her hands and smeared the mush across his face. "Better."

Tua's mouth gaped. "You can't rub poop all over a Big Man's face."

Dr. Callahan mashed some droppings between his own fingers. It was so thick that it coated the diamond ring on his right hand. He covered his bare arms and neck with the filth.

Ruby raised a triumphant eyebrow to Tua, who shook his head. She sniffed Dr. Callahan and nodded.

They waited. Ruby studied the web of Lines that traced the buffalo's path through the brush. Not just today's path, but every path he'd taken on this ridge each day for the last three years. He usually doubled back in the late morning, so long as nothing spooked him.

One of the Lines vibrated. Pricking her ears, she heard a soft swish of branches that sounded like the wind but was heavier. Ruby elbowed Dr. Callahan and pointed. The buffalo pushed out from behind a bush. Ruby's neck prickled at the sight of him. Five feet tall and all muscle. The air around the massive beast crackled with danger, sending pulses of energy careening down the Lines. The buffalo ducked his head and twitched his haunches, sensing something awry. Ruby's breath caught.

Soundlessly, Dr. Callahan raised his custom-made .416 Rigby rifle and squinted down the long double barrel. Ruby shook her head, disgusted that a Rigby belonged to such an idiot hunter.

"Wait, wait, wait," she whispered. They always fired too early. "Wait till he turns. Aim for his left shoulder."

Dr. Callahan's breathing slowed. The buffalo turned and he squeezed the trigger.

———

Tua pulled a cooler from the truck and unpacked it in the shade of a scrubby kiawe tree. He distributed sandwiches, kettle chips, and canned guava juice. Ruby sat cross-legged in the red, rocky dust, yanked off her hat, and unwrapped her lunch.

Dr. Callahan pulled out a pocketknife and delicately sliced his sandwich into two halves. The knife wasn't fancy, but there was something simple and graceful about its shape that caught Ruby's attention.

Noticing her stare, Dr. Callahan held it out to her. "Do you want to look at it?"

Ruby snatched it before he'd finished the sentence.

"Careful. It's very sharp."

"Knives usually are."

The handle was dark wood with dull chrome on the ends. It was worn a little on the left side where the right thumb rests. It fit perfectly in her palm. It was old, but the knife was clean and moved smoothly. She pulled the blade slowly across the ridges of her thumb. It was razor sharp. She wanted it.

"It was my father's," Dr. Callahan offered, though no one had asked. "Then my older brother's." His voice sounded tight.

Ruby stroked the smooth, lacquered wood handle and stopped when she felt the indentation of tiny letters. "The strength of the wolf is the pack," she read aloud.

"It's kind of like our family motto," Dr. Callahan said.

Ruby felt the words burn inside her, tasting their truth and their bitterness.

"Do you think Smit's group will bring back a bigger kill?" Dr. Callahan asked.

"No. We got the biggest on the island," Ruby said, nodding at the buffalo and reluctantly handing back the knife. "This year."

Dr. Callahan studied her. "You know the game individually?"

"It's my job." There was a long pause. "It's not like I have tea parties with them."

"Ruby!" Tua scolded.

"Ruby?" Dr. Callahan asked.

"I mean, Manakuke." Tua flushed.

Dr. Callahan squinted at her. "Wait. How old are you?"

"She's fourteen," Tua lied promptly.

Ruby tried not to roll her eyes. She knew she looked more like a nine-year-old than a twelve-year-old, but there was some law against hiring kids, so Tua always told the Big Men that she was fourteen. Most of them nodded thoughtfully, probably concluding that island-raised children aged differently than those on the mainland. But Ruby could see that Dr. Callahan didn't believe him. She tore a bite from her sandwich and smiled. Maybe he wasn't quite so stupid. She held up ten fingers, then two more for him when Tua wasn't looking. Dr. Callahan scrunched his eyes and forehead as if he were solving an equation. Never mind. Definitely stupid. He couldn't even count to twelve.

"Who are your parents?" he asked.

Ruby shrugged with automatic nonchalance. She was good at pretending to be indifferent to not having parents, good at hiding her daily fantasies about leaving Pan'wei and somehow tracking down the two people amazing enough to have created her, yet dumb enough to have left her here.

Dr. Callahan looked at her uncovered hair, probably noticing the blonde beneath the layers of dirt that she applied every day to cover her pale hair and skin. He looked at her eyes. There was no masking them. They were blue.

"Where were you born?" His voice was tense.

Ruby stood and walked to the truck. She leaned against it to finish her lunch alone, out of his sightline. She was paid to track animals, not to answer stupid questions.

———

Dr. Callahan must've given a good tip. Tua's face shone as he and Ruby braced against the helicopter wind.

A flash of desperate longing shot through Ruby as she

saw the outline of the pocketknife in Dr. Callahan's shirt pocket. Something about it intrigued her. She tried to imagine having something of her father's. Or having a father at all.

Dr. Callahan shook hands with Tua and then bent low and tried to say something to Ruby, but the sound of the rotor blades drowned out his voice. His shirt pocket was just inches away from her face. The knife was almost falling out of it, like it wanted to stay with her. In a flash, Ruby snatched the knife from his pocket and tucked it into her sleeve.

Dr. Callahan kept talking and she nodded, pretending to hear whatever farewell drivel he was saying.

Then Dr. Callahan patted her head. Ruby jerked back and felt a sharp pinch. When Dr. Callahan stood, Ruby saw that he held several strands of her fine blonde hair between his fingers. He folded the hair into his handkerchief and tucked it into his jacket, then waved a cheerful goodbye and boarded the helicopter.

"*What the...*" Ruby gaped at the retreating helicopter. Why would he take her hair?

"That was weird," Tua agreed as the noise faded. He shrugged. "Come eat with us tonight?"

Ruby considered.

"We're having spaghetti," he added.

She smiled.

2

The next time Ruby saw Dr. Callahan, he didn't arrive in a Hawaiian Hunting Holidays helicopter. He didn't hire Tua to guide him on an African cape buffalo hunt. But he still smelled like flowers and rubbing alcohol.

He stood outside the school, his face flushed with heat. Mr. Smit was with him.

"Ruby!" Mr. Smit called.

She stopped. She didn't know that Mr. Smit was back. Or that he knew her name.

"C'mon," urged Pika, one of the older boys, as he hurried up to Ruby.

"Just a minute," she said. Even Ruby knew that when the Owner showed up at school calling your name, you had to answer. She shuffled, feeling the weight of the stolen knife in her pocket. A bubble of fear swelled in her, but she pushed it down. There was no way this Big Man had come back all this way for a pocketknife.

"Ruby, this is Dr. Callahan," Mr. Smit said.

"I know." Her eyes drifted toward the boys running to the beach.

"Do you have a minute?" Mr. Smit asked, but it wasn't really a question.

She looked from his receding hairline to the receding students. Her leg twitched. Pika hung back for her. "Not really. There's a game," she said.

Dr. Callahan opened his mouth and squinted at Ruby, frozen with indecision. "Okay," Dr. Callahan finally said. "Can you come by Mr. Smit's house after the game?"

Ruby was already running away.

"It's important!" Mr. Smit barked after her.

———

STEPPING onto the beach's makeshift soccer field, Ruby forgot about the Owner, Dr. Callahan, and the stolen knife. She smiled. It felt like merging into a machine. Clear, bright Lines of energy crisscrossed around her, weaving together everything and everyone on the field. Whenever someone moved, the Lines tightened and slackened like puppet strings.

One of the brighter Lines quivered as Amoco, the biggest kid on the field, dribbled the ball down the beach.

Several Lines pulled, mapping the best route to interception. When Amoco was close, Ruby darted in and stole the ball. Easily dodging players, she drove toward the goal line. The goalie swallowed and shifted his feet. Ruby expertly aligned the Lines that ran between herself, the ball, and the goal. She kicked hard and watched the ball curve, crossing the goal just inches from the goalie's fingers.

Ruby's teammates patted her back and tousled her hair. One of the younger boys probed Ruby's head, trying to find the extra pair of eyes that were rumored to be there. Ruby knew it would only last through the game, but she smiled at the fleeting camaraderie.

Amoco glared across the centerline and puffed out his chest. Ruby smiled and raised three fingers, one for each goal she had scored.

Kikoei passed the ball to Amoco. Ruby watched the Lines, plotting her charge. But her head snapped up when she heard splashing. Amoco was dribbling through the ankle-deep water. Ruby's breath caught. There were no Lines in the ocean. Everyone but Ruby followed, splashing after the ball.

Ruby watched from the dry sand. Amoco was almost in scoring position. She sucked her hair and fumed, powerless just because they were ankle-deep in a little water. She tried to picture the Lines continuing beneath the ocean as she knew they must. *It's just wet sand.* She inched one foot forward, willing the Lines to come back, but they didn't.

The boys saw her and laughed. "Ruby is a baby," they taunted.

"Is wittle Wuby afwaid of the wa wa?" Amoco sang at her.

That was it. "Manakuke" was bad enough, but nobody called her "Wuby." She tightened her jaw and charged into the ocean. Amoco's face contorted in surprise, filling Ruby with satisfaction. But the moment she felt the water lap gently at her ankles, she screamed. The Lines were gone, replaced with confusion. She couldn't see Amoco or anyone else. All that existed was the thick, dark water swirling hungrily around her. Wet, cold oblivion.

Ruby stumbled and fell. The waves pelted her, coming again and again, stinging her eyes and invading her mouth. Death and darkness were only a breath away. She scuttled sideways like an injured crab until she felt dry sand and the horrible sea beat its retreat.

She gasped lungfuls of air, shuddering as the surf pounded nearby, stalking her like a bloodhound.

Amoco and the others howled with laughter. "Manakuke's crazy! Manakuke's crazy!" they yelled.

"What's the matter, lost your 'magical Lines'?" Kikoei asked.

Everyone laughed, even her teammates. Sometimes she wondered if they only let her play so they could taunt her from the water.

She turned away, cursing herself for ever telling anyone about the Lines. But when she was four she hadn't realized that no one else saw them. Or that they'd tease her about it forever.

A hand fell on her shoulder. Pika, Kikoei's older, non-jerk-face brother, sat down. "Manakuke," he said when she had stilled, "you're an idiot."

She sniffed and nodded. It was idiotic to be afraid of the ocean. Doubly idiotic to charge into it and expect the fear to disappear just because she wanted it to.

"A brave little idiot," he added.

"It's not fair. They know I can't go into the water, but they always make it so part of the field is in the ocean," Ruby said.

"How else is the other team supposed to have a chance?"

The game continued around them, the players circum-navigating the spot where they sat. Ruby dragged herself up, slapped the sand off her legs and hands, then surveyed the field. She knew they didn't want her, but she rejoined the game anyway.

3

Ruby could hear Dr. Callahan's and Mr. Smit's voices from outside the office door in Mr. Smit's house.

"This is it?" Dr. Callahan said, waving a single sheet of paper at Mr. Smit. "Where are her report cards? I can't show this to the Alexander Academy."

"Her standardized test scores," Mr. Smit said, passing a sheet to him.

Dr. Callahan frowned at it. "It's a year-round school?"

"No."

"But it's July. Why are they still in school?"

Mr. Smit swallowed hard. "Well, as I understand it, they had to delay school re-starting after Christmas break. One of the teachers was... detained for several weeks."

"Detained?"

Ruby smiled. Mr. Smit obviously did not want to explain to Dr. Callahan that the school's lead teacher had suddenly disappeared for all of January and February to surf.

"Unavoidably." Mr. Smit cleared his throat. "So they've had to run into the summer to make up the days."

"Where are her medical records?" Dr. Callahan asked.

"I guess she's never been sick," Mr. Smit said, his politeness straining.

"How would you know?" a woman's voice cut in. Ruby squinted and saw a slim female figure with gray hair fingering the crisp, white cuff of her sleeve over and over. "Honestly, Pinky. You knew we were looking. You could have at least checked the two hundred people living on your own private island."

Ruby covered her mouth so she wouldn't laugh. Had that woman just called Mr. Smit "Pinky"?

"Bertie arranged it. I was completely ignorant," Mr. Smit—*Pinky!*—said sullenly, clearly hating his nickname as much as Ruby hated hers.

"Bertie died seven years ago." The woman peered out the window. She looked elegant with her tailored suit and perfect posture, but she kept tugging her cuff. "Who's been taking care of her?"

"Our cook was raising her. But she died a few years ago—"

Ruby straightened. They were definitely talking about her.

"Why wasn't another guardian appointed?" Dr. Callahan cut in.

"Appointed?" Mr. Smit spat out the word. "Look around you. They don't 'appoint guardians' and sign contracts. They just do what needs to be done. It's a family."

"No. *We* are a family," the woman said, glancing out the window again. "I should've come to the school with you to meet her."

"Mom," Dr. Callahan said. "Another stranger might have startled her."

"I'm not a stranger." The woman's words fell like rocks into the silent room.

"She'll come," Dr. Callahan said.

"What if she gets a concussion? Or breaks her leg?" Dr. Callahan's mom asked.

"It's just soccer," Dr. Callahan said.

Ruby stifled a laugh. If this lady knew what Ruby's real job was, she'd be freaking out. The look of pale terror on the Owner's face told Ruby that he really didn't want this lady to find out he'd been taking Ruby on hunts for years now. Watching this woman terrify the Owner was the best thing that had happened on Pan'wei in years and, thanks to the Lines, Ruby could pretty much stay hidden as long as she wanted. Granted, stuff indoors was too static and boring, so the Lines just kind of drooped, fading into the background, like the hum the Owner's refrigerator made in the kitchen. Ruby thought about that refrigerator now, wondering if there was ice cream in the freezer.

"Don't tell me not to worry." The woman snapped at Dr. Callahan. "She's my granddaughter."

"I'm your what?" Ruby said, barging into the office.

Mrs. Callahan's blue eyes brimmed with a strange combination of relief and disbelief. She moved her mouth but no words came out.

"Hello again, Ruby." Dr. Callahan's voice was calm but his eyes burned.

"You're my grandmother?" Ruby turned Mrs. Callahan like it was an accusation, then rounded on Dr. Callahan. "And you're what, my uncle?"

"Yes."

Mrs. Callahan's eyes shimmered and she reached out her arms like she was going to hug Ruby.

But Ruby raised both of her hands. "This is no time for hugs."

Mrs. Callahan blinked and dropped her arms.

"Are you from my mom's side or my dad's? Do you know where they are? What happened? Who left me here?" Ruby saw Mrs. Callahan's face flinch with each question. "And what the heck is my last name?"

"Callahan," Dr. Callahan said. "I'm Miles." He extended his palm slowly.

Ruby shook it but didn't come closer. "Why did you steal my hair?"

"I had to confirm your identity, so I took some of your hair for a DNA test. I'm sorry if you found it unsettling."

Ruby frowned, shifting her weight. "It was a little weird."

The Owner scowled and tilted his head away from her.

Ruby knew she smelled bad after the game and from her general habit of not showering. But he should've thought of that before insisting that she come to his house.

"Ruby, this is my mother, Alice Callahan," Miles said.

"You're safe," Alice choked.

"Are you the ones who dumped me here nine years ago?"

"Certainly not," Alice said.

Miles squatted so that his blue eyes were level with Ruby's.

Ruby knew even before the faint thin Line flickered between their faces that he was her uncle. His eyes were identical to hers. Except his had little wrinkles.

"Ruby," he said evenly. "My brother..." He paused and screwed up his eyes as he sifted his words. "My brother, Rex Callahan... was your father."

"Yeah, no kidding. But where's—wait." Ruby stopped as

her brain chased to catch up with her mouth. "What do you mean '*was*'?"

"He disappeared. Nine years ago." Miles's voice was steady. The words were hard but he'd obviously said them enough times to wear down their edges. "We've been looking for him, but we haven't found him."

"Disappeared how?"

"Your mother and father left with you one night, in the middle of a party, and they never came back," Alice said, her voice quavering at the end.

Ruby hesitated. Tendrils of fear constricted her throat. But she had to know. "Where's my mother?"

"We haven't found her either," Alice said.

"How did I get here then?"

"I don't know," Miles said. "Mr. Smit's brother, Bertie, was a close friend of your father's. He apparently brought you here. But he died seven years ago. As you know."

A cavernous silence settled on the room. Ruby considered the new information as she looked at the three grownups. Uncle, Grandmother, a guy called "Pinky." But no mom or dad. She sighed. Her newfound family was disappointingly incompetent. "So you came all this way just to tell me that you don't know where my parents are?" she finally asked.

"We have tried," Alice said. "Maybe with your memories we'll be able to find them."

"My memories?"

Mr. Smit's mouth pulled into a smug line. "She doesn't remember her parents?"

"I was, like, three years old when they left me."

Mr. Smit smiled snakily. "She's a Trunc? How interesting. You can hardly blame me for not recognizing the first UnSighted Callahan in history."

Ruby didn't know what he was talking about, but the look on his face was ticking her off. "If I'm so 'UnSighted,' how come you use me to find animals on your safari hunts?" Ruby threw the words like a grenade, and Alice's reaction did not disappoint.

"You what!?" Alice spun on her heel and glared at him.

"Since I was ten." Ruby smiled triumphantly at the Owner's bright red face.

"Ten?" Miles asked, catching Alice by the shoulders, as if holding her back from charging the Owner.

"Get out." There was something dangerous in Alice's voice that frankly impressed Ruby.

"This is my office," the Owner said, but Ruby could already see the Line between him and the door tightening.

"That's it. I'm calling Nichols—"

"Okay, okay. Easy." He left, but not before mumbling audibly, "I warned Rex not to marry that UnSighted girl."

"Out!" Alice said. The door slammed at the exact same time, making it seem like her words alone had shut it.

"Um." Ruby didn't know where to start. "Who's Nichols?"

"Deputy Director of the FBI," Miles said.

"Oh. Okay." Ruby didn't know exactly what had just happened, but she understood that her grandmother and uncle had just kicked the Owner out of his own office. They were the biggest Big Men she'd ever seen. "What was that word he called me?"

Alice shuddered slightly.

"Trunc. Short for 'Truncant.' It's—" Miles looked to his mother as if for help, but she was rasping shallow breaths, and clearly in no state to speak. "It just means someone who isn't Sighted."

"But I see fine."

"Right. Um, it's a different kind of... Sighted people don't see *things* clearly, they see *time*."

Ruby squinted in concentration. "Huh?"

"They're called 'Sapients.' They see the past. And understand it perfectly. They have photographic memories and retain a thousand times more information than the average person."

"So, can they see how things are, like, connected?" Ruby didn't dare mention the Lines, but she was secretly hoping that Miles would, and then these strange words would name the uniqueness of her reality.

"Kind of." Miles smiled. "I guess they have to connect information as they organize it." He paused, searching for words. "It's like this filing cabinet." He stepped over to a large stack of drawers near the wall. He tugged on a handle and the drawer slid out at least two feet. Sheets and colored folders hung in neat, labeled rows. Miles ran his fingers over the tabbed folders and pulled one out. "Here's where Mr. Smit keeps his geological surveys of Pan'wei. Going back more than a hundred years."

"Whoa." Ruby felt a tinge of disappointment as she looked at the mass of papers. This was nothing like the Lines that she saw. "I didn't know Mr. Smit was so old."

Miles smiled. "These are from his grandfather and great-grandfather. But that's not the point. He has to keep paper copies so he can show them to other people. But Mr. Smit is a Sapient, so it's like his whole mind is full of these mental filing drawers, holding all the information he's ever learned. He could tell you from memory anything in these drawers."

Ruby looked up. The office had at least five other cabinets. She suddenly felt a little bad for the Sapients, having to haul all this boring information around with them all the time.

"Are you a Sapient?" she asked Miles.

He nodded. "All Callahans are."

"Except for me."

"Except for you."

Alice rose. "We don't know that. Ruby hasn't been tested."

But Ruby knew she wasn't a Sapi-whatever. Her brain was weird, but it wasn't crammed with a bunch of stupid drawers.

"She's not," Miles said gently.

"But—" Alice protested.

"Mom, she doesn't remember Rex or Emmeline." The words hung heavy in the air, sucking the color from Alice's cheeks.

"Rex and Emmeline are my parents, right?"

"Yes," Alice said.

"And they disappeared nine years ago, and you still haven't found them?"

"Yes."

"Okay. So, sounds like the trail's gone a little cold." Ruby tried not to let her displeasure show too much. They had probably tried their best with all their magical drawer thingies. But she'd seen Miles hunt. He wasn't exactly an expert at tracking things. "But I'm sure we can pick up the scent somehow. Where was the last place they were seen?"

"New York," Miles said. "But Ruby, you should know, we've exhausted every lead. We've used private investigators, the police, the FBI, the CIA, MI6."

Ruby waved away the string of nonsensical words he was spouting. "Doesn't matter. Let's start in New York."

"This isn't like tracking an animal, Ruby."

But Alice shushed him. "Quiet, Miles. Ruby just said she wants to come to New York with us." She turned to face Ruby, her clear eyes sparkling. "Ruby, we were hoping you would want that." Alice's body curved toward her and Ruby could tell she was resisting the urge to give her a hug.

Ruby let her keep on resisting. But since they would be working together, she gave Alice the congenial smile she gave to all Big Men before a hunt. Except for this time, Ruby actually meant it.

4

Ruby stared at the strange clothes on the Owner's guest bathroom counter—a pair of pressed pants and a stiff button-down shirt. It looked like a Big Man costume. A piece of paper lay on top with two words: "bathe first."

The bathtub stood shining and white in the corner. Ruby had been in Mr. Smit's house before, of course. Lots of times. He was gone so often and his house just sat there empty, practically begging for a visitor. She had watched his TV, eaten his food, and slept in his soft beds. But she had never thought about using his tub.

She peeled off her dirty clothes and sat on the edge of the tub, splashing some water onto her forearm. Trickles of mud ran down. She put her whole arm under and the dirt flowed off in torrents.

She turned on the shower and stepped in, tilting her face up. It felt like warm rain. What a shame the water in the ocean wasn't clear and harmless like the water in the bathroom. She shivered reflexively at the thought of the vast expanse of darkness just a few hundred yards away.

The dirt collected in a sludge at her feet. But eventually

the water coming off ran clear, as the last specks of Pan'wei disappeared down the drain.

When she looked in the mirror, she felt the usual chagrin at her skin color—pinky white like a pig's instead of rich nut brown like everyone else's.

Not everyone's. Miles and Alice had pink skin too.

———

IT WAS ALMOST DARK when they boarded the plane. Someone offered to take Ruby's luggage—a plastic grocery bag—but she refused, clutching it close. It only held a few clothes and a bag of candy corns. She was full from a big dinner and an even bigger dessert, but, still, candy corns were hard to come by and she wasn't taking any chances.

Mr. Smit stood at the edge of the tarmac, framed by the lights. A few villagers stood nearby, pointing and whispering. Ruby smiled as she felt the soft, thin fabric of the pants against her calves. They were probably amazed at how nice she looked.

She waved, feeling a swell of warmth for the people who had made up a sort of family the last nine years. Surely they would miss her, even like her, now that they could see she actually belonged to people. They were probably wishing they had been nicer to her when they'd had the chance. A few people waved back. But Ruby's heart sank as she realized that they were mostly staring at Alice and Miles instead of her. They weren't there to see her off. They'd come to get a look at what kind of people would go to all this trouble just to get Manakuke.

Ruby straightened her shoulders. She didn't need these people anymore. She had new people. People who wanted her. She fingered the pocketknife. *The strength of the wolf is the pack*, she repeated to herself.

A steep metal staircase hung outside the little plane. Ruby's foot hesitated above the first step. The plane was so small. Would it really be able to carry her safely across the dark, un-Lined depths of the Pacific Ocean? Her stomach turned. *It's just stairs*, she told herself, gripping the rail and ordering her legs to climb.

Inside, the plane was like a mini living room, with smooth beige couches, soft, cushy chairs, and little tables. There was a miniature sink and refrigerator in one corner and a large monitor hung above the cockpit door. Everything was cool and comfortable. Ruby relaxed a little as she shoved her plastic bag underneath a seat and sat down.

Miles maneuvered his and Alice's small bags through the door. A thin, middle-aged woman in a navy blue suit tried to help him, but he just smiled and waved her away. "I've got it, Doris," he said. "You can go up front." Miles opened the fridge and handed Alice a small green bottle and a crystal cup full of little ice cubes.

"Thank you," she said, holding the cool glass to her cheek as she sat down.

The plane's engines rumbled to life and Ruby's chest tightened. Ruby looked out the window to distract herself. The crowd of onlookers was slowly breaking up, but Ruby thought she saw Tua staring ruefully at the plane. At least one person might miss her.

"I'm sure it's hard to leave all your friends," Alice said.

Ruby shrugged, not wanting to explain that it wouldn't be hard because they weren't her friends.

"School starts in six weeks." Alice said. "But we can

delay enrollment. I know you'll need time to adjust. We'll have a tutor, and I'm still looking into childcare. Of course, there's always homeschooling."

Ruby straightened, her attention swinging between Alice's words and the impending flight. Why was Alice talking about homeschool and childcare?

"But there are other Academy kids who live in our building. So if you want more interaction with kids your own age—"

"What are you talking about?" Ruby asked. "What Academy?"

"The Alexander Academy. It's a school," Miles said. "For people like us."

"People like us?"

"Sighted people. Sapients," Miles said.

"But I'm not a Sapient," Ruby said.

"The Alexander Academy is for all types of Sighted people *and their families*." Alice said.

"Wait." Ruby straightened. "There's different kinds of Sights?"

"There are three." Miles buckled his seatbelt and motioned Ruby to do the same. "Each group sees time differently. Sapients see the past, 'Levants' see the present, and 'Providents' see the future."

"There are people who see the future?" That actually sounded cool. "Can I be one of them?"

Miles smiled. "We've never had a Provident in our family. But I guess it's possible. Have you ever had a dream or feeling about something happening and then it did?"

Ruby frowned and shook her head. "What about the other kind, the Lev...?"

"Levants are rare. Usually only one or two born in a generation."

"Hmph." Ruby slouched and twisted the seatbelt strap in her hands. "So do you, like, have friends who can see the future?" Maybe he could ask one of them if this plane would crash into the ocean.

Miles shrugged. "It's all pretty vague and unscientific. Providents claim they get glimpses or hints every now and then but it's hard to verify. Most of them were born UnSighted and pretend to be Provs because they don't want to be Truncants."

"Miles!" Alice said.

"Wait," Ruby said. "Didn't the Owner say *I* was a Truncant?"

"It doesn't matter," Alice said.

But Ruby looked at Miles's strained face and knew that it did matter.

"A Truncant is just an UnSighted child born into a Sighted family," Miles said.

Ruby sucked her hair and stared out the window. She was always Un-Something. "Is it because my mom wasn't Sighted?"

"I don't know," Miles said.

"Great," Ruby said. For someone with some secret super memory power, there was a lot he didn't know.

"You're very intelligent, Ruby," he said.

Ruby rolled her eyes. Adults only ever said that to stupid kids.

"I've seen your test scores. Academically, you're a little behind, but you're smart enough that you could catch up with a little tutoring. You'd be fine at the Academy, but—"

"But what?"

"There are other schools you could go to where no one's ever heard of Truncants or Sapients or Providents. You'd still need to catch up, but you wouldn't be 'UnSighted.'"

Ruby studied Miles's face. It was open, but she could sense unsaid words just below the surface. "Did my dad go to the Academy?" Ruby asked.

"Every Callahan has gone there since it opened in 1791," Alice said.

"Did my mom go there? Is that where they met?"

Alice straightened her skirt and stared at her drink.

"No." Miles put a soft hand on his mother's shoulder. "Rex met Emmeline abroad. We think."

"She said she was from Germany," Alice said.

"*She said?*"

"Your mother was..." Miles paused, squinting into the distance, "a little vague about some of the details of her personal life."

Alice snorted. "Like her name."

"You don't know her name?"

"She lied to us." There was something chilling about Alice's matter-of-fact tone. "About everything. Then she and Rex just disappeared with you one night. When we started looking for them," Alice continued, "we discovered that everything she'd told us, even her name, was a lie. 'Emmeline Gunther' never existed."

Ruby gaped. "Why did she lie? And then take me away in the middle of the night?" Ruby could feel the weight of the words as she said them. Her whole life was locked inside these questions.

"We don't know," Miles said. "She did have a vaccination scar on her left shoulder, so she might have been Russian, or Eastern European."

Ruby slumped in her chair, her confusion thickened by a growing anger at her mother.

"I suspect that Rex and Emmeline were in some kind of

trouble and they left you with Bertie for safekeeping. They no doubt intended to come back for you, but they didn't."

Ruby stared at the intersecting planes of Miles's unflinchingly honest face. "Do you think they're dead?" Her jaw tightened around the last word. In all her plotting and fantasizing about getting off of Pan'wei and finding her parents, she'd never allowed herself to even think that sentence.

Miles sipped calmly from his water bottle. "Statistically speaking, yes, they probably are."

"Miles!" Alice said. There was a warning in her voice that was sharp enough to make him shut his mouth. "That's enough."

Ruby slouched back into the soft sofa cushions, Miles's words swirling coldly around her. Her parents weren't dead. She would know. If she'd survived alone for nine years then so could they.

Suddenly the plane accelerated and Ruby felt the nose rise into the air. Her stomach plummeted. She pressed her face to the window, desperate to see the reassuring ground below, but there was only darkness and a little red light blinking on the wing.

Darkness. She tried to push her Lines beyond the window, but they wouldn't obey her. Ruby's heart pumped erratically and she closed her eyes, trying to tamp down the mounting panic she felt. *Not now. Not now.* Desperate for a distraction, she picked up a card on the seat. The card was full of cartoon images of passengers calmly exiting a burning plane or weirdly hugging seat cushions to their chests. She flipped it over. On the back was a picture of the passengers calmly bobbing in the ocean next to a wrecked plane. It was like someone had discovered her worst nightmare, drawn it out in cheesy, bright cartoon figures, then laminated it.

Ruby screamed.

"What is it?" Alice was kneeling in front of her, trying to catch Ruby's gaze.

Ruby stared at the monitor now, which showed a tiny plane hovering over the large expanse of blue between Hawaii and the mainland. She struggled to fill her lungs, but they were stiff.

"Ruby, take a deep breath," Miles said.

"Don't tell me what to do," she choked out.

"Do something," Alice pleaded to Miles.

Moments later Ruby felt the cold pressure of an icepack against the back of her neck.

"Ruby," Miles said, kneeling down. "Ruby, look at me." He still smelled weird as he scanned her face and pressed his fingers to her wrist. "Can you take a deep breath?"

She tried, but her lungs were too tight.

"Tell them to land the plane," Alice said.

"No!" Ruby screamed, remembering the cartoon people in the water. Tears ran down her cheeks and blackness edged her vision, as if the ocean was lapping at her face. She couldn't tell anymore if the plane was rising or falling. What if they were crashing into the sea right now?

"Ruby, look at me," Miles said. He held her chin firmly. His eyes shone with concern and maybe even fear. He pulled a deep breath through his nose and released it. "Ruby, can you do this with me?"

Ruby watched as his chest rose and fell rhythmically. But her own lungs wouldn't budge. "I can't."

Determination tightened Miles's eyes. "You have to try. Callahans don't give up."

Ruby closed her own eyes and listened to Miles's exaggerated breaths, but it didn't work. She was starting to feel dizzy. Then Alice shifted, pulling Ruby close to her. Ruby could feel Alice's small frame expand and deflate as she breathed. And she could feel Alice's heart beating fast but steady next to hers. Ruby's lungs loosened and she finally pulled in a deep breath, feeling relief flow in with it. She heaved a jagged sob, breathing so hard that she made a barking noise like a seal.

"It's okay," Alice said softly, patting her back.

Ruby flushed, ashamed at how good Alice's touch felt. "Are we crashing?" she finally asked.

"No. No, no, no," Alice said. "Is that what you're afraid of? We should've talked to you about it. Lots of people are afraid of flying."

Ruby sniffed. She wasn't afraid of flying, but she didn't correct Alice. Fear of flying sounded better than fear of water.

"Shhh," Alice said, "we're not going to crash."

Ruby knew Alice was right, but it didn't matter. She would never make it across the entire Pacific Ocean. They would have to go back, and then Ruby would be trapped on Pan'wei forever, and she'd never find her parents.

"Look," Alice said, tapping the window.

Ruby shook her head, afraid that if she looked, her lungs would close again.

"Can you see the stars?" Alice asked.

Ruby squinted at an upward angle, then nodded.

"Did you know that for thousands of years people used the stars as maps when they crossed the sea? Sailing into the unknown was so terrifying that they could only do it if they ignored the water and focused on the stars." Alice pulled a lever and Ruby's seat extended into a long soft bench. "Here," she said, patting it, "you're tired."

Ruby lay gingerly across the cushioned seat.

Alice pulled a thin blue blanket over her and then sat on the floor next to the seat, stroking Ruby's hair and humming softly.

Ruby looked at the stars, watching her Lines run in zig-zag patterns between them, as if they were looking for the map Alice had promised. Ruby was too tired to decipher their patterns, but she liked the gridded symmetry. Her shoulders relaxed and she listened to Alice's soft breathing. She was too old for bedtime songs and hair stroking, but she didn't care. She nestled into her blanket, eyes fixed on the steady stars and ears tuned to the steady vibration of Alice's voice beside her.

5

Ruby watched New York unfold from the car window, fascinated by the streets clogged with cars and the sidewalks jammed with people. Every inch of Manhattan was covered with buildings or concrete. The occasional tree or plant that did appear was carefully curated and cordoned off, as if they were latecomers to a land that had somehow sprouted cement from its soil instead of plants. Even the water that skirted the city seemed to have been tamed, lying walled in and still, with a delicate series of bridges arching over it.

Ruby had never been anywhere unfamiliar and her Lines raced around, sweeping up and down the long, straight stretches of asphalt, thrilling at the symmetry and the right angles. They wove a map for her that soon felt just as familiar as Pan'wei had been, despite the fact that she was just passing by in a car. Even the unseen streets and buildings were sketched in, the Lines reading the patterns of the grid and guessing at the unknowns. She rolled down the window and craned her neck out, wanting to see more.

A wave of warm, moist air blew over Ruby's face, smelling like coffee, wet plastic, and flowers.

The driver parked the car near Central Park West and Ruby jumped out. Evenly-spaced trees lined the sidewalk. Across the street lay an expanse of green space that was curiously empty of buildings.

"That's Central Park," Miles said to Ruby, pointing with his chin as he helped Alice from the car.

Ruby smiled. She was glad to have at least some nature nearby, even if it was landscaped and walled-in.

"Is this your house?" Ruby asked Alice, staring at the large building in front of them.

"Yes. But only part of it."

"It's huge."

"There are twenty-seven apartments in this building," Miles said. "I live in one. So does your Uncle Harlan."

Twenty-seven? The whole street was lined with buildings like this. Some were even bigger. There were more people on this street right now than lived on the entire island of Pan'wei. More people than she had ever met in her whole life. Her cheeks pushed up in a smile. And not a single one had ever heard the word *Manakuke*.

Inside the shiny lobby, a man nodded at them from behind a polished counter. "Good morning, Mrs. Callahan," he said, handing her a neat bundle of mail. "Miss Ruby."

"How do you know my name?" Ruby asked.

Before he could answer, a blur of color and fur raced past them. A woman teetering on precariously high heels whirred by, clinging to the leashes of four dogs.

"Sorry!" she said as she brushed between Alice and Ruby. "Oh, hi, Mrs. Callahan." She stopped so fast Ruby was certain there were skid marks on the marble floor. "Is this Ruby?"

"Seriously?" Ruby said. "Why does everyone here already know me?"

No one answered. Miles was too busy looking at the dog woman. And Alice was looking at Miles looking at the dog woman. The dog woman was looking at Ruby, offering a hand.

"I'm Chloe," she said. Her face was flushed and her eyes were bright. Her left cheek dimpled when she smiled and her wavy hair kept falling into her face.

"Ruby. But you already know that."

"I live in the building," Chloe said. "Just one floor up from Miles."

Blushing, Miles nodded to confirm.

"And Agamemnon," Chloe said, pulling a small, stocky, mustached dog from the tangle of leashes at her feet and offering him to Miles. Miles craned his head away but Agamemnon pursued him, covering his face in slobbery kisses.

"You have a dog?" Ruby asked, excited.

"Yes. This is Agamemnon," Miles said through tight lips, not wanting to ingest any of the canine saliva coating his cheeks.

"Aww. He missed you," Chloe said to Miles. "Didn't you miss your daddy?" she said to the dog.

"I think we had better get Ruby upstairs now. Harlan's waiting," Alice said.

"Here." Ruby reached for the dog, and he practically jumped into her arms, attacking her with the same ferocious affection he had slathered all over Miles. But Ruby held up her hand and looked straight into his eager brown eyes. "No," she said in a soft, firm voice. There were lots of stray dogs on Pan'wei, and Ruby was friends with most of them. Agamemnon cocked his head and stared at Ruby. She made a hushing noise and rubbed a circular pattern beneath his left ear and he stilled. "I'm Ruby," she said. The dog, at least, didn't already know her name. "I'm in charge." He slackened against her, nuzzling her elbow.

"Whoa," said Chloe. "That was amazing."

"Do you have a dog?" Ruby asked Alice hopefully.

"No."

"Can we get one?"

Alice looked horrified.

"Alice!" another female voice called out. A thin brunette woman scurried across the lobby toward them. She wore crisp white pants, a white blouse, and white sunglasses.

"Who's that?" Ruby whispered to Chloe.

"Mrs. Deckert."

Mrs. Deckert clasped Alice by the shoulders and kissed the air near each of her cheeks.

Alice pulled slightly back as though it was Agamemnon trying to kiss her.

"Hello, Veronica," Alice said.

"Are you that Ruby kid?" someone asked. Ruby craned her neck and saw a scrawny boy, half-hidden behind Mrs. Deckert's impeccably pressed pants. Tightening her lips, Ruby sized him up, ready for a confrontation.

"Who are you?" she asked.

"Winston Deckert. 6B."

"Hey 6B," she said.

Winston blushed.

"Winnie," his mother swooped down and hissed in his ear, "remember your typical peer interaction template."

Ruby winced. Winnie? Poor kid.

Winston blushed harder and held out his hand stiffly. "Hello. It's very nice to meet you."

"Okay," Ruby said, shaking his rigid little hand. They stood awkwardly for a moment while his mom talked to Alice. Or tried to. Alice didn't offer much encouragement. She kept one eye fixed on Miles, who was talking to Chloe. They both laughed as the three leashed dogs weaved in and out of their legs. Once, Chloe almost lost her balance and Miles grabbed her elbow to steady her.

"So, were you, like, kidnapped or something?" Winston said.

"No."

He clicked his teeth. "Where've you been all this time?"

"Pan'wei."

"Like in Hawaii?"

"Yeah."

"Weird."

"Yeah." Another silence, except for Winston clicking his teeth. "You go by 'Winnie'?" Ruby asked.

He shook his head adamantly.

"It's okay," Ruby said. "I hate my nickname too. Do you want to pet my dog?"

"Better not. Allergies."

"You're allergic to dogs?" This kid couldn't catch a break.

"Not specifically. But who knows what he's carrying in his pet dander, you know? July is one of the worst months for weed pollen and fungal allergens."

Mrs. Deckert inserted her face between theirs. "Winnie is the same age as you, Ruby. You'll both be going to the Alexander Academy in the fall."

"Yeah, but we won't have any classes together. I'm a Trunc," Winston said.

"Hey, so am I!"

Winston and Mrs. Deckert both looked at her as if she'd just confessed to a crime.

"So we could be friends then," Winston said quickly. "I mean, we live in the same building, that's geographic proximity"—he ticked off his fingers as he spoke—"and we'll be going to the same school, so we'll have a shared common experience. And we're part of the same socio-economic group. Even though your family is all Sape, so you're technically higher than we are—"

"Winnie!" his mother gasped.

"But we still have a lot of the major components of a mutually beneficial friendship—"

"We have to run." Mrs. Deckert simpered a smile at Alice. "We'd love to have Ruby over to play sometime. I'll call you."

"Gutterball," Winston said. "I have my Executive Skills Unstructured Play class today. So, you know..."

Ruby didn't know, but she nodded anyway.

"Goodbye, Ruby," Mrs. Deckert said. She tried to kiss Ruby's cheeks but Ruby raised Agamemnon defensively. The dog licked Winston's mom right across the mouth.

Mrs. Deckert shuddered, then pivoted toward the door, tugging on Winston's arm. He waved with his free hand.

Ruby smiled at Winston's retreating figure, wondering if she had really made a friend just ten minutes after arriving in New York.

———

ALICE'S APARTMENT was a lot like Mr. Smit's house: super clean with shiny wood floors, high ceilings, and lots of windows. A man with pale, wet-looking hair was waiting for them in the entry. His eyes flicked over Ruby once, fast and shrewd, like he was counting her. Then he blinked and his gaze warmed. "Ruby," he said.

"Hey."

"I'm Harlan." He stretched out his hand, which had a thick diamond ring just like Miles's. "I'm your older,  slightly-less-brilliant uncle." He winked when he said it, making Ruby feel like they'd somehow shared a secret joke.

"Hi Harlan," she said, smiling.

Harlan's smile deepened in return. He seemed determined to be delighted. "Welcome home."

Ruby smiled, her head starting to feel full of too many new names and faces.

"She's tired," Alice said. "Harlan, would you ask Elena if lunch is ready?"

Lunch was ready. Elena, the cook, served it on delicate-looking plates with cloth napkins at the spotless kitchen table. The fancy chicken was okay, but it was surrounded by weird purplish lettuce that looked like clumps of weeds. Ruby was glad she'd thought ahead and brought her candy corn stash.

"How come you guys all wear those rings?" Ruby asked Harlan halfway through the meal.

"They're Academy rings," he said. "They're presented to students at graduation."

Ruby smiled. "Really?" The school couldn't be too bad if they gave out bling like that. "On Pan'wei they just hand out leis."

"How lovely," Alice said. And she sounded sincere.

"Your dad had a ring too," Harlan said.

"Can I see it?" Ruby asked.

"He took it with him when he left," Alice said.

"I have a picture of it though." Harlan scooted his chair closer to hers and poked his phone twice, turning it so Ruby could see.

It was a wedding picture. The groom, who must be her father, stood straight and tall with brown wavy hair curling at his temples, his cheek dimpling affectionately as he looked at his wife tucked neatly under his arm. Emmeline smiled at the camera, her pale hair floating in loose curls around her shoulders. Ruby's free hand fingered her own scraggly hair as she looked at her parents' beautiful, happy faces.

"See." Harlan curled his hand around to poke at the picture. "It's on his finger."

"Oh, right." Ruby looked at Rex's left hand, which was wrapped around Emmeline's shoulder. His fourth finger was banded by a thick ring, like his brothers'. But Ruby barely noticed. These were her parents. She'd thought about them her whole life but she'd never been able to imagine their faces. They looked magazine-cover happy. Emmeline, or whoever she was, didn't look like a liar. And neither of them looked like they were planning to abandon their future kid.

"That's not the only diamond in the picture though," Harlan said after the silence had stretched out for almost a minute. "Do you see that necklace your mom is wearing?" Harlan asked, pointing to a large pendant hanging around Emmeline's neck. It was the shape and size of a quail egg.

"Harlan." Alice pinned him with a sharp look.

"What about it?" Ruby asked.

"Nothing. It's just a diamond pendant," Alice said.

Ruby's eyes widened. How could a diamond be so big? "Where did it come from?" she asked, unable to move her eyes from the picture.

"We don't know how she got it," Miles's even voice broke in. "We didn't even know what it was until after she left. She told us it was quartz."

Harlan's eyes glinted with excitement. "Do you want to see it?"

"Absolutely not." Alice glared at Harlan. "You know large diamonds can be dangerous."

"How?" Ruby asked, wanting to see it even more.

"Diamonds focus energy—" Miles began.

"It doesn't matter." Alice interrupted. "It's not worth the risk."

"Emmeline wore it constantly," Harlan said.

"Emmeline," Alice said, splicing the syllables in an unappealing way, "wasn't Sighted."

Ruby's heart was beating faster than on a hunt. "It won't hurt me. I'm not Sighted either."

"You're a Callahan." Alice clamped the words down fast against her argument. "That's close enough."

"I won't touch it," Ruby promised. "Miles?"

Miles stared into the distance, his lower jaw slowly rotating. "It's hers," he finally said. "She should see it."

―――――

 THERE WAS something strange about the office. It was different from the rest of Alice's apartment, with dark wood paneling and big, simple furniture. There were three ducks mounted on the wall, arranged as if they were migrating into the living room for the winter. An oddly docile stuffed grizzly bear stood in a corner. But the decor wasn't the weirdest part. As soon as

Miles unlocked the office door, Ruby's Lines banded together, forming one thick Line that thrummed with intense energy. The Line immediately shot toward a painting of fruit that hung near the desk.

Miles approached the painting and Ruby almost gasped, certain that he saw the bright ribbon of energy connecting her and the picture. But his face remained placid and he walked right through it. Alice's and Harlan's expressions didn't change either.

Miles swung back the painting, revealing a metal safe. He entered a long series of numbers into a keypad on the wall and a panel opened. Miles pressed his right thumb onto a thin rectangular pad and a blue light flashed. There was a slight gasping noise as the safe opened.

Ruby's Line tightened, nagging her toward the safe. Beside her, Harlan chewed his thumbnail, one hand tucked awkwardly into his pocket.

Miles reached in, pulling out a shiny cube from the safe that looked like it had been made from six black mirrors. He set it on the desk and lifted the thin magnetized lid, revealing a large diamond that glowed faintly blue. A thin silver necklace was attached to a delicate metal setting at the top.

Ruby stumbled forward as the Lines disconnected from her and rushed toward the diamond in a single electrified strand. The diamond absorbed the Lines, its own brilliance electrifyingly bright. Then, in less than a heartbeat, the Lines splintered out of the diamond, shining in strong, delicate streams from every facet and angle of the stone, pushing well beyond the walls and windows of the room. Ruby squinted against the explosion of light that only she could see.

"The night your mother disappeared, we found this on

her dresser," Miles said. "My father locked it in this safe and never opened it again. When he died two years ago, he left specific instructions for me to keep it secure until you or Emmeline came back."

There was a tugging sensation from the diamond, and Ruby's hand drifted toward the box but Miles caught her wrist.

"This is no ordinary diamond," he warned.

Ruby rolled her eyes. "I know."

"Be careful," Alice said, stepping toward Ruby. "Diamonds are pure crystallized carbon. And every living thing on earth is made of carbon."

"How can something be dangerous if it's made of the same stuff that I am?" Ruby asked.

"Carbon bonds with carbon," Alice said. "Diamonds amplify the light that passes through them. If they're big enough and clear enough, they can amplify other energies too. Like Sight."

"Allegedly," Miles said.

"But if they come into contact with too much negative energy, they can acquire a curse, like the Hope Diamond," Alice said.

"Allegedly," Miles repeated. "It's all very hocus-pocus."

It was all very awesome. Ruby felt like the diamond wanted her to touch it. Her arm crept up again.

"It's not cursed," Harlan said. "Emmeline wore it every day, and she was fine."

"Until she disappeared without a trace," Alice said flatly.

Ruby's arm dropped. Was this diamond somehow responsible for her mother's disappearance? She almost stepped back, but she couldn't bear to be any further away from it.

"She wore it every day and then just left it?"

"Yes," Alice said.

Miles removed the remaining four sides of the cube. Despite all his "allegedlys," he was careful not to touch the diamond.

Ruby raised her hand, stopping when her fingers were just an inch away. She wanted to touch it so badly. But her mother and the curse. Suddenly the diamond jumped into her open palm. Ruby gasped. An icy hot shock surged through her hand and up her shoulder. The diamond's surface was cold but a deep heat radiated from its core. Her skin tingled hot and cold together, as if she were sunburned and standing in a freezer.

The Lines inhabiting the diamond connected with her again, but they were different. Stronger and sharper. They moved faster and farther, and her mind reeled a little with the information they poured into her. Suddenly Ruby could read the spines of each book on the shelves and could tell that Miles owned them and had organized them twice, first by subject and then by the authors' last names. The whole office was his, but it hadn't always been. He had arranged the furniture, but he hadn't bought it. The desk was so old that she saw its finish was thinning on the window-facing side. Lavender patterns woven through the rugs told her that Alice had bought them. But not for Miles. For his father.

It felt like the Lines were suddenly three-dimensional. Instead of linking objects, they branched out, connecting people, things, and intentions through time. Every object in the room shouted its secrets at her and Ruby winced against the barrage of information.

But a new, inexplicably familiar feeling swept over her too. The diamond seemed to know her. She could feel its pull, almost like it wanted to be with her. Ruby had never belonged to anyone, but somehow she belonged to this ice-cold rock in her hand.

Harlan stood uncharacteristically stiff with one shoulder hitched. And now Ruby understood—Harlan didn't like this room. No, he liked it, but he didn't like *being* in it. He'd wanted it, but... her eyes moved to Miles, whose body language was simpler. Their father's office had passed to Miles, the youngest son, instead of to Harlan. Miles had the key and the safe was programmed for his thumb.

Ruby's pulse throbbed in her head and a cold, white-hot pain numbed the hand holding the diamond. She turned toward the window, but the sensations only intensified. She could see the faces of people all the way across the park, so clearly that she could count the freckles on a little girl's nose who was at least a quarter mile away. She closed her eyes but information kept screaming through her brain.

The Lines rushed away from the window, darting and scurrying around the desk. Especially the top left-hand drawer. She stepped forward, eager to open it, but then the Lines flared and the hairs on the back of Ruby's neck prickled in a sensation she knew well. Danger. There was something dangerous in the room. Her eyes flitted to the poor stuffed bear in the corner, but he was harmless.

The Lines had never acted with such complexity before. They had always been straightforward—ball: here, goal: there. But now they danced in intricate patterns, delicately inviting her toward the drawer but warning her at the same time. She followed their patterns in her mind, trying to decipher some meaning.

She turned toward Harlan and the warning intensified. Beneath his open, handsome smile lurked something dark and hungry. Miles's face looked the same as it always did, maybe more boring. Alice's face hadn't changed either, except that her concern had sharpened. But Harlan. Harlan almost looked like a different person.

"Ruby?" Miles said. His voice was soft and careful.

Ruby put down the diamond. Even though she'd only held it for a few seconds, her fingers stuck to it like syrup and she had to peel them off one at time. Instantly the room around her quieted.

"Are you alright?" Alice grabbed Ruby's shoulders and scanned her intently.

"Yeah. I..." Ruby didn't know where to start. She was fine. Better than fine. She felt energized, like she'd just stepped out of a cold shower.

"You're right," Harlan said. He quickly boxed up the diamond and put it back in the safe, closing and locking the door. "This was a bad idea."

"Wait," Ruby said, but she stopped. Alice looked like she was moments away from banning anyone from ever looking at the diamond again.

"Ruby, did... something happen?" Harlan's voice sounded nonchalant, but Ruby saw a flicker of intensity in his eyes that belied it.

"No." Ruby tried to smile reassuringly. "I've just—I've never seen a diamond that big before."

———

LATER THAT NIGHT, long after Alice was asleep, Ruby crept back to Miles's office. She knew she wouldn't be able to open the safe and touch the diamond, but she wanted to be near it, to feel the Lines intensify again. She

also needed to see what was in that
drawer. The lock on Miles's office door was easy to pick.
Ruby'd broken into the Owner's house countless times, and
Miles's lock was simple by comparison.

She stood barefoot on the plush carpet, tracing the
moonlit outlines of the migrating ducks and waited.
Nothing happened. The Lines barely moved, apparently
bored by a room they'd already mapped. Ruby stepped up
to the picture that hid the safe, expecting the Lines to jump
to life as she drew closer, but they didn't. Even in the darkness, Ruby could tell that the room was exactly the same as
it had been that afternoon. But it felt different. And the
Lines—

She walked over to the desk, slowly pulling open the
small drawer that the Lines had been so excited about
earlier. All she saw was papers, some pens, and a silver
letter opener. She reached back further, thinking maybe
there was a secret compartment or something.

Her fingers brushed against something smooth and
thick. Pulling it out she could see that it was a navy blue
passport, the kind the Big Men always used. On the first
page was a picture of a man, and his name: Rex Arthur
Callahan. Ruby traced the laminated image of her father.
The whole page was filled with information about him.
Squinting, Ruby read his birthdate and place of birth as fast
as her eyes could decipher the letters. Something tightened
in her chest. This little book had more information about
her father than she did.

She reached into the drawer again and found a second
passport, this one maroon. Ruby's breath caught as she
opened it. A picture of her mother—Emmeline Gunther
Callahan—or whoever she really was, smiled back at her.

6

———

Ruby frowned at the rows of clean clothes stacked neatly in her drawer. Technically, they were hers, but it looked like Alice had just shrunk her own clothes and put them in Ruby's dresser. There were delicate sweaters, crisp collared shirts, and pants with sharp creases in the front. Ruby grunted in frustration. She still couldn't find her old shorts, T-shirt, or flip flops anywhere. Not here. Not in the laundry room. Nowhere!

"Alice!" Ruby called.

"What's wrong?" Alice asked a few moments later, stepping into the room.

"Where are my clothes?"

Alice looked pointedly at the open drawer and the clothing strewn on the floor and bed. "Aren't they right here?"

"No. *My* clothes. The ones I brought with me."

Alice looked confused. "You didn't bring any luggage."

"They were in a white plastic bag."

"Oh." Alice frowned. "I didn't know—I threw that bag away."

"What?"

"I thought it was garbage."

Ruby didn't even know what to say. "Those were my clothes," she finally managed.

"I'm sorry, Ruby. But there are still lots of nice things to pick from." She pulled a pale pink blazer and a matching skirt from the closet. "This is pretty. And you could wear it to the musical tonight."

Ruby frowned, hoping that "musicals" were less boring than the ballet Alice had dragged her to last night. "That's way too fancy. I'm just going outside."

"Oh, I can't take you outside right now. I have a board meeting this afternoon. Maybe tomorrow."

"What?"

"I can't take you outside today."

"*Take* me outside? I don't need anyone to take me outside."

Alice paled. "This isn't Pan'wei. New York is big. And dangerous."

Ruby rolled her eyes, certain that nothing in New York was bigger or more dangerous than the cape buffalos she had tracked on Pan'wei. "I can handle it."

Alice's fist opened and closed. "I'll schedule some time to take you outside later this week," she finally said. Then she turned and left.

Ruby frowned and felt around her drawer for the softest pair of pants, which turned out to be khakis with weird pink flamingos embroidered all over them. She yanked them on. They were a little stiff, but at least they didn't itch. She found the least objectionable short-sleeved sweater and pulled it over her head. How could a person not have a single T-shirt?

Ruby flopped back onto the bed and reached under her

pillow for the pocketknife. It was sharp enough to transform these ugly pants into ugly shorts. But her fingers found her parents' passports instead, and she pulled them out. Flipping through her father's, she wondered how many times his own hands had held the little book. Probably a lot. Every page was full of colorful stamps from the countries he'd visited. There were even extra pages added in the middle. Every stamp had a date.

A small but bright Line skipped between the stamps until the tenth and eleventh pages. Then the Line stalled, ricocheting between the seven stamps on those pages. Ruby read the names of the cities: Rio de Janeiro, Lima, Mexico City, and Rome on page ten. Amman, Delhi, and Beijing on page eleven. The little Line jumped insistently from stamp to stamp in chronological order, but stalled and spun a little circle between Amman and Delhi. Ruby watched the pattern dozens of times until her eyes blurred.

Blinking, Ruby stared at the lush green park stretched out below her window. Her parents had travelled all over the world, but she was trapped in a room full of miniature grownup clothes. She reached under her pillow again and grabbed the pocketknife. Fingering the blade, Ruby stretched the khaki pants away from her leg and jammed the knife through the fabric. It pulled through the material easily. In less than a minute, a pool of pink flamingos lay at her ankle and the lower half of Ruby's left leg was liberated. She quickly did the other side, then looked in the mirror. The shorts were jagged and uneven, with threads poking out all over, but they felt perfect.

Ruby turned her attention to the Lines that ran limply around the boring four walls of her room. They hummed to life as she tasked them to find the best way out of the apartment undetected. The brightest Line led straight out the window. Cramming the passports and knife into the pocket of her newly made shorts, Ruby pushed open her window and stepped out onto the narrow decorative balcony. Her bedroom was on the twelfth story, which provided an excellent view of the park, but it also meant that she was over 100 feet up from the sidewalk.

Ruby studied the Lines. They ran straight off the balcony, but didn't go directly to the pavement. Instead, they gracefully cascaded down the row of ten balconies beneath Ruby's, then bounded across the street into the park. Ruby smiled and scuttled over her railing. Hanging by two hands, she swung herself back and forth a few times until she synced with the Line connecting her to the next balcony. She dropped, landing exactly where the Line had predicted. It was easy enough. The only tricky part was doing it fast before anyone in the apartments or on the street noticed. She repeated the maneuver several more times, swinging down the face of her building like a human slinky before dropping the last few feet to the sidewalk. Landing on the cement hurt a little, and a few pedestrians gawked, but Ruby was across the street before any of them could say anything.

Just in front of the park entrance, Ruby saw a little cart selling hot dogs. She went straight for it, thinking of all the weird, fancy food that appeared on Alice's table each mealtime. "One hot dog please," she said to the man behind the cart.

He picked up the meat with tongs and put it into a bun. "Two dollars."

"Oh. I don't have any money," Ruby explained.

"Then you can't buy a hot dog."

"What? But it's only two dollars."

"Exactly," the man said.

"Come on, I'm starving." Behind him, Ruby could see the park, waiting.

"Two dollars." He waggled two fat fingers at her.

"I'll bring you the money later," she pleaded, weighing the emptiness in her stomach against her eagerness to run on actual grass.

"No money, no hot dog," the man said.

A woman behind Ruby cleared her throat.

"It's one hot dog," Ruby said. "You have, like, thirty in there."

The woman made a louder sound and Ruby spun to face her.

"That's really distracting. I'm trying to get a hot dog here."

The woman opened her mouth in affronted surprise.

"Hey, do you have two dollars?" Ruby asked.

The woman grabbed the hand of the child beside her and huffed away.

"You are scaring away my customers," said the vendor.

"No, *you* are. No one wants to buy food from a man who lets kids starve," she yelled.

Two policemen walked over. "What's the problem?" the taller one asked.

"He won't give me a hot dog," Ruby said before the vendor could speak.

"Why won't you sell the kid a hot dog?" the policeman asked.

"Sell?" The man snorted. "She wants it for free."

"I said I would bring the money later," Ruby said. "Geesh."

"Ruby!" A familiar voice called from behind. Ruby turned. It was Chloe with the same four dogs from last time. "What's going on?"

"I'm trying to get a hot dog," Ruby said.

"Without paying," the vendor said.

Chloe looked from the man to the policemen to Ruby. She reached into her pocket and produced a ten dollar bill. "Here."

The man grabbed the bill and slammed a hot dog into a bun, slapping it into Ruby's hand and turning to the next customer.

"Excuse me," Ruby said. "You owe us four more hot dogs."

He glared at Ruby.

She glared back. "My friend gave you a ten."

He gritted his teeth and repeated the gesture four more times, anger mounting with each completed hot dog.

"Thanks," Ruby said, her mouth full before he'd even finished. She closed her eyes, savoring the bite. It was the best thing she'd eaten since arriving almost two weeks ago.

"Where's Alice?" Chloe asked, scanning the park as they left the stand.

Ruby shrugged. "Home."

"Does... she know where you are?"

Ruby shrugged again and handed a hot dog to Chloe.

"Ruby, you can't just—" Chloe took a bite and nodded her approval. "Umm. This is good." She pulled out her phone and walked toward a bench next to the park entrance. "Hey. It's me," she said into the phone. "I found Ruby by the park—" Chloe pulled the phone away and looked at it. "He hung up," she laughed. "He didn't even get the cross street." The phone buzzed and she answered it. "Hi. Eighty-first Street," she said. "And she's fine."

Ruby and Chloe sat on the bench, eating hot dogs while the four actual dogs tracked the food with laser focus.

"Why do you have so many dogs?" Ruby asked.

"They're not mine. Their owners hire me to walk them."

"Why do people have dogs if they don't want to walk them?" Ruby asked, tearing off four pieces of meat and tossing one into each dog's drooling mouth.

"Some people work all day and they don't want their dog to be home alone the whole time."

"Huh." Ruby stroked Agamemnon's ear. "Does Miles work all day?"

Chloe nodded.

"He doesn't really seem like a dog person," Ruby said. "How long have you been doing this?"

"Almost two years."

"When did Miles get Agamemnon?"

"About the same time, actually."

Ruby snorted, remembering how Miles had looked at Chloe in the lobby.

"What?" Chloe asked.

"Nothing."

"No really. What—" Chloe smiled then stopped, suddenly standing.

Ruby stood too, dropping her hot dog and sending the dogs into a feeding frenzy. Alice was crossing the street with Miles and Harlan.

"Ruby!" Alice hugged her tight, smooshing her small pearly buttons into Ruby's cheek as she choked out her name. "What happened?"

"Nothing," Ruby said cautiously. It was clear she was in trouble, but she wasn't sure why or how much.

"You just disappeared," Alice said.

There was an unspoken "again" at the end of the sentence that Ruby could feel, almost as real as Alice's tears against her neck.

"I just wanted to be outside," Ruby finally said, squirming free.

"Um, I better go," Chloe said.

"Thanks for your help," Miles said, turning back to Ruby and taking in her appearance, pausing momentarily on the ragged ends of her makeshift shorts. "How did you get out of the building? The doorman said he hadn't seen you in the lobby."

Ruby frowned. Alice was not going to like the answer. "Um, just, you know. Through the window."

Alice's face blanched.

"But that's twelve stories high," Miles said, a hint of astonishment in his voice.

"Yeah, but all the balconies line up." Ruby pointed to the front of their building. "It was just like stairs. Why is everyone freaking out?"

Miles crouched down so his face was level with Ruby's. "You can't just sneak out a window when you want to go outside. You have to ask permission."

"You're telling me I'm supposed to *ask permission* to go outside?" Ruby said the words slowly so he would hear how crazy he sounded. But his face didn't register the irony. Neither did Alice's. Ruby scanned the three adults staring at her, stopping at Harlan. He looked relaxed and harmless in his shorts, sweatshirt, and flip-flops. Whatever beef the Lines had had with him in the office, she knew that he was her best shot at freedom right now. She looked at him, silently asking for help.

"Everyone just relax," Harlan said. "She's fine."

Ruby's eyes wandered to the green trees in the park. She hadn't even gotten there and she was already in trouble just for using the wrong door.

"Come on, Ruby. We're going home." Alice turned and reached for Ruby's hand but Ruby stepped back.

"No. I've been inside all day."

Alice just stared at her.

"Why don't we all take a walk?" Miles said. "Together."

Alice squinted at the park like she didn't know what it was. Then she looked at her son and finally at her own feet, which were clad in thin little slippers. "I'm not wearing any shoes," she said.

"Miles, you take Mom home," Harlan said. "And I'll take Ruby for a walk."

Miles nodded and put an arm behind his mother's shoulders.

Alice's eyes stayed on Ruby. "One hour," she finally said.

Harlan nodded and Ruby sighed in relief as he turned toward the park. "You could've gotten hurt, you know," he said after a couple minutes.

Ruby thought about the Lines, guiding her between the balcony grates like a rope. "Eh. Not really."

"You have to think about other people. Your grand-mother almost had a heart attack when she couldn't find you."

Ruby sighed. "I'm twelve years old."

"Exactly."

Ruby sucked on her hair. "I thought you were going to be the fun uncle," she muttered.

"I am."

Ruby snorted.

"What, you think *Miles* is more fun?"

"At least he has a dog."

"You have to be more responsible," Harlan lectured.

"This isn't an island with a few dozen people. Over eight million people live in this city."

Harlan kept talking, but Ruby tuned him out. She wasn't about to take family advice from a dogless man who couldn't even find his own niece for nine years. Instead she watched her Lines running along the paths and around the trees, mapping the new space.

"Ruby?"

Ruby blinked. Harlan had obviously just asked her something, but she had no idea what. "Huh?"

"Do you want to go through the maze?"

Maze? Ruby looked around, wondering if this park had one of those hedge mazes like castles had in the movies. But there were no hedges. Just a sign reading "Reflection Point."

"It's a public art installation. They set up a maze made out of mirrors. It's supposed to be cool."

"Okay." Ruby liked mazes, but she'd only ever done them on paper. The Lines always guided her pencil to the end in record time. The thought of actually walking through one, of feeling the Lines rush into and around the space, was exciting.

She followed Harlan to a ticket booth, where she saw a flat, grassy field filled with hundreds of tall, reflective columns. It was huge—more of a labyrinth than a maze. Disembodied slashes of green grass and blue sky were refracted and reflected so many times that it looked like the park had been turned into a giant jigsaw puzzle. It was impossible to tell which rectangles were actual mirrors and which were just the spaces between them. Well, almost impossible. The Lines were not fooled as they buzzed energetically around, weaving between the mirrors and showing Ruby most of the way through the maze before she'd even entered it.

"Should we race?" Harlan asked, his eyes glittering as they approached the entry point.

Ruby tried to suppress the smile pushing up her mouth, shrugging one shoulder casually as if there would be a true contest. "Sure."

He handed their tickets to a teenager who tore off the bottom half. "How long does it usually take people to get through?" Harlan asked him.

"Fifteen minutes. Ten if you're good," the boy said.

Harlan smiled wryly at Ruby. "You want the right side or the left?" Harlan asked as they stepped into the mirror-lined path.

"Right," Ruby said, even though she could already tell that the left path offered the more direct route. Harlan deserved at least a fighting chance.

"Okay. Ready?"

Ruby nodded, smiling at the playful glint in his eye.

"Set, go!" Harlan took off.

Ruby sprinted into the maze, glad she'd cut her own pants off into shorts. It felt so good to run, to feel fresh air in her face as the Lines spread out, careening through the space almost faster than she could follow.

Two minutes later, Ruby skidded to a stop, returning to a mirror she'd just passed. She could see Harlan's figure, reflected two turns ahead. But he wasn't running anymore. He wasn't even going the right way. Confused, Ruby followed him. He was heading back to the entrance. Maybe he'd forgotten something or he was trying to be nice and let her win. But Harlan hadn't been carrying anything, and he didn't seem like the kind of person who let other people win.

She watched Harlan exit the maze and walk purposefully around its perimeter, his legs intersected and truncated by the multiple mirrors, making him look a little bit like a centipede. When he had passed her field of vision, Ruby wove her way through the maze, letting the Lines lead her to the next vantage point. She peeked out between two narrow columns and saw Harlan hovering at the finish line, looking at his phone like it was a stopwatch. Was he *timing* how long it took her to do the maze?

Ruby sighed. This was ridiculous. Whatever game Harlan was playing, she wasn't going along with it. If he wanted to secretly time her, she'd secretly make him wait.

She walked slowly, watching her reflections follow each other like a legion of identical soldiers. Ruby wandered to the center of the maze, an open square of concrete with a small round pool in the middle. The water reflected the maze upside-down, making it look like a portal to another dimension. It might have been beautiful if it weren't for the Lines stopping abruptly at the water's edge, looking like they'd fallen off a cliff. Shivering, Ruby slunk away from the pool, melting back into the mirrored pillars of the maze.

After Ruby had explored the entire maze, she sat down between two columns and pulled out the passports. Emmeline's had the same seven stamps as Rex's, so they'd obviously taken the trip together, two years before Ruby had been born.

Ruby visualized a world map and marked each city— Rio de Janeiro, Lima, Mexico City, Rome, Amman, Delhi, and Beijing. Seven cities in thirty-two days. It was a big trip. So why did she feel like something was missing? In the office, the diamond had led her to the passports. As if it was trying to tell her something. But no matter how many times she looked at the Line bouncing purposefully between the stamps, she couldn't figure it out.

Finally, she stood, shoved the passports into her pocket,

and asked a passerby for the time. It was 12:50. Twenty minutes in the maze was probably long enough to make Harlan wait. Brushing off her shorts, Ruby sprinted for the exit, following the bright Lines as they led her to the end.

Harlan pocketed his phone immediately and smiled at Ruby as she approached.

"You beat me," she said between breaths.

Harlan's smile broadened. "Old-man luck."

Ruby smiled back. He seemed so good-natured that it was hard for Ruby to remember that he'd been messing with her. Maybe it was just some kind of joke or prank and her delay had ruined it.

"Ice cream?" he asked.

"They sell ice cream here too?"

"Yeah," he smiled. "Of course."

"Perfect," she smiled back.

7

"Hey," Winston said to Ruby as he opened his front door.

Mrs. Deckert popped up behind him and pointedly cleared her throat.

"I mean, hello. It's nice to see you. Thank you for inviting me to accompany you on your walk." Winston rolled his eyes and Ruby giggled.

"Here." Ruby handed him a leash. A Yorkshire terrier named Cleopatra was attached to the other end.

"Whoa." He backed away. "Gross."

"You said you'd help." Ruby nodded at Chloe, who was trying to untangle herself from a sleek Dachshund named Cyrus. "So take a leash."

"People literally pick up dog poop while they're holding that."

"Unless you're planning to carry the dog, you'll need the leash."

"Fine." Winston disappeared into the apartment.

Ruby followed him in and waited. The apartment was kind of like Alice's, except there was a lot more gold stuff.

Classical music drifted in from the living room. Peeking around the wall, Ruby saw a skinny boy hunched over the keys of a large grand piano. His arms shot jerkily across the keyboard as he played. He flinched when he saw her, crushing a dissonant chord.

"Hey," Ruby said, smiling.

The boy gaped at her, but Mrs. Deckert swooped in before he could reply.

"Winnie will just be a minute," she said. "Charlie, you still have ninety minutes of practicing left."

"Eighty-three minutes," Charlie mumbled as Mrs. Deckert guided Ruby back to the entry.

She hovered, tapping an envelope in her hand. "How are you adjusting to New York?" Mrs. Deckert asked, her face pursed in sympathy.

Ruby shrugged. It had only been three weeks, but she was already tired of the question.

"Sometimes big changes can be hard," said Mrs. Deckert.

Ruby squinted at her. Did Mrs. Deckert really think that having a bed and food and a family was harder than not having those things?

"I'm sure compared to Hawaii, New York feels big and confusing." Mrs. Deckert was using the kind of voice adults used with preschoolers.

"It's not confusing," Ruby said. "The streets are straight and run in numerical and alphabetical order."

"Alphabetical order?" Mrs. Deckert furrowed her brow.

"Amsterdam, Broadway, Columbus." Ruby made three chopping motions with her hand and Cleopatra shifted in her arms.

"Oh. Right." They stood in awkward silence for several moments, listening to Charlie's practicing and Mrs. Deckert's envelope thudding against her palm. Ruby stared at the ceiling, wishing Winston would show up so they could leave.

"Do you like it?" Mrs. Deckert finally said, motioning to the enormous crystal chandelier above them.

"Um, sure." Ruby adjusted her pants and wished she'd worn her newly cut shorts.

"It belonged to Catherine de Medici."

"Oh. Okay," Ruby said, confused. Why was Mrs. Deckert bragging about some light she'd gotten at a garage sale?

"I mean—" Mrs. Deckert reddened and there was a glint of panic in her eyes. "The fixture your parents had was lovely too. Of course. But, you know, Catherine de Medici. She was queen of France—"

Winston finally returned wearing leather gloves. He raised an eyebrow as he took in his mother's flustered face and Ruby's confused expression. "See you," he said to his mom as he and Ruby left.

"Are you living in my parents' apartment?" Ruby asked as soon as the door closed.

"Um, yeah, kind of. My parents are just subletting it though. Temporarily. Until... you know."

"Oh." Whatever emotion had been pooling in Ruby's chest dissipated at the word "temporarily." "Okay. But just so you know, when I find my parents, you'll have to move out."

"Course."

"Why was your mom bragging about that stupid light?"

Winston sighed and plucked the leash from Ruby with two gloved fingers. "She's trying to impress you."

Ruby snorted. "Why?"

"You know."

"No, I don't."

Chloe's heeled boots clacked down the corridor, but Ruby and Winston lagged behind. He scratched his nose. "My mom's obsessed with all the old Sighted families, like yours. She wants to prove we're as good as everyone else."

"Sounds exhausting," Ruby said, remembering how impossible it had been to fit in on Pan'wei.

Winston's small brown eyes flicked up to hers. "It is."

Chloe waited for them in front of Miles's apartment.

"Was that your brother on the piano?" Ruby asked.

"Yeah. Charlie. He's two years older. But he's a Sape, so..." He shrugged one shoulder.

Ruby could hear Agamemnon's paws skittering on the other side of the door before Miles opened it. The dog launched himself straight into Ruby's arms. She rubbed his belly and felt him calm against her.

"Hey," Miles said, running a hand through his perfectly combed hair.

"Hello, Dr. Callahan. It's nice to see you," Winston began. "Thank you for allowing me to accompany your dog on his walk."

"Dude," Ruby said to Winston. "Cut it out. That's creepy."

Miles bent down and picked something up. It was the passports. They must've fallen out of Ruby's pocket when she'd picked up Agamemnon.

"Oh, those are mine." Ruby reached for them, passing the dog to Winston, who took a startled step backwards at the sudden contact with fur.

"May I?" Miles asked Ruby, nodding to the little books.

Ruby swallowed. "Okay."

Miles opened the pages with careful fingers. "These are Rex's and Emmeline's." His eyes softened as he looked through the pages, holding them so that Ruby could see them too. He lingered on his brother's picture for several moments. "He looks so young."

Ruby nodded, though she really had nothing to compare the picture to.

"A lot of these trips we took together." Miles's voice was normal, but his fingers quivered.

Ruby stopped him when he landed on pages ten and eleven. "Did you go with them on this trip?"

"No," he smiled. "That was their honeymoon. They took a tour of the seven wonders of the world. See? Christ the Redeemer, Machu Picchu, Chichen Itza." He pointed to the stamps for Rio de Janeiro, Lima, and Mexico City. "Then the Colosseum, Petra, the Taj Mahal, and the Great Wall of China."

Ruby watched the Line follow his finger around the two pages, spinning on the empty space between Amman and Delhi.

"They skipped Egypt?" Chloe asked.

The Line brightened, spiraling faster.

"Wait. You said seven wonders, and there are seven stamps," Ruby said. "So how did they skip something?"

"Most tours include the pyramids, since they're the last remaining wonder of the ancient world," Miles said.

"So there should be a stamp for Cairo right here?" Ruby pointed to the blank spot and the Line relaxed, curling around her finger with satisfaction.

"Theoretically." Miles handed the passports back to Ruby. "But Emmeline didn't want to go to Egypt."

Ruby sucked on a piece of hair, still not certain why the diamond and the Lines were so obsessed with a missing stamp in a pair of expired passports.

"I'll pick you up around five for the game," Miles said to Ruby.

Ruby wrenched her thoughts away from the passports. "Oh right. The baseball game. Hey, can Winston come?"

"No thanks," Winston said quickly. "I don't like baseball."

"Do you like hot dogs and soda and being outside?" Ruby asked, knowing that his life was sadly short on all three things.

"How do you know what's at a baseball game?" He sounded weirdly defensive. "You've never been to one."

"I've seen them on TV. We had TV on Pan'wei, you know. It's not Antarctica."

"Actually, they have TV on Antarctica," Miles interjected.

"See?" Ruby said.

"I just don't like baseball," Winston said.

"Fine." Ruby turned to Miles. "Can Chloe come then?"

Miles's cheeks pinkened. "Um, sure. If she wants to."

Chloe smiled. "I wish I could, but I have to—"

"Sure. Of course." Miles nodded his head quickly. "Um, so have a good walk." He bent down and patted Agamemnon's head three times. Then he gave three identical pats to Ruby's head. She scowled as he shut the door.

———

 RUBY BARELY FELT the warm sunshine on her face as they strolled down Broadway. Her mind was too busy churning over the passports. Why Egypt? Maybe the diamond was trying to tell her the places where her

parents *weren't*. Ruby hoped that wasn't it. The world was big and it would take forever to find them by process of elimination. Still, it had to be some kind of clue.

"Ooh, look, a street fair," Chloe interrupted Ruby's thoughts, pointing to the mass of people flooding Broadway. Canopied food carts lined the sidewalk, filling the air with sweet, salty smoke.

Winston stopped, then suddenly jerked forward as Cleopatra lunged off her leash and sprinted into the throng of people, disappearing immediately.

"Cleopatra!" Chloe yelled.

Winston pulled up the empty end of his leash and stared at it, disbelieving. "Gutterball."

Ruby passed Agamemnon's leash to Chloe and ran into the crowd after the dog, but Cleopatra was gone. Ruby tried to find a Line connecting her to Cleopatra but it was hard to pick out among the thousands of other Lines she felt at the same time. Breathing deep, she crouched down and imagined that she was a dog. A dog who wanted something badly enough to yank out of a leash. She detected the savory smell of cooked meat and suddenly one of the Lines brightened, tugging a little. Ruby sprang up and ran through the crush of people, bobbing and weaving her way through as she followed the Line.

The Line led to a kebab stand surrounded by a low, blue picket fence. Cleopatra stood whimpering at the man grilling the meat. Ruby's heart panged in sympathy. Her own mouth was watering now too, but, again she didn't have any money. And New Yorkers were weird about that. She wondered if she could just take one and run. But the crowd was too thick to make a clean escape. She surveyed the man. He was busy, but he looked nicer than that hot dog guy.

Ruby sniffed loudly. "It's okay, girl," she said, scooping

up Cleopatra. "I'm sure we'll find something to eat in that garbage over there." Cleopatra whined pathetically. "I know it smells good. But you have to *buy* them," Ruby said loudly. "And we don't have any money."

"Hey, kid," the man said. "Here." He dropped a kebab into a napkin and handed it to her.

"Wow. Thanks, Mister." Ruby tried to sound like a grateful, half-starved orphan.

The man waved her off. "Now go collect your Oscar."

Ruby pulled off a chunk of beef and fed it to Cleopatra and then took a bite for herself. The strips of meat pulled off, salty and soft. Juice ran down her chin onto the dog's shiny coat as she threaded through the crowd.

"Hey," she said when she made her way back to Winston.

He started and then threw his scrawny arms around her in a brief, awkward hug.

Chloe's hug lasted longer. She was surprisingly soft for someone so skinny. And warm. No wonder Miles had bought a dog. "I can't... Alice would kill me if I lost you," Chloe said.

Ruby scoffed. "Please. I never get lost." She offered Winston a piece of the kebab.

He shook his head, staring at her with a squinty, appraising look.

Ruby shrugged and popped the meat into her own mouth.

———

"You're not hiding it very well," Winston finally said after several minutes of silence. They sat cross-legged on the floor of her bedroom, Ruby thumbing through her parents' passports and Winston nervously yanking out tufts of carpet.

"Hiding what?"

"The fact that you're a Levant."

Ruby snorted. "What?"

Winston rolled his eyes. "A Levant. A Sighted person who sees the present."

"I know what a Levant is." Ruby frowned. "But I'm not—"

"It's okay. I won't tell anyone. But if I figured it out then other people will too."

"You're joking," Ruby said, even though Winston wasn't really big on jokes.

"You found that dog in, like, three minutes."

"So?"

"So, only a Levant could do that. Do you see these, like, 'Lines' everywhere?"

Ruby met his gaze. "How do you know about that?" she whispered.

"All Levants see them."

Ruby was tempted for a moment to believe him. It would be nice to finally have an explanation for the Lines. But it just wasn't possible. She shook her head. "This is ridiculous."

"Don't you think it's weird that you've never gotten lost?"

"Nobody ever got lost on Pan'wei."

"Yeah but—" He squinted. "Huh."

"What?"

"Nothing. It's just... ironic that you were living in the one place where you wouldn't stand out."

Ruby grunted. "I stood out."

Winston's eyes alighted on her hair and he smiled. "I

mean, your abilities wouldn't stand out." He shivered. "But all that water. That must have been terrible."

She stiffened. "What do you mean?"

"Levants are afraid of water. It's one of the signs."

Something inside Ruby loosened. "Really?"

"Levants see everything, all the time. Where things came from, where they are, and where they're heading. It's why they're so good at sports. Everything they see is plotted on a perfect, moving map of Lines. Except for water. The Lines don't work there, so water is this dark, unmappable abyss. It's supposedly terrifying."

Goosebumps raised on Ruby's forearm. That was exactly how she felt about water. About all of it, actually. "Maybe you're right. Maybe I'm a... Levant," she said slowly, trying the words out. She felt their truth even though she still struggled to believe them. Her life seemed to fracture and reassemble in a way that made more sense. A warm relief settled on her. "So, I'm Sighted?"

"Yeah."

"Like all the other Callahans," Ruby said. She couldn't wait to see Alice's face when she found out.

"No. This is something totally different."

"But it's good, right? I mean—Oh shoot." She suddenly remembered Harlan sweating outside the maze in Central Park. "Now Harlan's going to know that I was messing with him in that maze." She laughed, wondering whether Harlan would be mad or amused when she told him.

"Wait." Winston grabbed her forearm. "Harlan took you to a maze?"

"Yeah." She shrugged. "That one in Central Park."

"Gutterball." Winston covered his face with his hands. "Ruby, that's a classic test for Levantancy. You shouldn't—" he looked around and stopped. "You can't let anyone know.

Levants are valuable. They can find things. Things that bad people would do anything to find. Did anyone notice how fast you finished?"

"No. I pretended to get lost and took, like, twenty minutes." Ruby wanted to laugh, but her smile faded when she looked at Winston's lined forehead. "Relax. You worry too much."

"No, I worry the exact right amount. Think about it. Just as easily as you found that dog in a street fair, you could get into a bank vault, down a mineshaft, or through a prison. Anywhere."

An icy tingle of danger shivered down Ruby's spine. He was right. The whole world seemed to stretch itself before her, new and dark. "What should I do?"

"You have to pretend you're ordinary. Someone who's terrible with directions, bad at sports, and definitely bad at mazes."

Ruby sucked her hair, trying to ignore the heaviness collecting in her chest. "But what if I can't hide it?"

"You can." He took a deep breath. "I've been doing it for five years."

"Doing what?"

"Hiding the fact that I'm Sapient."

"You're a Sape? But why would you hide that?" Ruby cocked her head, confused.

His jaw hardened uncharacteristically. "When they found out Charlie was a Sape, everything changed. Now every minute of his day is meticulously planned by my parents and a team of experts hired to 'maximize his potential.'"

Ruby scowled. "That's terrible."

"It's like he's not even a kid anymore. I didn't want that."

"I'm not very good at lying," Ruby said, running her thumb over the laminated passport picture of her mother. She was a stranger, but delicate Lines twined between her face and Ruby's, connecting their shared features. Even as Ruby's mind twisted through all the new problems and dangers that came with being a Levant, it simultaneously wound through the mysteries and secrets surrounding Emmeline, finding nothing but frustration on each front.

"I'll help you."

"Thanks." Ruby smiled, her chest easing a little at his sincerity. Right now at least, in this room with Winston, she was safe. "What if—" Ruby stopped, pulling the words from the dark tangle that always surrounded her thoughts of Emmeline. "Do you think my mom was a Levant too?"

Winston gasped. "Holy smokey-jokies! Of course!" He leaned forward, tapping the passports. *"That's* why she wouldn't go to Egypt!"

"What's why?"

"She was avoiding the Azarians."

The Lines twanged like popping rubber bands at his words. Whatever he was talking about, they agreed with him. Ruby scooted closer. "The *What-ians?*"

"Azarians. They're this secret ancient order obsessed with capturing Levants. They're why Levants hide their Sight. And they're headquartered in Cairo. No Levant would ever go there."

Ruby was still for several heartbeats, watching the Lines thread through the echoes of Winston's words and then wind around the fractured picture she had of her mother. "Alice said that my mom lied to them about who she was and where she came from. Even her name was fake."

Winston's eyebrow propped up. "I bet she did it to hide the fact that she's from a Levant family."

"You think so?"

"Yeah. She probably knew that you were a Levant too. The signs manifest really early." He stopped, wincing. "Oof."

"What?"

"I just can't imagine a Levant leaving another Levant on a tiny island surrounded by water."

8
_____

Ruby traced the Nile River through the map of Africa in the open textbook. Her head slumped on her hand and she looked wistfully out the window of Alice's library.

"And where did Solomon source the building materials for his temple?" Sterling asked. Ruby ignored him. Even though it was summer, he still came every morning to teach her, wearing his red Sape blazer, as if he were a university professor instead of a sixteen-year-old tutor.

Winston's hand shot up. "Lebanon and Syria."

"You don't have to raise your hand, Winston," Ruby said. "There are only two of us." Mrs. Deckert had asked if Winston could join Ruby's daily tutoring sessions, claiming that he needed an "organic, low-pressure, one-to-one peer interaction session." Which apparently meant that he needed to raise his hand every ten seconds.

"That's right." Sterling smiled. "Do you know why?"

Winston's hand went up again.

"Ruby?" Sterling never stopped asking her even though she had not once, in the four weeks of tutoring, answered.

"Dunno," Ruby said mechanically. She did know that there were exactly forty-two minutes left until this session ended and Chloe showed up with the dogs for their daily walk. "Hey," Ruby whispered to Winston. "Do you think your mom will let us watch *Ghostbusters* after we walk the dogs?"

Winston flushed, glancing furtively at Sterling. "I only have fifty-four minutes of screen-time left for the week."

"Okay," Ruby said, ignoring the impatient look Sterling was leveling at them. "I'll tell her that I need to watch movies that are set in New York in order to feel more comfortable in the city."

"But you don't," Winston hissed.

It was true. Levants apparently acclimated more quickly to new environments than most people. "But your mom doesn't know that—" Sterling cleared his throat loudly and flipped the pages of Ruby's textbook. "Around 950 BC, Solomon, the king of Israel, built a temple," he said pointedly.

Ruby rolled her eyes and turned back to the book. This Solomon guy looked like a weirdo.

"And I know what you're thinking," Sterling said.

"That Solomon shouldn't be wearing a dress?" Ruby asked.

"You're wondering what this ancient temple has to do with us."

Ruby had not been wondering that. She had been wondering if she could talk Chloe into an ice cream stop on their walk.

"Well, Solomon was a Levant."

Ruby straightened. A Levant? She reconsidered the illustration. Maybe Solomon wasn't so bad. Maybe he was only wearing that dress thingy because no one would buy him proper shorts.

"Do you know what this is?" Sterling pointed to a square with twelve round stones in it.

Winston's hand sprang up. "It's the high priest's ephod," he said, as if he'd been holding his breath. "Each stone represents one of the twelve tribes of Israel."

"Right. And the sixth stone was a diamond," Sterling said. "Most Sight Scholars believe that this is the first written record of a Sight Stone."

Ruby stared at the picture, her heart quickening. It was her diamond. The one in Miles's safe. She would know it anywhere.

"The Sighted have always been fascinated with diamonds." Sterling rubbed the diamond in his own class ring. "The crowned heads of Europe were generally Sighted, which is why they were obsessed with hoarding large jewels. And while it's true that most large diamonds enhance Sight, this one, known as the 'Solomon Stone,' is special. It doesn't just amplify Sight. There's strong evidence that it can be used to connect the energy fields of multiple diamonds."

Ruby frowned at the illustration. She hadn't exactly "connected" with the "energy fields" of any other diamonds in Miles's office. Well, she'd connected to each visible object, and understood the patterns of time and space that had brought it there, which was pretty cool. But the diamonds in her uncle's rings hadn't been singled out. "What happened to it?" she asked.

Sterling smiled and flipped ahead in the textbook. "Good question. Egypt sacked Jerusalem in 925 BC. They took the Solomon Stone and it eventually fell into the hands of Alexander the Great, another Levant."

Ruby looked at the picture of Alexander the Great, posed heroically in front of an army, wearing... an even shorter dress. Sheesh.

"The Solomon Stone protected him. That's why he never lost in battle, right?" Winston asked.

"That's what the legends say. But," Sterling flicked his eyes around the library, "some people believe that when a Levant uses the Solomon Stone, something unusual happens. There are legends of Levants using the Solomon Stone to '*Render*.'"

Even Winston looked baffled now. "'Render'?"

"The Solomon Stone amplifies a Levant's abilities so much that the Sight actually morphs into something else. Instead of seeing Lines connecting space and time, they can actually access the traces of another person's energy. Given the right circumstances."

"Access energy?" Ruby asked. "What does that even mean?"

Sterling shrugged, but his eyes gleamed. "No one knows exactly, but there are ancient accounts of Levants doing amazing things with the Solomon Stone." Sterling pulled an old leather-bound book from his messenger bag. It looked like it was flaking away into dust. He opened it gently and handed it to Ruby. "For example, there's this story about Alexander the Great and his conquest of India."

She looked at the brown-yellow pages, but the print was small and hard to read.

Sterling's eyes shot upwards for several seconds, reminding Ruby of a computer downloading a file. Too bad his eyes didn't spin in rainbow circles like her laptop did. That would be awesome. "While invading India, Alexander the Great encountered King Porus and his army," Sterling said, obviously reciting from memory the text from the unreadable page. "Porus retreated and Alexander followed. Every day Porus and his men woke at dawn and rode until dark. But every day Alexander and his men drew closer, unrelenting, like a deadly disease you've already contracted."

"The king led his men through the unforgiving jungle that no foreigner had ever survived. But Alexander followed. Porus led his men across the perilous Jade River full of man-eating crocodiles. But Alexander followed, gaining on him each day." Sterling paused for a moment and blinked rapidly, probably scanning his massive memory bank for the next thread of the story.

"King Porus wasn't worried. He knew his own territory. But Porus didn't know that Alexander was a Levant, let alone a Levant who possessed the Solomon Stone. Alexander could've tracked a gnat through the Sahara Desert."

Ruby's hand tightened on the fragile book, remembering how her own senses had sharpened when she'd held the Solomon Stone.

"So, Alexander followed Porus through every jungle and glade in India, dogged as death," Sterling continued. "Porus grew desperate and veered north through the treacherous Kahill Mountains. King Porus always carried his own cache of diamonds with him for protection in battle, but they were so heavy they slowed his flight. He knew he couldn't carry them through the steep mountain pass, but he couldn't bear to leave them either. Deep in the mountains was a ravine. Too steep to climb out of and filled with deadly snakes."

"Were they venomous?" Winston asked.

"Let him finish!" Ruby snapped. Everything she was or wanted seemed locked inside this strange little story.

"Worse than venomous." Sterling said. "They had glassy black-red eyes that could turn man or beast alike into stone with a single glance. Porus threw each of his huge diamonds into the ravine, trusting the snakes would guard them until he could return. Alexander arrived at the ravine just hours later. He saw the glimmer of the diamonds deep in the crevasse. Several brave men volunteered to retrieve the diamonds, but Alexander sensed danger. He polished his shield with sand until it shone like a mirror, then he threw it into the snake pit. When one of the snakes drew close, it saw its own reflection and turned to stone."

Ruby and Winston both gasped and the corner of Sterling's mouth twitched up before he continued.

"Alexander knew that diamonds hold their masters' secrets and he wanted them, but he was unwilling to risk the lives of his men," Sterling said. "So he killed a mule and threw the chunks of raw flesh into the crevasse. The meat stuck to Porus's diamonds. Then the sky blackened as ravens, eagles, and crows gathered, drawn by the meat. The birds swooped into the ravine and devoured the flesh in great, greedy gulps, diamonds and all."

"When the birds flew away, Alexander and his archers tracked them, shooting them from the sky. They cut the birds open and retrieved the diamonds. Now that Alexander held Porus's diamonds, the Solomon Stone Rendered," he paused, letting the word hang in the air a moment before continuing, "Porus's heart to him. The diamonds spilled their master's secrets like a cracked cup—his love, his fear, his ambition, and, most importantly, his plan. Nothing—no horse, no sword, and no soldier is as valuable to a general as his strategy."

Ruby and Winston leaned forward, as if being closer to Sterling would somehow speed up the story.

Sterling's eyes glinted as he continued. "Alexander learned that the king intended to lure him to Belai, his capital city, and there make his stand. The diamonds also told him that the people of Belai were angry with Porus for plundering the diamonds from their temple before his campaign."

"Two days later, Porus finally arrived at his precious capital, only to find his own gates shut against him. His tower guards were now loyal to the brave young conqueror who had come the day before, bearing the city's treasures back to her. Alexander won the city without shedding a single drop of blood."

"Wait." Winston blurted. "So Alexander *Rendered* Porus's diamonds?"

Sterling's eyes flickered. "It's an old story, but we think that's what happened."

"Who's 'we'?" Ruby asked.

"I've been doing research with Dr. Pierce. He's a Solomon Stone expert. He's found dozens of ancient stories like this, where Levants use the Solomon Stone to Render diamonds. It's easy to see if you know what to look for."

"Where is it now?" Ruby asked, though she knew the answer.

"No one knows." Sterling sighed. "The last known owner was Tsarina Alexandra of Russia. But it hasn't been seen since she was captured and killed by the Bolsheviks in 1918."

"So," Ruby fingered the musty pages of the book, "Levants are good at finding things, but a Levant with the Solomon Stone could find, like, *anything*, right?"

"Basically," Sterling said.

Ruby's whole body tingled with excitement as she struggled to stay quiet. She was a Levant and she owned the

Solomon Stone. And there were two people she very much wanted to find.

———

RUBY COULD BARELY WAIT for Sterling to leave before she pounced on Winston. "I have it!"

Winston, who now had Ruby crouched over him like a mountain lion with both hands on his shoulders, flushed red. "Have what?" he stammered.

"The Solomon Stone. I have it. They showed it to me a few weeks ago. It's in the safe in Miles's office. And the Lines went, like, crazy. And then I touched it and it was like —I can't even explain."

Winston searched her face. "*The* Solomon Stone?"

"Yes! And I'm," Ruby lowered her whisper-scream a few decibels, "a Levant, which means I can do that Render-thingy and find my parents!"

Winston blinked a few times, his enormous Sape brain apparently processing all the information. "I mean, the Solomon Stone *does* pull Levants to it. And I'm pretty sure your mom was a Levant."

Ruby nodded furiously, barely able to stand how slow he was talking.

"But," Winston sat up now, shaking free of Ruby's feline grip, "it's been lost since the Russian revolution."

"Miles thinks my mom might be Russian! She has, like, a Russian baby-shot scar on her arm or something." Ruby's hands batted the air with excitement and Winston frowned, edging away. "I'll show you!"

Ruby dragged Winston from the library to Miles's office. It was Monday, and Miles always came over on Monday afternoons to work in there. He sat at the desk, reading a thick stack of papers and rocking gently. The Lines, familiar with every room in Alice's house by now, hung slack.

"Miles?"

"Hmm?" He looked up at her with his intense blue eyes.

"Um, can I look at my mom's diamond again?" Ruby tried to still her fidgeting body and sound calm.

Miles rocked for several moments, his eyes trained on her face. The silence stretched out so long that Ruby started to wonder if he'd heard her.

"I suppose so," Miles finally said, rising and stepping over to the safe.

It felt like he was moving in slow motion as he pressed his thumb to the scanner and pulled out the black mirrored box.

Something tight and dark grew beside Ruby's gurgling impatience. The Lines. They weren't doing anything. She sucked her hair and shuffled a little as she waited for Miles to slowly open the box.

The diamond glittered against the red velvet, just as it had before, but Ruby felt nothing. The Lines stayed as they were, limp and loose at her feet. She raised her hand toward the diamond, but there was no pull. It was as if the diamond had forgotten her. She folded her hand around it. No icy heat burned from the center.

"Ruby," Miles said. "You're not supposed to touch it."

"Sorry." Ruby let go. Her fingers didn't even stick. She stared at the diamond. It looked exactly the same, but it wasn't. No wonder the Lines were so lethargic.

"Whoa," Winston said. "That is huge."

"Is this..." Ruby trailed off, the words *Is this a fake?* seeming so silly, but she couldn't think of any other explanation.

"Hmm?" Miles asked.

"Nothing."

Ruby felt hollow and deflated as the truth seeped into her. It was gone. The Solomon Stone, the only thing she had from her mother, and her best chance at tracking her parents, was gone.

9

Every single store on Forty-seventh Street sold diamonds. The display windows were jammed with so many that the air itself shimmered. Even the pavement glistened. It was so bright that Ruby had to squint. She sighed. There must be thousands of diamonds just on this block. Maybe hundreds of thousands. But not the Solomon Stone.

She shifted the heavy shopping bag which held her brand new, totally boring school uniform. Truncs wore navy woolen blazers paired with weird, itchy plaid skirts. The bag's weight was a constant reminder that school started in just five days. Five days until her life turned into one giant, boring tutoring session. Even Ruby's Lines seems apprehensive, lethargically meandering around the street.

Her stomach flipped as she was hit with the smell of roasting caramelized nuts from a sidewalk vendor.

"Come on," Alice said, heading toward a shop.

Ruby nodded, but she couldn't take her eyes off the cart. Why did New York always smell so delicious?

Alice paused, following Ruby's gaze. "You're hungry,"

she said.

Ruby shook her head. Alice liked to have lunch at fancy restaurants. She wouldn't want to buy food off the street.

Alice pursed her lips, studying the cart for several moments. "Here." She pulled a twenty dollar bill from her wallet.

"Oh." Ruby blinked. She wasn't used to other people worrying about her stomach. "Thanks."

Apparently, actual money made a big difference, because the nut vendor happily handed Ruby a packet of candied pecans and her change. Ruby offered some to Alice, but she delicately declined, which was a shame, because they were perfect—warm, salty, and sweet.

Ruby finished the bag, then followed Alice into a small shop labeled "Steiner's Jewelers." Inside, she pressed her face against the glass display cases, staring at the shimmering rings, bracelets, and necklaces that sparkled like the ocean in full sun. Suddenly the Lines tugged her upright. They had banded together, just like they'd done in Miles's office, forming a thick, bright ribbon running from Ruby to a small door behind the counter that was slightly ajar.

A small, irrational part of her wanted to rush through the door and use the Lines to find her diamond. The Lines themselves seemed to like the idea, straining toward the door like dogs against a leash. Ruby blinked hard, trying to ignore them. There was only one Solomon Stone, and there was no way it was just sitting in the back room of some random shop.

A short man in a gray suit came through the door, carefully shutting it behind him. Ruby's shoulders relaxed as the Lines slackened and returned to normal. The man wore a welcoming smile, but it slipped for a second when he saw them. Something like surprise or even fear crossed his face, but then he was smiling again as if they were all best friends.

"Mrs. Callahan," he said warmly. "My favorite client." He clasped Alice's hand in both of his.

"Ben," Alice said, "this is my granddaughter, Ruby. Ruby, this is Benjamin Steiner."

Steiner looked at Ruby, his eye shrewd. "Ah," he effused as his gaze loosened. "Finally, a Callahan girl." He reached to pat Ruby's cheek, but she stepped back. Steiner chuckled and raised his index finger. "Wonderful. A true Callahan woman is not easily won over." He winked at Alice, but she didn't respond. Her eyes were fixed on a ruby pendant in the display case. Steiner smiled and pulled out the necklace. "Do you like it?"

The red stone glistened like a crystallized drop of lava. Alice cupped it in her hand.

"It's not a diamond," Steiner said. "But rubies are known for their strength and resilience."

Alice's mouth curved up slightly. "And their inner fire," she said, holding it close so Ruby could see the slight red glow emanating from its center.

"Will you try it on?" Steiner asked.

"No." Alice returned the necklace reluctantly. "We're here for Ruby. She needs a pair of earrings."

"I do," Ruby said. It was supposed to be a question, but the words felt true as she said them.

"Of course," Steiner said. "She will start the Academy in less than a week, yes? And nothing complements the red blazer like a pair of diamond earrings."

"Blue blazer," Ruby said.

"Ah. Blue." He rested his eyes on her and smiled gently. "She is unique in every way." He pulled out a black velvet tray lined with pairs of diamond studs.

Ruby inspected each set carefully. Her eyes were drawn to a pair that were smaller than the rest but shone the brightest. She picked them up and watched the light refract off their tiny facets. They were beautiful.

Steiner and Alice exchanged a look. "She has excellent taste," he said. "Those are practically flawless and have perfect clarity. Most would pass them over because of their size. But Ruby has a good eye."

"But my ears aren't pierced," Ruby said. She looked at Mr. Steiner, hoping he would have an equally nice pair of clip-on diamond earrings.

Alice smiled. "We can do that here."

"Really?" Ruby asked.

"Tabitha," Steiner called to the back room. "We need you."

A young woman appeared from the back with a serious suit and tight ponytail. She brought a tray with cotton balls, rubbing alcohol, a pen, and something that looked like a toy gun.

She drew Ruby to a chair and marked her ears with the pen. Then she carefully loaded one of the studs into the plastic gun-thing. "This might hurt for a second."

Ruby nodded. Alice patted her hand and Ruby's fingers somehow intertwined around hers. She was too embarrassed to look at Alice, but she didn't let go. It was over in an instant. Two orbs of pure light shone on Ruby's throbbing earlobes. They were so beautiful that Ruby's throat constricted as she looked at her reflection.

"Do you like them?" Alice asked.

Ruby nodded, unsure if she could speak. Her eyes glistened as though they were reflecting the diamonds' own inner fire.

10

On the morning of the first day of school, black cars lined Fifth Avenue for five solid blocks. Ruby stared out the window as the driver eased forward four more inches. She sighed. Her Lines swirled and tugged in frustration. The Academy was only half a block away. "We could just walk from here," she said.

"We have plenty of time," Alice said, tugging her shiny black purse strap over and over.

Ruby shifted, her heart racing with idle energy. She raked her fingers up and down her calf. No one had warned her about tights—wooly, itchy things that were somehow too big and too small at the same time. Her stiff white button-down shirt bunched uncomfortably beneath her blue blazer. Only the two small diamonds twinkling on her earlobes felt right.

Alice's foot tapped against the seat. "We could still homeschool—"

"No." Ruby rolled her eyes.

"Stephen," Alice said to the driver.

"Two more minutes, Ma'am," he said.

But it wasn't two more minutes. It was at least four minutes. And that wasn't even counting the time Ruby had to sit and wait for Stephen to put the car in park, get out, open Alice's door, and then walk around to open Ruby's door. As if she and Alice couldn't lift a door handle.

Ruby hefted her backpack and her muscles instinctively tightened, ready for battle. She took one deep breath, clenched her teeth, and turned to face her new school.

Kids streamed down the sidewalk, almost all of them wearing bright red Sapient blazers. Some had on hunter green Provident jackets. They all looked like they were wearing little lawyer or banker costumes. There were adults too. A few dads, but mostly moms, balancing on spiky heels with red soles. They looked polished, clean, and expensive. Like Barbies straight from the box. Ruby wondered for a second if her mom would've put on high heels and lipstick just to bring Ruby to school.

Some of the kids stared at Ruby. Even some of the moms darted covert glances at her. The hairs on the back of her neck prickled. She was obviously an outsider. Again. She caught each stare with hard eyes and tight lips.

Ruby's Lines avoided the red coats and the Barbie moms as they flowed up the stairs into the Academy. They pulled to the left instead, where the navy coats drifted toward a small side door: the Truncant entrance. But Alice defied the unseen Lines and led Ruby through the main entrance.

Inside, the school looked like a castle with stone walls, wood floors, and huge windows. A chandelier hung from the high ceiling, softly illuminating the oil paintings on the walls.

"Good morning, Mrs. Callahan," the secretary said as they walked into the main office.

Alice nodded. "Hello, Nigel." They began exchanging papers and boring words.

Ruby glanced around. It looked more like a fancy living room than a school office. A boy in a blue blazer popped up from one of the seats and came over, hand outstretched.

"Hi. I'm James," he said, smiling. A patch of large freckles bridged his nose, some of them so big they looked like flakes of fish food.

"Okay," Ruby said, staring at his hand. Was he some kind of scout, inspecting the new kid so he could report back to his classmates?

"James Whipple," he said, raising his hand to his forehead and fluffing his bangs, as if that were the original reason he'd extended it. "Alice probably mentioned me."

Ruby sucked on her hair and shook her head.

"We're cousins," he said. "Well, third cousins."

Ruby frowned.

"Third cousins once removed, actually. My great-grandmother was your great-grandfather's aunt."

"Huh?" Ruby said, finding his friendliness as confusing as the information.

He sighed. "I'm here to take you to class."

Turning, Alice looked at James without confidence, then scanned the hallway. "Maybe I should take you," she said to Ruby.

"I'll be fine." Even Ruby knew that showing up to your first day of sixth grade with your grandma was a bad idea. At any school. "I can find my class."

"Right." Alice nodded but she didn't move toward the door. "Here." She pulled something black and flat from her pocket and slipped it to Ruby. "It's a phone. In case of an emergency. It has my number and Miles's and Harlan's."

Ruby's fingers tightened around it, thrilling at the

smoothness of the sleek rectangle. "It's mine?" she said, trying to keep her voice flat, even as excitement coursed through her.

"They're not allowed at school," Alice said, standing up and smoothing her unwrinkled skirt. "But if you need it..."

Ruby nodded and slipped it into her pocket next to the pocketknife, which was probably not allowed at school either.

Alice pulled Ruby into a tight hug followed by a very obvious kiss on the cheek. Then she straightened and pulled out a tissue to wipe her eyes.

Ruby looked around, bracing for the jeering that such a public display of affection would bring, but James just smiled.

"Alright," Alice finally said. "I'll be off then."

Something tightened in Ruby's chest as she watched Alice's straight back retreat through the door. Tears tingled in the corners of her eyes. Horrified, she blinked them back. A hug from your grandma was one thing, but crying when she left? That was social suicide. She clutched the knife in her pocket, waiting for her breath to slow. *The strength of the wolf is the pack. The strength of the wolf is the pack.* Her shoulders relaxed and she started walking, following the Line that led to the Trunc wing.

"Hey!" James ran after her. "Where are you going?"

"To class."

"But you don't know where it is yet."

"Umm, that's right." *Gutterball.* Hiding her Sight might be even harder than she'd thought. "I definitely do *not* know where my class is and I need you to show me."

"It's this way." He indicated the direction she had been headed and they started walking together. James kept pushing his hair back and unbuttoning and re-buttoning his jacket. "So, do you have all your books and everything?" he finally asked.

Ruby nodded. "Alice checked my backpack three times last night."

He smiled. "She's a perfectionist. All Callahans are."

Ruby tried to return his smile, pretending that she too knew what "all Callahans" were like.

"So, there are eight Truncs in sixth grade this year. We have all our classes together."

They turned a corner and Ruby blinked. The wood floor ended and a monkey-puke-green linoleum began. Rows of dingy plastic fluorescent lights lit the low-ceilinged hallway.

"This is the Trunc wing?" she asked, scowling. Different colored blazers was one thing, but this was ridiculous.

"Yes."

Their classroom was small with just one window overlooking the park and a blackboard with "History of Civilization" scrawled gloomily across it. Four blue-blazered boys stood around or sat on desktops. They all looked up when she entered, curious. No, not curious exactly. Were they nervous? Some shot wary glances at Winston, who sat in the middle of a small semicircle of desks, alone, his hand resting purposefully on the desk beside him.

"This is it. Our classroom," James said, nodding a greeting to the various boys.

"Where are the girls?" Ruby said.

James laughed as if she'd made a joke. "Exactly." The other boys joined in, their eyes darting to hers shyly.

Ruby smiled back, as if she'd intended to be funny. Each of them flushed under her gaze.

Winston smiled at Ruby, then glared at James.

"Hey," Ruby said, sliding into the desk beside him.

"Good morning, Ruby. It's nice to—" he began, but she cut him off with a skeptical look.

"Hey," she repeated.

He blushed and smiled. "Hey."

"So are you that Callahan kid?" a voice said from behind.

"Her name is Ruby," Winston said possessively, as if he hadn't asked her the exact same question six weeks ago.

"I'm Harrison," the boy said, extending his hand.

"Hi," Ruby said, cautiously shaking his hand. He was the largest in the class, probably the Alpha, except for the fact that he seemed really friendly instead of aggressive. Why were they all acting so nice? She didn't know whether to be relieved or suspicious.

A middle-aged man carrying a leather satchel and a steaming coffee cup strode in. Sterling trailed him, wearing his red Sapient blazer. He winked at Winston and Ruby as he sat down. A second boy followed. He wasn't as cute as Sterling, but he was taller and his face looked older, with signs of stubble shadowing his neck. He wore a red blazer and a cocky smile.

"Oh, gutterball," Winston moaned as the remaining students found their seats. "Dr. Pierce."

"Good morning," Dr. Pierce began, "I apologize for being late. All my other classes are in the Sape wing." He took a self-important sip from his deli coffee cup that Ruby suspected was the real reason he was late. He wore slacks, glasses, a turtleneck, and a brown corduroy blazer, like a teacher from TV. But the clothes looked wrong on him. He had a broad chest, long legs, and big arms that seemed barely contained in his professor getup. Most Big Men moved with a carelessness that came from over-trained minds in under-trained bodies. But there was nothing careless about Pierce. Something sharp lay beneath the muted layers of corduroy and faded jersey knit. He wore the same style of diamond ring that Miles and Harlan did. Ruby looked around and noticed that each boy in the room wore some version of the ring.

"I'm Dr. Pierce and this is the Truncant block of History of Civilization. These are my TAs, Octavius Chesterfield," he gestured at the taller boy, who was perched atop an empty desk with a toothy smile, "and Sterling Hancock. This year we will study the origins of our civilization, starting with the ancient Greeks. Please pull out your *Campbell Anthology*. We begin with the Socratic dialogues—"

Ruby scratched her calf. She didn't pay attention to the lecture, but she could tell from the dazed, glass-eyed looks of the other students that whatever he was saying was dead dull.

"We have some housekeeping to take care of," he said sometime later. Ruby started and looked groggily at the clock. Class was almost over. Had she fallen asleep?

"As you know, fall team tryouts are this week."

Ruby was suddenly alert. "Like soccer?" she blurted.

Dr. Pierce pressed his lips and ignored her. "For those of you who are interested, we have permission slips and forms for your physicals."

"What's a permission slip?" Ruby whispered to James.

He cocked his head and looked at her strangely. "It's a paper that your parent signs to give you permission to play," he said slowly.

"Oh yeah." She tried to look nonchalant as she struggled to imagine a world where kids had to get notes from their parents before they could play soccer. "And the physical is just..."

"Your doctor has to sign off that you're healthy enough to play." He passed the papers to her.

"Right."

"And of course, Camp Ketchikan is in three weeks," Pierce continued. "You'll need to return your permission slips for that too."

"What's Camp Ketchikan?" Ruby whispered to Winston.

"It's torture," he groaned. "Seriously, we should notify the United Nations." Worry lines creased his brow. "They make you stay in the woods and run around outside all day learning useless things like how to build fires and shoot a bow and arrow and stuff."

"Oh," Ruby said, stuffing the forms into her backpack. For his sake she tried to suppress the smile that was creeping up her cheeks. It didn't sound like torture at all.

11

When Ruby heard a sea lion barking halfway through Geography class, she thought she'd fallen asleep again and was dreaming. But she wasn't. Craning her neck, she saw that right outside the classroom window, just twenty yards from the building, lay an octagon-shaped pool chock full of fat sea lions.

Ruby was out of the classroom before the bell even stopped ringing. Two and a half minutes later, she stood at the fenced pool perimeter, staring at the sea lions' sleek brown bodies, eating a hot dog and trying to reconcile the presence of marine mammals in the middle of Manhattan. A tangy pop of juice squirted onto her tongue when she bit through the hot dog's skin. Mixed with ketchup and the sun on her face, it was perfect.

Nearby, a woman held a chubby toddler on her hip. Their arms were extended out together, pointing at the animals. The mother's hand was clenched, gentle and tight, around the child's waist.

Ruby snorted. The girl was at least three, old enough to stand by herself. Kids here were so babied.

"Mommy, Daddy," the girl said.

"That's right, Ainsley," the woman said in a sing-song voice. "There's the mommy seal and the daddy seal."

"Daddy seal," Ainsley repeated.

"They're not seals," Ruby interrupted, her mouth full of hot dog and derision. "They're sea lions. And they're all females. And none of them are moms."

The human mother smiled stiffly and turned away. Ainsley gurgled again, "Daddy seal."

"You're living in a fantasy world if you think there's a daddy seal," Ruby yelled to the woman's retreating back.

Heavy footfalls came up behind her. "You're not supposed to leave school," Sterling huffed.

Ruby sighed. How come no one ever let her eat a hot dog in peace? "It was an emergency."

"Going to the zoo and getting a hot dog is not an emergency."

"It is if you're starving."

"Lunch is in an hour."

"Exactly."

"There're only eight kids in your class, and you're the only girl. You'll be missed. You could get in really big trouble."

"Just so you know, I don't really care if I get in trouble." Ruby licked the grease off her fingers. "Hey, how come I'm the only girl in that class?"

"Very few girls are born Sightless."

"So there must be more girls than boys in the Sape sections."

"Quit stalling. You're not allowed to leave campus without permission." He tried prodding her arm but she yanked it away.

"You're skipping too. Aren't you worried you'll get into trouble?"

"It's my research period."

"Right. Me too. I'm researching which vendors have the best hot dogs."

Sterling rolled his eyes but his cheek dimpled. "I'm Dr. Pierce's research assistant. It's my Social Science credit."

"You're his TA *and* his research assistant? Don't you get bored?"

"No. Dr. Pierce is a genius." Sterling's eyes shone with a faraway wonder as he spoke.

"If he's so smart," Ruby scoffed, "how come I fell asleep in his class?"

"He's one of the world's leading Sight Stone scholars. We're lucky to have him."

"Huh. Well, I guess he's not that bad if he lets you skip your research period."

"Uhh," Sterling smoothed the front of his unwrinkled shirt, "he's at a meeting, so I sort of snuck out."

"Cool," Ruby said, feeling admiration for him for the first time. "If he catches you, you can tell him that I got lost and you had to rescue me."

He smiled. "Thanks, I guess. But he'll be gone for a while. He's in the Diamond District."

At the corner of Ruby's eye, some of the Lines were starting to tighten and twang, pulling south toward Forty-seventh Street, and Steiner's Jewelers. Ruby's muscles tensed, flooding her with an intense urge to follow the Lines' pull. "What's he doing in the Diamond District?"

Sterling cocked his head, apparently amused at her question. "He had a meeting with a guy named Ben Steiner—"

Ruby didn't wait for him to finish. She sprinted south as if his words had been a race-starting gunshot.

"Hey!" Sterling called after her, but she didn't stop.

Fifth Avenue was crowded, but, with the Lines, Ruby easily threaded through the people. She was on Forty-seventh Street in eight and a half minutes. She pretended to examine the window displays of the shop next door to Steiner's as she caught her breath, hiding behind two men in black coats who were speaking in a language she didn't understand. Through the window, Ruby could see Pierce shake hands with Steiner and a third, taller man whose face was blocked. Steiner flipped the "open" sign to "closed" and they all disappeared through that little black door behind the counter.

Ruby's Lines raced after them, nudging at the door. She pressed her fingers to the outside glass and felt a pulsing energy pull on her. Her fingertips prickled in recognition. It was here. The Solomon Stone was in Steiner's shop. But how? Her chest tightened as she remembered the faint blue glow on Miles's thumb when he'd opened the safe. The other man in the shop had been tall, just like Miles.

Ruby yanked at the shop door but it didn't budge. She pounded the glass until her hand hurt but that didn't open the door either. "Gutterball," she grunted, inspecting the door's six different locks—two thick manual ones and four computer-activated pads. Some of the Lines spun around them, but they offered no solutions.

Ruby paused. Several people on the street were staring at her. Suddenly aware that she'd just been pounding the window of a jewelry store like a maniac, she took a step backwards, wincing at the pang of longing in her chest. "I'm coming back for you," she whispered.

Across the street she found a shadowy nook. Leaning

against the wall, she stared at Steiner's store, feeling the relentless pull of the Lines. She panted at the effort of holding still. It started raining but she still didn't move.

After twenty minutes, the Lines loosened. Steiner returned to the front of the shop and flipped the "closed" sign to "open." Ruby tensed, certain that Pierce and Miles would come out. But they didn't. She waited ten full minutes more, but they never appeared.

Finally she headed back to Fifth Avenue, wet and disappointed. *Miles.* Miles must have stolen the Solomon Stone. Only he and Alice could open the safe. And it couldn't be Alice. It just couldn't. She sighed. Why was she even surprised? Why *wouldn't* Miles betray her? Her own parents had abandoned her. That's just what people did.

It took her over twenty minutes to walk the one mile back to the Academy, her legs seeming to move slower the closer she got.

"Ruby?" Dr. Pierce's voice snagged her as soon as she walked in, making her jump.

"Oh... um..." she stuttered. How had Pierce gotten back before her?

"Are you feeling better?"

"Uhh," Ruby said, her mind racing in circles. Maybe he'd taken a taxi back to school. But that still didn't explain why he was completely dry.

"Sterling said you weren't feeling well and went to the nurse's office."

"Oh... yeah." She had enough of her wits about her to grab at the cover story Sterling had so thoughtfully invented for her. "I just—"

"First day jitters, huh?" He smirked, baring a mouth full of weirdly straight teeth.

"Yeah. First day jitters," she lied.

12

"Be sure to walk Ruby right to the entrance," Alice said to Chloe, who was standing in the apartment entryway, nodding at the steady stream of instructions that had been pouring out of Alice for the last four minutes. "Maybe hold her hand, just to be sure."

Chloe nodded again, but sneaked a wink at Ruby that said she had no intention of holding her hand on the walk to school.

Ruby exhaled. That was something at least. Every morning for the last two weeks Alice had delivered her to the Sape entrance, fussing over her like she was a kindergartener while all the red-jacketed jerks stared. Being walked to school by Chloe would still be embarrassing—especially since all of Chloe's other clients were dogs—but at least she wouldn't rub invisible dirt off of Ruby's face with a spit-licked thumb in front of half the school.

"And make sure you're there to pick her up right at three o'clock," Alice continued. "At the Academy door. I don't want her wandering around looking for you. Be at least five minutes early, just in case. You have her phone number if there's a problem—"

"Okay," Ruby said, impatiently tugging her backpack straps.

Alice surveyed the entry, probably looking for more stupid things to worry about. "And see that she finishes this." Alice handed Chloe a clear plastic cup containing the green gooey smoothie that was Ruby's untouched breakfast. Slimy little lumps floated in it. Alice scraped her cuticles with her thumb. "You have your backpack?" she asked, even though the straps were clearly visible on Ruby's shoulders.

"I'm fine," Ruby said. "I just need you to sign something." Ruby fished out the Camp Ketchikan permission slip, then dug around in her backpack for the soccer papers.

Alice put on her reading glasses and frowned.

Ruby's stomach tightened. "Winston said that even the Truncs get to go."

Alice pressed her lips but signed the slip.

Ruby handed her the soccer permission slip.

"What's this?" Alice asked.

"It's for soccer."

"Soccer?" Alice sounded appalled.

"Yeah."

Alice took off her glasses with a sigh. "Ruby, soccer is dangerous. People can get concussions. Or worse."

Ruby stared at her. "I've never gotten hurt playing soccer."

"Doctors recommend that children avoid high-contact sports until their brains are more developed."

"How developed?" Ruby could barely believe she was having this conversation. Her brain was just fine.

"The brain finishes developing around age twenty-five."

"You don't want me to play soccer until I'm twenty-five?"

"We'll find you a safer sport," Alice said, handing back the flier. "Something indoors. Like ping pong. Or chess."

"Chess isn't a sport."

"One of the safest sports is swimming."

The last word hit Ruby like a punch in the gut, transforming her frustration into fear. Swimming? It hadn't occurred to her that people would swim in New York.

"The Academy has a good swim team."

The room spun and darkness edged Ruby's vision. She took a deep breath, forcing down the panic that was rising in her throat like bile. She yanked open the door, desperate to get outside.

"Your father was an excellent swimmer," Alice said.

"Well, good for him," Ruby called back from the elevator bank. Her heart didn't slow until she and Chloe were inside the elevator.

"You should have Miles talk to her," Chloe said. "He might be able to change her mind."

Ruby glared at the doors, shoving the unsigned permission slip back into her backpack. She wasn't going to ask Miles-the-thief for anything.

"So what's in this?" Chloe held the smoothie cup up to the light.

"I dunno. Like, weeds and stuff."

Chloe took a tentative sip. She immediately spit it out, spraying the interior of the elevator with dark green speckles. "Oh my gosh," she said. "It tastes like... like..."

"Seaweed and dandelions?"

Chloe nodded, her body convulsing from the aftershocks of the taste. "And rhubarb."

"I usually pour it down the toilet, but I didn't get a chance this morning."

"I feel sorry for your toilet." Chloe held the cup at arm's length as if it were radioactive. "So what do you eat for breakfast?" she asked as they stepped outside.

Ruby shrugged. "Nothing." As soon as they rounded the corner, Chloe dropped the cup into a trash can.

"C'mon," she said.

"Where are we going?"

"You'll see." They walked for several blocks before Chloe finally yanked open the door to a fast food restaurant.

Ruby had never been inside a restaurant like this before. It smelled amazing. Bright plastic tables lined the wall. A huge crowd of people were packed in front of the counter so tightly that Ruby couldn't even tell where one line ended and another began. "Do we have time for this?" she asked as her stomach rumbled.

Chloe consulted her watch. "We'll be okay." She stood on her tiptoes, looking over the crowd, but made no move to get into line. One of the cashiers smiled at her and she held up three fingers, then two. Ruby saw him nod, then say something to another worker.

A few seconds later, a younger kid came out from behind the counter carrying two white bags. "Here you go, Miss Chloe," he said.

"Thanks, Blake." Chloe returned his smile and handed him some cash.

"That's the coolest thing I've ever seen anyone do," Ruby said as they stepped out the door. "You're, like, the queen of that place."

Chloe snorted and handed her a little round package.

Ruby peeled the yellow wrapper off, revealing a biscuit

sandwich with a sausage patty and some egg inside. Just the smell made her mouth water.

"C'mon," Chloe said, eating as she walked. "Follow your queen."

Ruby scrambled after her. But she stopped short after taking a bite. "Whoa." It was the best thing she'd had since she'd left the island. Maybe since she'd been born. The way the fluffy, sweet biscuit mixed with the chewy, savory sausage and egg was somehow perfect.

Chloe smiled. "Right?"

"Why would anyone ever eat anything else?" Ruby said, spraying crumbs everywhere.

Chloe giggled.

Ruby laughed too, but stopped when it was clear she would snort the biscuit crumbs up her nose. Which would be a terrible waste.

"Okay, slow down." Chloe fished a little orange cup from the bag. "Wash it down with this."

Ruby sipped the orange juice. She hadn't thought the meal could get any better, but she was wrong. Just as she was draining the last drops from the weirdly small cup, she saw Dr. Pierce come out of a bodega half a block away, holding a steaming cup of coffee. Ruby ducked behind Chloe.

"What is it?" Chloe asked, licking the last crumbs off her fingers.

"That guy up there. He's one of my teachers."

Chloe squinted. "Dr. Pierce?"

"You *know* him?"

"He taught at the Academy when I was there."

"But Sterling told me he only started two years ago." Ruby's eyes tracked Pierce, watching him like prey.

"He came *back* two years ago. But he was here before. He left about nine years ago."

"Really?" The Lines crackled and brightened as Chloe spoke about Pierce, almost like they were trying to remember something. "He left the year I disappeared?"

"Yeah. The same week, actually. All the parents were mad because he left in the middle of the year and the Academy had to scramble to replace him. I'm surprised they brought him back."

"Huh." Ruby sucked on her hair. Nine years ago and two years ago. Nine and two, nine and two. In her mind, thread-thin Lines bounced around four points: nine years, two years, the Academy, and Steiner's shop, charting Pierce's movements through space and time. But four data points wasn't much. Ruby watched Pierce walk away, waiting for the Lines to slacken, but they didn't.

She finished the last bite just two blocks before they reached the Academy. Ruby checked the Lines, mapping the path that would avoid the most red jackets as she was accompanied to their entrance like a prisoner under guard. At least it was Chloe today instead of Alice. But still.

"You can make it from here on your own, right?" Chloe asked.

"Really?" A thrill ran down Ruby's spine.

Chloe nodded and smiled.

Ruby sprinted to the Trunc entrance before Chloe could change her mind.

———

"I'm telling you guys. It's the best restaurant in New York." Ruby raised her voice to be heard over the noise coming from the Sape side of the cafeteria. She took a bite of her cafeteria chicken, which wasn't bad, but it was no sausage biscuit with egg.

Winston, Harrison, and James made incredulous noises in her direction.

Ruby's eyes flicked to the hallway and back. Her fingers grazed the folded notebook page in her pocket where she had sketched out her mental map of Pierce's movements onto paper.

Suddenly a cluster of Sapes burst into laughter. Ruby looked and saw a group of red-blazered boys laughing at someone. Squinting, she saw that it was Winston's brother, Charlie, who sat red-faced and rigid. Something inside her crumbled. She knew that look. Their eyes met and she nodded in perfect understanding.

"McDonald's?" Winston said, dragging her attention back. "Like *McDonald's*, McDonald's?"

"Isn't there an ironic McDonald's in Brooklyn?" James asked.

"Just McDonald's. It's a few blocks down from my building," Ruby said, glancing at the hall again. Still no sign of Pierce.

"Hey." Charlie was suddenly hovering awkwardly behind Winston.

"Hey, Charlie," Ruby said, carefully ignoring his splotchy face and the fact that he was the first Sape she'd ever seen cross to the Trunc side of the cafeteria.

"Hey, I just, um... needed..." Charlie's fingers bunched and un-bunched the edge of his red blazer. "Something... from your locker."

"What?" Winston scowled, but Ruby elbowed him over and patted the bench next to her. A grateful sigh escaped

Charlie as he sat down. "He doesn't really need something from my locker," Winston grumbled.

"So what?" Ruby hissed back.

"Hey, Charlie," Harrison said. "How do *you* feel about McDonald's?"

Charlie's eyes bulged in panic. "You mean as a restaurant or as a symbol of capitalistic hegemonization of our vulnerable food culture?"

The Truncs, apparently assuming that Charlie was being ironic, erupted in appreciative laughter. "Nice one. 'Capitalistic hegemonization!'" Harrison wheezed.

Charlie blushed, his mouth turning up, obviously enjoying laughter that wasn't directed at him.

"Dude, you Sapes are hilarious," James laughed.

"Not really," Charlie said softly.

"What are you doing here?" Winston hissed to Charlie around Ruby's back.

"He's sitting," Ruby said. "You would want a break from those guys too." She nodded at the north end of the cafeteria where the group of large boys in red blazers laughed and tossed bits of food at each other.

"You trying out for soccer after school?" Harrison asked James, backhanding his friend's chest.

"Yeah," James said, turning to Ruby. "How about you?"

Ruby frowned, remembering the unsigned permission slip in her backpack. "Yeah, of course." She fished the permission slip out and uncrinkled it on the table. "Hey, I need a pen," she said to Winston.

Winston handed her one of the many writing utensils that he kept in every pocket on his person. But when he saw that she was about to sign her own permission slip, he tried to grab it back. "You can't do that! It's forgery."

"Stop it." Ruby pulled the pen away and then tapped

her teeth with it. "Does anyone know what Alice's signature looks like?"

"You're getting spit on my pen!" Winston huffed.

"Sign Miles's name," Charlie suggested. "He's a doctor. They have terrible handwriting." He scrawled something on a napkin that looked more like pointy scribbles than actual letters.

"That's perfect," Ruby said, sliding the paper to him. "Can you sign it?"

Charlie smiled triumphantly at Winston. "Sure. Happy to help," Charlie said.

Ruby pulled her phone out, holding it beneath the table as she texted Alice. *Can I stay after school for chess club?*

"You're not supposed to have phones at school," Winston whisper-yelled as he read the text over her shoulder. "Why don't you just ask her to come sign the slip for you?"

"Alice said I couldn't play soccer until I was twenty-five."

"Well, that is when the brain finishes develop—"

"She wants me to do swimming instead."

Winston's mouth shut. "Oh. Well, good luck then I guess." He leaned close to her ear to whisper, "Just, don't be *too* good at soccer, you know?"

Ruby nodded. Maybe she could pretend that the goal post was the target instead of the goal itself. Most of the time, anyway.

Just then Pierce passed, holding a white takeout bag. Ruby pulled the folded paper from her pocket. "12:24, lunch," she wrote, filling an empty square on her tracking chart. There were still more empty spaces than full ones. Tracking someone who spent most of his time in the Sape wing wasn't easy.

"What's that?" Charlie asked.

She glanced up the table. The other boys were engrossed in a conversation about soccer cleats. "I'm tracking Dr. Pierce," she whispered.

"Why?" Charlie asked.

Ruby looked at Charlie with his little neck poking out of his red rumpled blazer. Could she trust him? He was Winston's brother, but family didn't always mean what it should. She looked at Winston, her question clear on her face.

Winston's little eyes rolled with reluctant approval. "You can tell him," he sighed. "He doesn't have any friends to tell anyway."

Charlie glared at him.

Ruby hunched forward, checking again that no one else could hear. Charlie leaned in and so did Winston, even though he already knew about the chart. "Dr. Pierce has something of mine, and I'm going to get it back."

"What does he have?" Charlie asked.

"The Solomon Stone," Ruby said.

Charlie's hands stopped fidgeting and his eyes widened. "What? That's impossible."

Ruby flicked to her parents' wedding photo on her phone and showed it to him. "No, it's not."

Charlie's mouth fell open as he stared at the diamond dangling loosely from Emmeline's neck. "Holy gutterball," he whispered. "Your mom's necklace was the... how?"

"Some long story about the Romanovs. But it's the real thing. I saw it. And touched it."

Charlie screwed his eyes, as if trying to calculate the possibility of what she said.

"Miles had it in his safe at the apartment, but someone took it, then Ruby figured out it was in Steiner's store, and she saw Pierce there," Winston said impatiently, as if these were obvious facts.

Charlie's eyes rounded. "Seriously?" Ruby felt something warm in her chest. He believed her, just like Winston had. "How did they get it out of Miles's safe?"

Ruby squirmed against the tightness in her throat. "Probably an inside job."

"Shouldn't you call the police or something?" Charlie asked.

"That's what I said," Winston muttered.

"The police won't do anything," Ruby said.

"Why?" both boys asked.

"They're grownups. Grownups never listen to kids."

"Maybe a stranger broke into the house and took it," Charlie said.

"Those biometric safes are impossible to break into," Winston said.

"But maybe..." Charlie's eyes lit up. "Maybe someone vibrated their hand at the same frequency as the walls, then slipped their hand through the safe's wall."

Ruby cocked her head. "Huh?"

"You know," Charlie said. "Like how The Flash can do that thing?" He shook his hand to illustrate.

"Charlie, we've talked about this. No real person can do that," Winston said.

"What if there was, like, a vibrating drone—" Charlie said.

"I still don't get how tracking Dr. Pierce helps you get the Solomon Stone back," Winston interrupted.

Ruby pressed her lips together, staring at the chart. She wasn't totally sure either, but her hunter's instincts told her it was the right thing to do. "Chloe told me that Pierce taught at the Academy when she was a student, but then he left Suddenly nine years ago. Right after my parents disappeared." She spoke slowly, tracking the Lines which flickered between the paper chart and the map in her head, webbing out in their search for patterns. "After my grandfather locked the Solomon Stone in his safe."

Winston's eyes widened. "When Pierce came back two years ago, it was just eight days after your grandfather's funeral."

"Eight days? Really?" Ruby asked, the Lines thrumming faster now.

"Do you think that means something?" Charlie asked.

"I don't know. Maybe Pierce was hoping someone would open the safe after my grandfather died. I need to search his office."

Winston scowled. "That's way too dangerous."

"Not if I know exactly when he's gone." Ruby waved the paper.

"He teaches my Global Narratives class at 2:30," Charlie offered, pointing at a blank square.

"Thanks," Ruby said.

"Here, let me see that." Charlie pulled the paper over and started systematically filling in the blank squares, occasionally pausing and blinking as if flipping through imaginary files.

"Ruby." Winston's eyes were wide and pleading. "If Pierce *was* involved in stealing the Solomon Stone, he could be dangerous."

Ruby was about to scoff. Pierce was a balding, middle-aged, corduroy-clad history teacher. But then she remembered how he walked, confident but careful, with too many muscles moving beneath his tweedy jacket and suddenly Winston's words didn't sound so scoffable. "Well," she said as Charlie handed back the paper to her, almost completely filled in. "I'm dangerous too."

———

Ruby paced back and forth on the Academy steps, shoving her damp hair out of her eyes and scratching her legs. Putting her tights back on after she was sweaty from soccer practice had made them extra itchy. She checked the time on her phone. Chloe should be here any second. She hoped the cold air prickling against her face would help erase the signs of soccer practice. Ruby didn't know much about chess, but she didn't think people got sweaty playing it. She tried to look bored but her heart raced. Soccer had been amazing. Even the other girls, who were all Sapes, had been friendly.

"Did you get out early?" Chloe asked as she came up the Academy steps.

"No." Ruby slouched and turned away from Jane, a girl from soccer tryouts who was waving at her.

"Well?" Chloe asked, raising an eyebrow at the exchange. "How was chess club?"

Ruby shrugged. "It was okay, I guess."

"I can never keep the names of the pieces straight."

"Yeah." Ruby's throat tightened. Chess pieces had different names? This might be harder than she'd thought.

"Sorry soccer didn't work out." Chloe's voice was soft. "Alice is just scared."

"Of what?"

"You were gone for nine years. That doesn't just vanish overnight."

Ruby sighed. "So what, now I can never do anything just because—"

Chloe's phone buzzed and she pulled it out. Her face broke into a warm smile. "It's Miles."

Ruby scowled.

"He says Agamemnon is having a midlife crisis." Chloe laughed, showing the phone to Ruby. There was an admittedly adorable picture of Miles's dog looking longingly at a child-sized, cherry red Ferrari in the window of a toy store. Chloe texted back, speaking the words slowly as she typed. "He better... not... dump... me... for... a younger... dog walker."

"You know you can do way better than Miles, right?"

"What?" Chloe gave Ruby a distracted, baffled look. "Miles is nice, and smart, and it doesn't even matter that he's amazing or whatever because we're not—" her face flushed when she read Miles's response.

We would never.

Ruby frowned. It was bad enough that Miles had stolen Ruby's diamond. Now he was trying to steal Chloe. And he was using his innocent dog as bait.

13

"**R**uby!" Winston hissed.

"What?" Ruby froze midway through opening a drawer in Pierce's desk. Her heart thudded in her ears as she scanned the office, reading the Lines for the best hiding place. Definitely the corner closet.

"I don't think this is a good idea."

"Winston! Don't do that. I thought someone was coming." Ruby continued searching the drawers. Nothing.

"But what if someone *does* come?"

"They won't. I've been charting his movements for two weeks now."

"But someone could still—"

"You're supposed to be the lookout guy. Not the point-out-everything-that-could-go-wrong guy," Ruby said.

"What are we looking for, anyway?"

"I don't know yet. That's why I'm looking."

"We could get in so much trouble." Winston hopped between his feet like he had to go to the bathroom.

Ruby ignored him and opened a console cupboard beneath the window, sighing when she saw that it was mostly empty. She sucked her hair. There had to be something in the office.

"Someone's coming!" Winston sputtered.

"What?" Panic rose again in Ruby's throat. "For reals?"

"Yes!"

"Who?"

"Pierce and Octavius," he hissed.

"Gutterball." Ruby rushed for the closet, but stopped suddenly when she saw that the Lines were now veering away from it. Tracking the brightest Line, Ruby dove for the large console cupboard, yanking open the shutter-slatted door. She shoved the books and papers aside and squished herself onto the upper shelf, while Winston folded his small frame onto the lower shelf. He made a gasping whine as she hooked her finger into the round doorhold and slid it shut.

It wasn't dark in the console. The slatted door let in light and Ruby could see the office door open as Pierce came in, followed by Octavius.

"Steiner and Callahan will be here soon," Pierce said, tightening the blinds around his office windows so that no one could see in.

"Okay." Octavius's voice cracked.

A scraping, thump-like noise came from the closet. The Lines paused for a split second, as if standing at attention, then rushed toward the sound. Suddenly Ruby saw Steiner walking toward Pierce. Behind him, carrying a black velvet pouch that Ruby was certain contained her diamond, was Harlan.

The Lines swirled in a frenzied eddy around the pouch, but Ruby ignored them. *Harlan?* Where was Miles? How could Harlan have stolen the Solomon Stone from Miles's safe? Then the Lines in her head spun and she suddenly remembered her first day in New York. It was Harlan who had suggested showing Ruby the Solomon Stone. And afterwards, Harlan had put the diamond back in the safe. Only he must have switched it for the decoy. Ruby closed her eyes. How could she have missed that?

"Any problems?" Pierce asked.

"No," Harlan said.

Ruby's mind raced. Where had they come from? The closet had been empty a few minutes ago.

Harlan placed the velvet sack on a table in front of Octavius, gingerly loosening the pouch strings and sliding the Solomon Stone onto the tabletop.

The Lines pulled free from Ruby, disappearing into the Solomon Stone, only to burst out again in a firework of brilliant fibers. Several strands connected to Ruby, and her hand rose to the console door, like some Line-strung marionette. It took some effort to pull it back to her side.

Octavius, oblivious to the frenzied web of Lines surrounding him, wiped his hands with an antiseptic wipe.

"No need to be nervous," Pierce said. "People have been using the Solomon Stone to Render for thousands of years."

"It's just that I've only read accounts of Levants Rendering," Octavius said.

"Levants have their Lines—they don't need the Solomon Stone. It's the Sapes who need help," Harlan said.

"Help? From who? We already run everything," Octavius said.

Harlan scoffed. "We *used* to run everything. Do you know how many Sapes were elected to the first session of Congress in 1789?"

"Sixty-eight."

"That's right. Eighty-four percent of the members. Today, it's only thirteen percent. Forty years ago, almost every CEO in the country was a Sape. Now it's less than ten percent. Our influence is plummeting. If we don't evolve, Sapience will become irrelevant in ten years." Harlan sounded fervent.

"But how could having perfect recall be irrelevant?" Octavius was obviously skeptical, but his tone was polite.

Harlan made a frustrated grunting sound. "We spend years in school training our minds to organize and catalogue vast amounts of information. But now, any idiot with a smart phone can instantly access as much data as you or I could accumulate in a lifetime, and they don't have to worry about storing it in their heads."

Ruby sucked on her hair, picturing a huge mess of facts sloshing around in Winston's head. No wonder he always looked a little lost.

"Millions of people wear diamonds every day," Pierce whispered conspiratorially. "Senators, presidents, CEOs, spies. Imagine being able to access all that information with just a handshake. Once you learn to Render, you'll be able to do whatever you want; have whatever you want; be whatever you want." Pierce's voice was silky, but Ruby cringed at the deceit she heard beneath it.

Octavius nodded, still scrubbing his hands with the wipe.

Steiner finished whatever he had been doing at the desk and inspected Octavius's hands without touching them. Nodding, Steiner pulled on a pair of tight black gloves and produced a small diamond pendant. "It's vital to keep the carbon sources simple," he said. "Since it was mined, this diamond has been handled only by people wearing special inorganic gloves." He wiggled his own gloved fingers.

Octavius gulped and nodded.

Ruby watched as the Lines nervously raced between

the Solomon Stone and the pendant, crackling with anticipation.

"It has touched living carbon just once. My niece wore it for just fifteen minutes this weekend, at her birthday party, so the information on it should be pleasant." Steiner placed the pendant next to the Solomon Stone and eyed Octavius sternly. "Interference from life forms other than you and the Rendered subject could be—"

"Frustrating," Pierce cut in.

Steiner said nothing, but Ruby could tell from his pursed lips that "frustrating" was not the right word.

"Once you have contact with both diamonds, be sure to verbalize what you see," Harlan said to Octavius.

Octavius was breathing hard, his chest trembling as it rose and fell.

"You have to touch both diamonds simultaneously, like you're completing an electric circuit," Pierce said, holding two fists in front of himself to demonstrate.

Ruby shivered. There was something cold and hard about Pierce that made it easier to imagine that Winston was right about him being dangerous.

"Right." Octavius said, slowly extending his left hand over the Solomon Stone and his right hand over the pendant.

Beneath Ruby, Winston shifted and the shelf creaked. Pierce's head ticked toward them, but he didn't turn. Ruby lay completely still and waited, silently begging Winston to do the same. She didn't want to imagine what would happen to them if they got caught.

Octavius took several shallow breaths, grabbing a diamond with each hand. A sharp pang shot through Ruby's temple and there was a buzzing, ringing sound. She covered her mouth to stifle the cry that was brimming in her throat.

One word occupied her whole mind: *Mine*. She gritted her teeth and concentrated on holding still.

Several thin Lines shot between Octavius's closed fists, throbbing with an energy Ruby had never seen. Octavius's face flushed and his eyes were closed tight in a contorted wince. "I see... I see," he said through puffed cheeks.

Steiner, Harlan, and Pierce leaned in.

Ruby squinted against the intensity of the energy running between Octavius's hands.

"A table and faces. Everyone's holding up drinks and laughing and singing Happy Birthday." The words flowed out of Octavius's mouth, but they seemed detached from him, as if he was a speaker playing a recording. "There are books everywhere. I wish for Ethan Holloway to be in my Language Arts class next semester, even though I'm too old to believe in wishes. I blow out the candles." Octavius exhaled as if he were blowing out candles.

An excited look passed among the three men.

Octavius's left hand began to tremble and Ruby saw that the Lines running between his hands looked lopsided, as if more were flowing into his left hand than were coming out of his right. "Mom gives me a blue box with an orange ribbon," he continued in a strange, high voice. "Some woman I don't even know is talking about oysters and someone else is arguing with her." Octavius winced. "Oysters? Seriously? Why can't I have my friends at my own party? It's always Mom and Dad's friends."

He clenched his eyes tighter and Ruby saw that his arms were shaking and his left shoulder twitched in time with the pulsing Lines, as if he were getting shocked repeatedly. The Lines buzzed and crackled, and Ruby could feel their agitation. Something was wrong. She felt like the buzzing would solidify inside her, take over her limbs, and force her to grab the diamond from Octavius. Tears of frustration ran down her cheeks as her muscles cramped from the effort of holding still.

"They're all talking about it." Octavius's voice strained. "Best oysters are in Maine... no, Prince Edward Island... no, Japan—Shut up! Shut up! Shut up! No!" He convulsed once and his eyes slid up so that only the whites were visible.

Harlan lurched toward Octavius but Pierce held him back. "You'll get pulled into it," Pierce hissed.

Then Octavius screeched in pain and collapsed onto the floor. His body jerked and twitched for several seconds. Then he finally stilled, his face lolling toward the console where Ruby and Winston were hidden, his mouth open and his eyes half shut. His listless hands relaxed and opened, releasing the two diamonds onto the floor.

14

For a heartbeat, no one moved. Ruby could almost smell the panic coming from Winston, but he didn't make a sound. Ruby stared at Octavius's lifeless form through the space between the console doors, willing him to get up, but he didn't.

Pierce, Harlan, and Steiner crouched around Octavius. Steiner's gloved hands fluttered between Octavius's neck and wrist, looking for a pulse, as his lips muttered nonsensical syllables, unable to find words.

Harlan's wide eyes stared blankly at the boy.

Both men looked to Pierce, who snaked his hand to Octavius's wrist. "He's alive," Pierce said calmly.

Ruby's lungs loosened.

Steiner slackened, almost leaning against Pierce in relief. "Okay. We should call—"

"Put it away," Pierce ordered.

Steiner looked around, confused, until he saw the Solomon Stone. With shaking gloved hands he eased it back into the velvet bag and handed it to Harlan.

Ruby felt the Lines slip away from the diamond and reattach to her. They resumed their normal behavior, though they still seemed agitated by proximity to the Solomon Stone.

Steiner put the small diamond pendant into a smaller pouch and stood, removing his gloves and stealing a glance at Octavius's prone figure. "Well, that was—"

"It worked," Harlan said, inspecting Octavius's face and hands. He rubbed his thumb against something on Octavius's palm and winced. "Right?"

Pierce grinned at Harlan across his student's unconscious body. "Yes."

"I can't believe it," Harlan said as they both stood. His face was flushed and his eyes danced with excitement. "It actually worked. Exactly like we'd predicted."

"An unmitigated success," Pierce agreed.

"The boy is lying unconscious on the floor," Steiner said slowly, apparently confused.

Pierce waved a hand. "Comas do happen sometimes with non-Levants."

Harlan grimaced. "If we had a Levant—"

"We don't," Pierce said, cutting Harlan off with a shadowed look full of some shared secret menace that made goosebumps erupt on Ruby's arm. There was a hard glint in his eye that reminded Ruby of a bull about to charge.

"So, he's in a coma?" Steiner asked.

"We need to tweak a few variables, obviously," Harlan said, breaking Pierce's intense gaze. "But the thing works." Harlan frowned at Octavius. "We should go, before..." He looked at Steiner, then at the closet.

Steiner straightened, obviously reluctant to leave Octavius.

"I'll handle this," Pierce said, his voice infused with an

experienced confidence that made Ruby wonder how many unconscious bodies he'd dealt with.

Nodding, Harlan led Steiner into the closet and closed the door. Ruby squinted after them. She couldn't see anything, but the Lines lingered strangely around the closet door until Ruby heard a scraping bump. Then the Lines slackened and Ruby knew that Steiner, Harlan, and the Solomon Stone were gone. Every muscle in her body strained as she resisted a desperate urge to follow after her diamond.

"Nurse Cardon?" Pierce said into his phone. His voice sounded worried, but his face showed no emotion as he idly inspected one of his fingernails. "There's been an accident with a student. In my office. You'll need the gurney." Pierce hung up and lazily observed Octavius. He lifted the boy's eyelids, shined a light into his eyes, checked his pulse, felt behind his neck, and checked Octavius's palm.

A minute later, the door flew open and Ruby heard the screeching of wheels against polished marble. Nurse Cardon, the burly man who handled student illnesses in the office, skidded in behind a beige gurney. "What happened?" he barked, checking Octavius's vitals.

Pierce instantly assumed a concerned stance, hunching over Octavius. "I don't know. He just collapsed."

Ruby's stomach churned. Why was Pierce so good at lying?

"Help me lift him," Nurse Cardon said.

Both men heaved and grunted as they maneuvered Octavius's body onto the gurney.

"Take this end," Nurse Cardon said. He was simultaneously holding open the door, dialing his phone, and pushing the gurney. "Hello? 911?" Ruby heard him say as he and

Pierce disappeared down the hallway, the door swinging slowly shut behind them.

"Ruby!" Winston gasped.

"Shhhh," she said, listening. The room was silent. A minute passed and the motion-sensor lights switched off. She pushed open the cupboard and tumbled out, unable to stand on her prickling feet.

"Did you... What just happened?" Winston spluttered.

"I don't know." Ruby was already at the closet. This time she studied the walls carefully. Nothing. No panels or false shelves. But the Lines were swirling strangely on the floor. Ruby bent down and found a curving line contrasted against the angular floorboards. A hatch.

"It was like..." Winston stopped and squinted. "Like he was re-living that girl's birthday. Was he Rendering?"

"That's what it sounded like." Ruby traced the Line until she found a fingerhold. She hefted up the heavy hinged lid, revealing a dark, round hole. Ruby shined her phone's flashlight into the darkness, revealing a smooth cement tunnel reaching straight down, with skinny metal rungs fastened to the wall.

"Whoa," Winston breathed.

Ruby dipped her arm into it. The air was cool and the Lines dove past, rushing southward. She lowered herself onto the ladder. "C'mon."

"What? Ruby, no."

"They have my diamond." She was halfway down the ladder when she heard the office door open.

Winston made a squeaking noise and clambered down after her, closing the hatch behind him.

When they reached the bottom, they stood in the darkness, waiting and listening. Nothing. Winston trembled beside her.

"It's okay," she said, tapping the light on her phone. They were in a tunnel, narrow and long with tiled walls and a cement floor.

"Do you think Octavius is going to be okay?" Winston whispered.

Ruby shivered as she remembered Nurse Cardon's face. "No."

"What?" Panic edged Winston's voice.

"You saw him." She wasn't going to lie to Winston, even to make him feel better. She squinted, looking as far into the darkness as she could. "C'mon," she said, snatching Winston's hand and following the Lines.

The air was damp in her nose, even though the paved floor was dry. Suddenly the walls and floor started to shake as a rumbling sound filled the tunnel. Ruby froze with terror, clinging to Winston's arm and praying that the tunnel wouldn't collapse on top of them.

"It's just the subway," Winston whispered.

"Oh, yeah." Ruby shook her head sheepishly as the noise subsided. The subway. She'd felt the same rumble beneath the sidewalk hundreds of times. "Let's go."

"Wait." Winton took in the dingy tiles and wet darkness around them. "Do you know where we are?" he asked.

"We're under Fifth Avenue."

Winston's eyes widened owlishly in the dim light. "Your Lines work down here?"

"Of course."

"Is Steiner or Harlan nearby?" Winston whispered.

Ruby stilled, checking again for his sake. The Lines stretched out straight in both directions, finding nothing but empty space. "No, but they definitely came this way. So come on." Ruby could feel Winston's hand, sweaty and cold in hers.

Winston gulped. "But we don't know where this tunnel goes."

Ruby rolled her eyes. She could feel the Lines tugging. Their urgency seeped into her voice. "We can't go back to Pierce's office anyway. Someone's there."

Winston shuffled forward. "Fine."

"You know I won't get lost."

"That doesn't mean we won't get into trouble."

"We're already in trouble for missing class. Might as well make it count." Ruby started walking, slower than she wanted, for Winston's sake. She tracked the streets above them in her head and fought the urge to run. She held Winston's hand, shining her phone light for him.

"So I guess it was Harlan who stole the diamond?" Winston said eventually.

Ruby sucked on a strand of hair. "Yeah. I guess so."

"That sucks. I was hoping it was The Flash."

Ruby snorted, the joke catching her off guard.

"Kind of messed up that your own uncle robbed you."

"Yeah." Ruby sniffed. "Messed up" was an understatement. It was cold, hard betrayal. "Worst 'fun uncle' ever." A shiver went down her spine when she remembered how Harlan had looked, prowling in front of the maze exit, waiting for her. "You don't think he's, like, an Azarian, do you?"

"Who, Harlan? No," said Winston.

Something loosened in Ruby's chest. Apparently she was relieved that her uncle was just a thief and not an operative for an international crime conglomerate. "You're sure?"

"Your family doesn't have ties to the Azarians. Harlan's lived here his whole life," Winston said, scratching his nose. "Besides, he lived in the same building as your mom for five years and never realized that she was a Levant. An Azarian would've figured that out."

"So, Harlan stole the Solomon Stone so that he and Pierce could learn how to Render?" Ruby asked.

Winston puffed out a breath. "Yeah. I guess it's good that they're not Azarians. But they're still—I mean, they used Octavius like a guinea pig."

"Yeah." Ruby tried to push back the image of Harlan's face staring indifferently at the kid he'd just put into a coma. Then the tunnel turned sharply to the right at Forty-seventh Street, veering straight into the Diamond District. It widened considerably, stretching to match the size of the street above them.

"Where are we?" Winston asked.

"Forty-seventh Street."

"These must be the Rockefeller tunnels." Winston inspected one of the vault-like doors that lined the wall. "There's this rumor that when John D. Rockefeller built Rockefeller Center, he added secret tunnels so that merchants could move diamonds without worrying about robberies. I bet armored trucks can drive right through here."

"Why is there a tunnel to the Academy?" Ruby tried to imagine a millionaire strolling through the dank passageway they'd just left.

"Rockefeller's daughter was headmistress of the Academy. He wanted to be able to visit her without dealing with crowded streets or bad weather."

"If I was a millionaire, I'd dig a tunnel from our building to McDonald's," Ruby said, laughing, but she stopped suddenly at another padded, steel-reinforced door. "This is Steiner's shop." The door had a large spindly wheel in the middle, just like bank vaults in the movies. Ruby drew close to inspect. The Lines weaved in and out of the spokes, as if trying to figure out exactly how it had been turned less than an hour ago. Ruby grabbed one of the handles and spun the wheel.

"Ruby!" Winston hissed, pulling her back from the door.

"What—" Ruby spluttered.

"Look." Winston pointed to a series of very technical-looking devices attached to the right-hand side. She recognized one as a biometric reader.

"Urgh," Ruby grunted, tightening her lips against this unwelcome truth. Of course. This wasn't the 1800s. This door would be riddled with security. She pulled out her pocketknife and ran it along the hinged edge, looking for a place to pry something apart.

"Ruby!" Winston's whisper was saturated with exasperation. "What if they hear you?"

"They stole my diamond." She squinted at the locks. "We'll just have to break in from the street."

"*Just*? Ruby, you can't *just* break into a jewelry store and steal an enormous diamond," Winston said. "This is the Diamond District. There's more security on this street than at the White House."

"But they stole my diamond," she repeated the words like a mantra.

"Ruby, even if you could get inside, there would just be more security. Sensors and cameras and silent alarms that automatically call the police. You could end up in jail. Or worse."

Ruby realized he was right. "But they stole my diamond," she still said softly.

It was Winston who had to slow his pace for Ruby as she dragged herself away from the secure door to Steiner's shop. Her feet and mind felt thick and slow as she walked to the west end of the passageway where they found a door, another tunnel, more doors, and finally stairs to the street. Ruby barely noticed, following the Lines in a daze until she was suddenly blinking against the bright sun on the corner of Forty-eighth Street and Sixth Avenue.

Winston smiled and breathed deeply. "Feels good to be above ground." He looked at Ruby with concern when she didn't respond.

She stared south, trance-like, as if she could see through the block of buildings standing between them and the Diamond District.

Winston sighed. "Ruby, maybe you should just let it go."

"Let what go?"

"The diamond." Her neck slowly pivoted toward him and he swallowed. "It's too dangerous to steal it back."

"What's the point of being a Levant if you can't get your own property back?"

"Ruby, you know you're more important than that diamond, right?"

"Then how come I was dumped on some island and the diamond was locked away in a safe?"

He didn't have any response.

15

Ruby stared at the fractions until they looked blurry. She had been doing homework for seventeen minutes and her brain hurt. Elena's knife thunked steadily against the cutting board as she chopped vegetables for dinner.

Ruby glanced across the table, where Alice seemed engrossed in a small pile of papers. Quietly, Ruby tugged out the notebook page with the map she had been making of the Diamond District. Winston and Charlie had helped supply the names of each shop, along with a brief history of every building. She sucked on her hair, studying the small rectangle that was Steiner's shop. Her Lines ran laps around it, but they offered no suggestions for how to get in.

Ruby rubbed her toes against her ankle where a blister had formed from wearing Jane's old soccer cleats. She thought again about telling Alice and asking for a new pair. But then Ruby remembered Alice's face when she'd seen the permission slip.

"Can I borrow your laptop?" Ruby asked. "Mine's out of battery."

"It's on my desk," Alice said.

Ruby retrieved the laptop and opened it, carefully positioning the screen out of Alice's sightline. She pulled up the Amazon homepage.

The front door opened. "Hello?" Harlan called from the entry.

Ruby's stomach tightened. Harlan. She hadn't seen her un-fun uncle since he'd put Octavius into a coma last week. She tucked her map inside her notebook.

"Hi Mom," Harlan said as he entered the kitchen and kissed Alice's cheek. "Hi Ruby."

A tremor of disgust and terror convulsed through Ruby, making the hairs on her neck prickle in alarm. She didn't answer, unable to shake the image of Harlan smiling excitedly over Octavius's unconscious body.

"Are you staying for dinner?" Alice asked, folding her hand over Harlan's.

"No. Miles just needs me to sign something. Is he in the office?"

Ruby drummed her fingers on the laptop, willing Harlan to leave. *Yes, go away to the office.* But he sat next to Alice instead, pulling over a bowl with some remnants of nuts in it and started shelling them.

Elena made a *tsking* sound and placed a frosted sugar cookie and a glass of milk in front of him.

Ruby's lips tightened. Those were her favorite cookies. Elena made them especially for her with extra frosting and sprinkles. Was there anything of hers he wouldn't steal? She dug her phone and earbuds from her backpack and shoved them into her ears, drowning out her uncle's voice with whatever music popped up first on her playlist.

There were at least thirty different kinds of cleats. Ruby scrolled through them, trying to decide which ones to buy.

She selected an expensive fluorescent pink pair and put them in Alice's shopping cart. Then she searched for soccer socks. She picked a pair of black socks and a pair of fluorescent orange ones, then checked out. A smile tugged at her mouth as Amazon automatically charged Alice's credit card.

"Ruby."

Ruby looked up to meet Alice's intense gaze.

"Huh? Sorry." Ruby popped out her earbuds and tried not to look at Harlan, who was already on his second cookie.

Alice's fingers were tensed like a claw around her shiny black phone. Elena was nowhere to be seen. A tingle of anxiety ran down Ruby's spine.

"Do you know who that was on the phone?" Alice's voice was calm but tight.

Ruby shook her head.

"That was Mrs. Linklater." Alice paused as if that should mean something to Ruby. "She's the president of the Academy girls' soccer booster association."

Ruby closed her eyes as a heavy lump of dread formed in her throat.

"She wanted to know if I would host a pre-game dinner for the soccer team. The team that my granddaughter is apparently a member of."

Ruby braced herself. This was going to be bad.

"I told her she must be mistaken, because you're not on the soccer team. But she said that you have been attending practice every day for the last three weeks." Alice's eyes were locked fast on Ruby's. "Is that true?"

"Yes," Ruby said in a small voice.

Annoyingly, Harlan continued to enjoy his cookie.

Alice's eyes tightened. "You told me you'd joined the chess club."

Ruby shook her head.

"So you've been lying to me?"

Ruby nodded.

"And playing soccer?"

Ruby nodded again.

"Even after I specifically forbade you."

Ruby flinched. *Forbade?*

"Soccer is dangerous." Alice's voice climbed as she spoke and was now uncharacteristically loud. "You could've gotten hurt."

Miles strolled in, looking curious, and selected an apple from the bowl on the counter. Then he started rubbing his shoulders back and forth across the doorframe, like a big dumb horse with an unreachable itch.

"You've betrayed my trust," Alice said.

Ruby snorted. "Trust? You don't trust me. I can't even go outside by myself."

"I'm afraid I'll have to ground you."

"What?" Ruby and Harlan said at the same time.

Ruby glared at him before turning back to Alice. "You're grounding me? For playing soccer? That's not fair."

"No more soccer. No more anything for..." Alice paused for a millisecond, and Ruby could feel her whole life hanging in the balance. "For six weeks."

"Six weeks?" Tears burned in Ruby's eyes, as she pulled hot, angry breath through her nostrils. "I wish I were back on Pan'wei," she yelled. "At least there I wasn't a prisoner!"

Alice flinched as if Ruby had struck her. Then her phone pinged and she flipped it over. Her face reddened as she stared at it. "Your Amazon order of girls' soccer cleats has been shipped?" she read aloud, then stared at Ruby.

"Gutterball," Ruby whispered.

"You ordered cleats? On my account?" Alice's astonishment eclipsed her anger, which was saying something.

"I have blisters," Ruby whimpered, pulling off her sock and showing Alice her swollen red foot. Maybe sympathy would work.

"I... I don't even..." Alice stuttered, looking at Ruby's foot and then at her two sons in turn.

"I don't understand." Miles's voice rose quietly from the corner. "How did you get on the team?"

"I tried out. I'm really good," Ruby said.

"You have to have permission from a guardian. And clearance from a doctor," Miles said.

Ruby pressed her lips together tight as a flush spread across her face.

"I signed your name on the slips," she lied, not wanting to get Charlie in trouble too.

"Ruby," Harlan chided. "That's dishonest. And illegal."

Ruby glared at him. She was not about to be lectured by a thief.

"Ruby!" Alice sounded scandalized. "That's it. I'm grounding you from Camp Ketchikan too."

"What? No!" Ruby said. Stupid Miles bringing up the stupid permission slips.

Miles, apparently satisfied with the damage he had done, put his phone to his ear.

"Whoa. You can't keep her home from Camp Ketchikan," Harlan said. "It's tradition."

"She secretly joined the soccer team, lied about it for three weeks, forged signatures on the permission slips, and then ordered herself new cleats without permission." Alice ticked off the offenses on her fingers.

"Alice, please," Ruby pleaded. "You can't keep me home from Ketchikan. Please. Everyone is going. Even Winston. It's the only cool thing they let the Truncs do."

Alice's eyes softened but her mouth remained tight.

Mortifying tears streamed down Ruby's cheeks, but she couldn't stop them. "I'm sorry. I thought you would change your mind and I didn't want to miss tryouts. I didn't know it was a big deal."

Alice winced. She looked like she might cry too. "Camp is too dangerous, and far away—"

"You could come," Ruby said.

Alice and Harlan gaped in surprise. Then Harlan laughed.

"You could," Ruby said. "Then you wouldn't have to worry about me. You could be a counselor or something. Sterling's going as one."

"You could wear khakis and a polo shirt," Harlan huffed between laughs. "Braid your hair, maybe."

Alice looked as if she were lost in her own kitchen. "I... I can't go as a counselor," she fumbled, pushing three fingers against her forehead.

"Maybe you could get a whistle." Harlan's eyes were closed, he was laughing so hard.

"That's enough, Harlan," Alice said.

He stopped laughing and straightened. Then he full-on winked at Ruby, as if they were friends sharing an inside joke instead of a thief and his victim. "C'mon, Mom. We've all been to Ketchikan. Even you went when you were a kid."

"Ruby's different," Alice said.

"Why?" Ruby asked. "Because I'm a Trunc? Because my mom was UnSighted?"

"No!" Alice answered. But she didn't seem to be able to find any follow-up words. She stood and started pacing as if she were trapped by the countertops.

Ruby sensed that Alice was close to caving.

"We just got her back," Alice said to Harlan in a small voice. "I can't—"

"Ruby." Miles pocketed his phone as he returned to the kitchen.

"What?"

Miles sat in the chair beside her. "I think Alice is right about soccer. Not because it's dangerous, but because you lied. If you had just come and talked to us about it..."

Ruby rolled her eyes. She *had* talked to Alice about it.

He reached for her foot but she yanked it back. "What are you doing?"

"Your blisters could get infected."

Ruby winced. Infection sounded bad. And they did hurt like crazy. Reluctantly she put her foot on Miles's chair, hoping they still stank from soccer practice.

Miles pulled out some bandages and ointment from the cupboard next to him. "As for Ketchikan..." he said, carefully examining and bandaging the worst blister.

Alice's shoulders stiffened.

"I just talked to Anton Banduk, the camp director. He said I could come up as one of the camp doctors."

Ruby blinked. "What?"

Alice turned and stared at him too. "What about your surgery schedule? Ketchikan is next week."

"Amelia will cover for me. And Jim can reschedule some of my appointments. If I went up, would you be comfortable sending Ruby?"

Not that the field was very competitive, but, at that moment, Miles was Ruby's favorite uncle.

Alice straightened her shoulders and looked at Miles with grateful relief. "Yes," she relented.

16

—————

At Camp Ketchikan, the Truncs, Sapes, and Provs divided into separate cabins, mess halls, and even firepits. But every day there was one school-wide wilderness survival challenge. And every day the challenge was won by a team of smug Sapes.

Ruby had signed up for the first two challenges, but had had to drop out when she learned that they involved orienteering, and that "orienteering" was a fancy word for not getting lost. Pretending to lose to Sapes would be harder than standing on the sidelines and watching them win.

But day three was fire building, and Ruby signed up again, adding Winston's and James's names too, since the challenge required teams of three. But six minutes into the challenge, she was re-thinking her choice of teammates.

"This doesn't look right," James said, scuttling around as if he were trying to ignite the fire with the friction of his shoes alone.

"What doesn't look right?" Winston asked, frowning at Ruby's arrangement of steel wool and kindling.

"I don't know. Everyone else's looks different."

"So what?" Ruby slid her pocketknife down a stick, curling thin strips along its length. Miles stood on the edge of the clearing, chatting with another adult. He was too far away to recognize his knife, but Ruby hunched a protective shoulder over it anyway.

"Do you think we could get into Steiner's store if we somehow turned off the power to the whole block?" Ruby murmured to Winston softly, trying to recall all the robberies she'd seen in movies. "Then the security cameras would be down, along with the digital locks and everything else."

"It wouldn't work," Winston whispered, scanning the other twelve fire-building teams, all in red Sape T-shirts. "There's probably a backup analog system."

"Do we need more sticks?" James interrupted. "The other teams have more sticks. We never should've tried to compete against Sapes."

"It's fire building," Ruby said. "Their super memories won't help them."

"I dunno." James squinted at the other teams' intricate configurations of sticks. Ruby looked too and wondered if they had actually memorized some fire-building technique from a book.

All the Truncs were bunched a few yards away, anxiously watching every move Ruby made.

James gnawed the corner of his lip. "I told you, Truncs never compete in these events."

"And I told *you* that we're not going to just sit back and let those walking Wikipedias take everything."

"But if we lose—" James said.

"We won't lose." She whittled faster, determined to make the sentence true. "I've done this a thousand times. Just go get me more sticks like this one." They had plenty of wood, but James's constant fretting was making it hard to plan a diamond heist.

"The store is locked down too tight," she said to Winston when James was out of earshot. "We have to wait until it's out of the store, then take it." She carefully arranged the strands of steel wool around their kindling.

"But there's no way to know the next time they take it out."

Ruby frowned and struck the flint, showering sparks onto the nest of steel wool. It started to smolder and a fat beetle scurried away from the smoke, a thin tendril of a Line following it. Ruby gasped and grabbed Winston's arm, almost knocking him off balance. "What if we flushed them out?" she said.

"Huh?"

"If there was like... a fire in Steiner's store, he'd take out the Solomon Stone and run with it, right?" Ruby carefully blew onto the sparse cluster of sparks as she consulted the complicated map of the Diamond District that she kept in her head, the one that was overlaid with all of Winston's historical data and everything she knew about Steiner's and Pierce's schedules. The Lines no longer circled Steiner's shop in useless agitation. They were sharp and alert.

"You mean arson?"

"No. Not a real fire. Something *like* a fire."

"So, like a... metaphorical fire?" Winston sounded baffled.

"A 'metaphorical fire'?" James interrupted, startling Ruby as he suddenly crouched beside her. "We need an *actual* fire to cook an *actual* egg."

"I know. Quit bugging me and go..." Ruby tried to think of a task she could give him that would get him out of the way. "Go get us a better pan."

James frowned and then left, nervously tapping his leg and scanning the other teams.

Ruby carefully poked one of her feathered kindling sticks into the center of the pile so its shaved edges would catch the flames and carry them to the thicker part of the stick.

"We just need something to scare him out of the store with the diamond," she said to Winston. "Maybe we could, like, pretend to break in—"

Winston rubbed his forehead, smearing grime across it. "Like a 'metaphorical robbery'? I doubt the police will see the difference."

"Hmm." Ruby sucked her hair as she blew the baby flames, coaxing them further up the sticks. There must be some way to flush Steiner out.

"You guys, you guys!" James ran up, panting and swinging the new pan. "No one else has flames. We're winning!" he whisper-shouted as he shoved the pan over the fire. Excited murmurs rippled through the Trunc spectators.

Ruby smiled as she fanned the fire and Winston cracked the egg into the pan.

James bounced back and forth on the balls of his feet, shaking the pan as Winston tried to stir the egg.

"You've got it! You've got it!" Harrison yelled from the sidelines.

"Go! Go! Go!" the other Truncs cheered.

Ruby focused on the congealing golden glob in their pan. Then her hand shot up. "Finished!" she yelled.

All the Sape teams turned and glared in shocked disbelief.

Ruby smiled and shrugged. Did they really think they would always win everything?

Miss Mason, a woman who looked like she'd spent about as much time outdoors as a pet goldfish, came over to inspect. She took a miniscule bite of the egg and nodded, astonished.

Cheers erupted from the Truncs as an angry murmur coursed through the Sapes.

"That's not fair," an older Sape girl said. "They didn't use any of the standard fire-building matrices."

Ruby stared at her. Fire-building matrices?

Miss Mason nodded, uncertain, and scanned the other adult spectators, all of whom were Sapes. An angry knot roiled in Ruby's stomach and her hands clenched into fists. Everyone looked upset except the pocket of Truncs gathered around Ruby's fire.

"Look at that mess!" Another Sape yelled. "It's just a burning pile of sticks!"

"You know that's what a 'fire' is, right?" Ruby said.

"She's right," Miles said from behind Miss Mason, his voice calm and authoritative.

Miss Mason looked at him in complete confusion. "But... the matrices—"

"The rules just say no matches," Miles said.

Miss Mason cleared her throat. "Team Thirteen wins," she said in a wobbly voice, as if it were a question. She passed Ruby some kind of certificate, but it didn't matter. The look of defeat on the Sapes around her was all the proof of victory Ruby needed.

"Bunch up so I can get a picture," Harrison said, extending his phone out with his right arm.

Ruby felt James's, Harrison's, and Winston's arms wrap around her shoulders. Most of the Truncs crowded in behind and Winston raised his free hand in a skinny victory fist.

"I can't wait for the water races!" Harrison said as he snapped the picture.

Ruby's stomach lurched. "What?"

"Today's Water Day at the lake," he said.

"I bet you can swim circles around everyone else," James said.

"Um—" Ruby's throat was tight and dry.

"Yeah," someone said. "She practically grew up in the ocean."

Ruby felt like throwing up.

Winston squeezed her shoulder. "Don't worry," he whispered.

Ruby shoved her shaking hands into her pockets. The air felt thick and black spots danced at the borders of her vision. *Not here, not here,* she told herself.

Suddenly Winston started running across the field. "Race you to the mess hall," he yelled over his shoulder.

Ruby stared at him, confused. Winston never voluntarily ran anywhere.

"Hey!" James and Harrison tore after him.

Ruby followed too, even though she felt like curling up in a ball. As she was passing Winston, his leg swept out, tripping Ruby and knocking her flat on the ground.

"Ruby!" he yelled, crouching beside her. "Are you okay?"

"What the—" Ruby sputtered, pushing him away. "You tripped me!"

"Play along," he whispered. He sucked in a loud breath and said loudly, "Oooh, that ankle looks bad. Does it hurt?"

"What? No." Ruby started to stand, but Winston pushed her shoulders down.

"Does... it... hurt?" he said slowly, between gritted teeth, giving her a look like she was supposed to know what he was talking about. Harrison and James had circled back and were staring at her, and a crowd of other kids was forming behind them.

"Umm," she said, uncertain.

"I hope it isn't *sprained*," Winston said tightly. "Then you'd have to *miss Water Day*."

Ruby finally caught on. "Oh. Yeah," she said. "Ouch!"

"I'll take you to the First Aid hut." Winston helped her to her feet.

Ruby nodded, pretending to scowl at him. "Thanks a lot," she said, faking sarcasm.

He smiled. "You're welcome," he said under his breath.

———

RUBY'S TOES curled on the grass at the edge of the dock. Dark lake water sloshed beneath the wooden slats, devouring her Lines and drowning out all other sounds. Dozens of kids swarmed around, jumping in and out of the water like seals. Eliza, a Sape from Ruby's former soccer team, dove in gracefully and resurfaced, smiling and rubbing the water off her face. At the far end of the dock, Dr. Pierce presided over the chaos with a whistle and a clipboard.

Ruby dragged her Ace-bandage-wrapped foot onto the dock, where there were no Lines. Her leg trembled and her vision blurred. *Don't be a baby!* Her chest constricted and she struggled for breath, digging her fingernails into Winston's skinny forearm.

"Hey, it's okay," he said.

She tried to nod, but a cowardly tear rolled down her face instead.

"Dr. Pierce!" Winston yelled, stepping Ruby back from the dock.

"I was fine," she muttered, even though her heart was still racing.

"Liar."

The Lines wrapped possessively around Ruby as she closed her eyes and felt the rocky sand on her bare feet. Another tear streamed down her cheek and onto her lips, tasting like failure.

"What is it?" Dr. Pierce called as he stepped over.

"Ruby can't swim today," Winston said.

"What happened?" He was wearing swim trunks and a white tank top instead of his regular teacher clothes. Ruby shuddered at the downy tufts of brown hair quivering on his shoulders. Gross.

"I sprained my ankle," she said.

Pierce's eyes clicked onto her. "Okay. You can watch from the shore." He pointed at a grassy hill by the lake.

Ruby nodded and walked up the little hillside, leaning on Winston, even though her ankle didn't actually hurt. He helped her sit down and then ran down the hill, straight to the end of the dock where he dove in like it was nothing. Ruby sighed. At least no one had called her "Manakuke."

17

———

Ruby squished the mud between her fingers. It felt refreshingly warm in the chilly night air. She rubbed it through her fluffy white-blonde hair, smearing her face until only the whites of her eyes showed.

Winston did the same, gagging at the feel of slime on his skin.

When they were thoroughly covered, they crept to the ridge Ruby had chosen to hide their team's flag. The Truncs had not officially named Ruby as their captain when a camp-wide game of Capture the Flag began, but her ideas were so good that within ten minutes they were all just following her instructions.

Ruby heaved herself over the ridge and a light glared into her eyes.

"What the—" James said.

"It's us," Ruby hissed.

James panned the beam over their faces. "Holy snakes. What happened to you guys?"

"Camouflage," Winston said.

"Turn off the light before you give away our position!"

"Sorry," James said, flicking off the light.

Ruby scrambled up a tree on the south edge of the ridge, easily hoisting her muddy body through the branches.

Winston grunted in the tree beside her.

"Hey," she called when she'd climbed as high as the branches would hold her. "What can you see?" She only heard heavy breathing. "Winston?"

"Wow," he said softly, "it's beautiful up here. And super dangerous."

Ruby smiled. That sounded about right. Pinpricks of light jostled through the forest in regular linear formations. Ruby's Lines attached to each light, following them as the Lines interpreted the movements. Probably Sape patrols looking for Truncants. Ruby sucked on a dirty strand of hair. There really were a lot of them. And the precise patrol patterns reflected their perfect knowledge of the terrain. No wonder they always won Capture the Flag.

"They've already hidden their flag and the guards have turned off their lights," she said.

"We should've climbed the tree first," Winston said.

"Yeah." The flashlight specks looked like a swarm of fireflies. But the Lines were pushing at the dark boundaries of the orderly Sape patrol patterns. "Wait. We don't know where their flag is, but they do."

"Yeah. So?"

"So that's the one place they won't patrol. Look for a spot the lights avoid. There have to be a hundred flashlights out there. It gives us good odds." They watched, still in the quiet darkness. The Lines started running the perimeter of a dark space in the middle back of their territory. "There." She pointed. "In the middle. Did you see how that light just turned?"

"Yeah. And that whole area is dark. But it looks really far. And dirty."

"C'mon." Ruby smiled. "We're already dirty."

———

 ONCE THEY CROSSED into Sape territory, Winston and Ruby were silent. Well, Ruby was. Winston couldn't even breathe quietly. Ruby made him turn off his flashlight and he stumbled every other step. She finally grabbed his hand just to keep him upright.

"We really shouldn't be using your Sight for this," Winston whispered.

"Hmmm?"

"If the Truncs suddenly win Capture the Flag for the first time in living memory, people might get suspicious."

"You don't need Sight to figure out that they're keeping their flag in the one weirdly dark spot on the grid. That's just common sense."

Winston snorted. "Grid? You know that most people don't see the world in grids, right? And common sense or not, only a Levant could navigate through a thick forest in the dead of night without a flashlight."

Ruby sucked her hair. She was getting tired of pretending to be lame. "You wanna go back?"

Winston sighed. "No." He sounded guilty. "I can't stand how they just assume they're going to win everything. Always."

Ruby nodded. "They're the worst."

"But when we get back to school you have to keep pretending to be bad at soccer."

"Soccer won't be a problem," she said heavily. Suddenly there was a rustling noise that made Ruby freeze in attention.

"What is it?" Winston whispered.

Ruby's ears tracked the sounds as her Lines connected to a new figure creeping through the woods about fifty yards away. She was about to crouch and hide from a potential Sape enemy, but there was something familiar about the footsteps that sent a shiver of real danger down her spine. Pierce moved like that. She stepped closer, trailing him, careful to stay within the cover of the brush. Fortunately, Pierce was following a small stream, and its noise masked Winston's occasional twig snaps and branch swishing as he followed Ruby.

After several silent minutes, Pierce stopped, hands in his pockets, waiting. A second figure emerged from the trees, and Ruby's heart froze when she realized who it was. Sterling.

"You weren't followed?" Pierce asked.

"No sir."

"Good. I've just heard from Steiner. He's managed to source a completely untouched diamond that he believes is suitable for Rendering."

Even in the dark, Ruby could see Sterling's posture go rigid.

"I... I thought Octavius was going to Render," Sterling said.

"He was." Pierce was creepily casual. "But as you know, Octavius has unfortunately fallen ill."

Ruby's forehead tightened, remembering Octavius's body crumpled on Pierce's floor.

"Which is why," Pierce continued, "I'd like you to take his place."

"Me?" Fear and excitement churned in Sterling's voice. "When?"

Pierce shrugged. "It takes time to cut and polish a diamond without it ever coming into contact with organic carbon. Then Steiner has to get someone to wear it for a few minutes. Just be ready."

"But Octavius spent months preparing to Render."

"Only because it took us months to source the Solomon Stone."

Ruby scowled. They hadn't *sourced* the Solomon Stone. They'd stolen it. From her.

"But Rendering itself is relatively straightforward," Pierce said. "And very safe. People have been doing it for thousands of years."

Ruby had to swallow the scoff that tried to push through her nose.

Sterling nodded, but Ruby could read the reluctance in his posture. She silently willed him to say "no" and walk away.

"You'll get to hold the actual Solomon Stone in your hand," Pierce said. "Harness the ancient power that shaped so much of our world. It's absolutely breathtaking."

Yeah. Breathtakingly coma-inducing. Ruby's hand curled into a fist against the tree trunk as she remembered how carefully Pierce had avoided touching the Solomon Stone himself.

"We'll start your training first thing tomorrow," Pierce said.

Ruby's stomach lurched when she saw Sterling nod. "Yeah. Okay."

"It'll be fine." Pierce clapped Sterling's shoulder as they walked away into the darkness, "I promise."

Ruby stood motionless in the darkness, listening to

Winston breathing beside her and idly watching the Lines that traced Sterling's and Pierce's departure.

"Are they gone?" Winston finally whispered. His eyes were closed tight, as if that would make him invisible.

"Yeah." Ruby's mind spun, picturing the diamond moving in a continual loop from Steiner's store through the tunnel to Pierce's office.

"They're going to do the same thing to Sterling soon." Panic pulled his voice up an octave.

"I know."

"What should we do?"

Ruby's jaw hardened. "What we've been planning to do. Steal it back. Fast."

18

The Sapes' flag was well hidden. The trees were so thick around it that Ruby didn't see the guards until they were just twenty feet away. She studied her Lines as they surrounded the scrap of red fabric lying crumpled on the ground next to a stump. She sucked her hair. Snatch and run seemed like the best option. Ruby cupped her hand around Winston's ear and whispered, "You distract them and I'll grab the flag."

Winston's eyes grew wide, but he nodded solemnly.

"I'll sneak around behind them. Once I'm there, I'll need ten seconds."

"What if they catch me sooner?" he asked.

"Then we'll lose."

Following her Lines, Ruby slipped through the trees until she saw the backs of the guards. Closing her eyes, she matched her breathing with the wind.

Suddenly Winston's flashlight appeared. "I found it! Over here, guys! I found it!" he shouted. A Sape guard ran after him. Winston switched directions, drawing two of the three guards after him. They were fast. Ruby might only get eight seconds.

Ruby dashed forward, grabbed the flag, and ran back into the trees.

Behind her someone yelled, "The flag's gone! The flag's gone!"

Then the woods burst into commotion. Scores of flashlight beams jerked as their owners raced toward her. Voices clamored from almost every side. Ruby sprinted flat out, switching from Line to Line as she swerved away from Sapes and trees. Her legs and lungs strained, but the possibility of winning propelled her forward.

Ruby steadily snaked her way back toward the boundary line until she could see the flagpole, just fifty feet away. But in front of the flagpole was a big problem.

The Sapes had regrouped and formed a huge human boundary line that was thirty feet from the actual one. Each stood about four feet apart, hands joined as if they were about to play Red Rover. They were too close together for her to break through.

Ruby's Lines combed over the row of Sapes for a weak link. But each of the small Sapes stood next to a large one. She gnawed a piece of muddy hair. There were no good options.

"Ruby!" a voice called through the darkness. It was Harrison. Ruby smiled. At least she wasn't alone in enemy territory.

"Harrison!" she answered.

The Sapes squinted into the darkness, trying to locate her. "Hold the line!" someone barked. It was obvious that their confidence had drained and that they were not accustomed to the sensation.

"Ruby! Me, thirty-four. You, thirty-two. In ten, nine, eight," Harrison yelled.

The Sapes shifted and glanced around, confused.

Ruby was not confused. She continued Harrison's countdown in her head while she counted the line of Sapes until she found the thirty-second child. It was a girl, small like Ruby. And kid thirty-three wasn't so huge, but kid thirty-four was. She winced. Harrison would be sore tomorrow.

The Sapes swiveled their heads, some looking into the woods, others looking at each other. Some were counting, but not fast enough.

"Five, four, three," Ruby thought. "Two, one." She and Harrison burst from the trees at the same time. Some Sapes saw her but most were focused on the huge mass of blue charging straight for the thirty-fourth Sape. Harrison wasn't alone. James and Winston were right behind him. They all barreled straight into the big kid, knocking him over. Sapes rushed to catch Harrison, leaving the line in tatters.

Ruby shot through the widening gap between kid thirty-two and thirty-three. A tall boy saw her and ran after her, but she was faster. Another boy grabbed for her but she swerved.

She ran for the boundary at a dead sprint, feet crashing behind her. Her legs and lungs burned in protest. Just twenty-five feet, twenty, fifteen.

Some boy caught the sleeve of her left arm. Ten feet. His fingers found purchase, pinching the fabric. Just one touch from his other hand and she'd be captured. She wrenched her arm hard and twisted out of his grip. Behind him, half a dozen more Sapes were coming for her.

Ruby crossed the boundary line and a second Sape

grabbed her. "It's over!" she said, shoving him away and pointing to the boundary line behind them. "We won."

He looked at her like she was speaking a foreign language. All the Sapes' faces were a mess of horror and astonishment as they realized that they'd lost.

Ruby winked at them as she dusted herself off. Harrison rushed toward her with a huge smile and a massive bloody nose. A swarm of blue shirts followed. She saw James and Winston, their faces shocked and red but triumphant. Ruby pulled the flag from her shirt and waved it over her head. "Trun-cant!" she yelled at full voice while she pumped her fist. "Trunc! Trunc! Trunc!" The voices of every blue-shirted kid joined in, echoing around the clearing as they hugged each other and hoisted Ruby onto their shoulders.

Ruby laughed as she tried to keep her balance while being marched around the clearing. The Sapes watched, huddled in a miserable mass. Even the teachers gawked, a shock that bordered on rudeness etched on their faces.

Only Dr. Pierce seemed unaffected by the Trunc victory, watching passively with his hands in his pockets, looking decidedly unimpressed with Ruby's flag-snatching. Probably because he was used to stealing real things in the real world. His mouth curled into a lazy smile as he raised a mocking, semi-congratulatory salute at her.

19

Ruby leaned against the Academy's ivy-clad brick wall, cartwheeling her phone between her fingers as she watched the after-school crowd of Sapes moving around her. Her phone buzzed with a text from Chloe.

Sorry. Running late. Be there soon.

Ruby opened the maps app, scrolling back until the small screen was filled with a map of the world. Sucking on her hair, she stared intently. Hidden somewhere between the four brightly colored corners of this screen were her parents. She tried pushing the Lines onto the map, hoping some part of it would excite them or draw their attention. But the Lines just laid there like limp threads on the static screen. She'd been trying to get the Lines to conjure her parents' location on world maps since she was a kid. It had never actually worked.

Ruby looked at the actual Fifth Avenue in front of her, watching her own Lines run toward the Diamond District, but they just circled in an endless loop between the school and Steiner's shop. Ruby rested her head against the cold brick wall. Why was she so bad at this? Levants were supposed to be able to find anything. But she'd been home from Ketchikan for over a week and she still had no clue how to flush Steiner and the diamond out of the store.

"Ruby!" someone called. A Truncant boy she didn't know walked by with his hand out. She high-fived him automatically, already accustomed to her popularity since camp. Someone tousled her hair from the opposite side. Ruby jerked away before she saw that it was Sterling. Her mouth curved into a weak smile as a tight knot twisted in her chest.

"Hey," he said, winking at her before he merged with a group of Sape girls in soccer uniforms heading toward the park.

Ruby frowned at his retreating figure, trying not to picture his friendly face writhing on the floor of Pierce's office.

"Hey," Chloe said, emerging, slightly breathless, from the crowd. "Sorry I'm late."

"Hey." Ruby's eyes stayed on Sterling and the group of soccer players.

Chloe followed Ruby's gaze and winced sympathetically. "I'm sorry about soccer."

Ruby shrugged, not bothering to tell Chloe that her frustration stemmed from her friend's impending doom. Soccer stress was simpler.

"Maybe next year—"

Ruby snorted. "Alice said I can't play until I'm twenty-five."

Chloe winced, pulling out her phone. "You know what? I have an errand to run downtown. Do you want to come with me? It'll help get your mind off of things."

"What's the errand?" Unless it was robbing a jewelry store, it probably wouldn't help much.

"I have to pick up my paycheck from work."

"I thought *I* was your work."

Chloe smiled. "You're just my day job."

"You have a night job?"

"I'm an actor."

"Like on TV?" Ruby straightened. "What show are you on? Are we going to a TV studio? Can I be on TV too?"

"No. I work for a theatre company. We do modern adaptations of Shakespearean plays."

"Oh." Ruby's shoulders sagged. "Sounds boring. No offense."

"We can get donuts after."

"With milk? Miles never lets me get milk."

Chloe's cheek dimpled. "With milk. Lemme just text Alice."

Ruby snorted.

"She's not that bad. C'mon." Chloe walked toward Fifth Avenue and Ruby followed. At the corner of Fifty-ninth and Lexington, Chloe handed Ruby a flimsy yellow plastic card with "MetroCard" printed in large blue letters across it.

Ruby's pulse quickened. "We're taking the subway?"

Nodding, Chloe disappeared down a staircase that descended directly into the sidewalk.

Ruby followed. She had never actually been inside the subway, and it was hard to imagine that a whole system of trains really ran beneath the city.

The subway station smelled sweaty and had white tiled walls like a bathroom. On the platform, swarms of people flowed in all directions. Ruby's Lines tracked all the movements, energized by the complexity of the task. The ground trembled as a low rumble shook the platform. Ruby peered down the track and saw a wall of steel heading straight toward her, its two headlights shining through the dark.

The sheer power of the approaching train constricted her lungs.

The train screeched to a stop and opened its doors with a sigh. A crowd of bored-looking people stepped off and an equally nonchalant group stepped on as if there were nothing remarkable about a train suddenly emerging from the underground darkness. Then the doors closed and the train lurched away, leaving the platform, and everything inside Ruby, trembling.

"We're getting on a train?" Ruby asked. It was a stupid question. And she knew she was gawking, the one thing New Yorkers never did. But she couldn't help it.

"Yeah, but not that one." Chloe directed Ruby to a map, bright and cartoonish, mounted on a wall behind thick glass. "We'll take the 6 train to Canal Street." She pointed to a green line that ran down the spine of Manhattan.

Ruby traced her fingers over the glass, amazed. Her Lines raced over the image, shifting her concept of the city, adding a three-dimensional layer of information beneath the roads she already knew.

"You can go anywhere on here," Ruby whispered as her eyes ran from the Bronx to Staten Island. Some of the place names sounded strange, like "Jamaica Van Wyck" or "Euclid Avenue," but each of them slotted neatly into her mental map of the city.

Ruby's heart quickened when they stepped onto the next train and sat in bright blue seats at the end. As the train rumbled away from the platform, Ruby exhaled, her whole body tingling with excitement as her Lines careened through the underground tunnels.

"Miles told me that you beat the Sapes at Capture the Flag at Ketchikan," Chloe said.

Ruby smiled. "We destroyed them."

"I bet they were mad. They're not used to losing."

"Some of them were so upset that their parents had to come and pick them up early."

"No!"

"Yeah. It was bad. I was, like, embarrassed for them."

"Stop." Chloe was laughing hard now.

"No, for reals. They're such babies. If I'd been born a Sape, I'd pretend that I wasn't."

Chloe smiled. "That's impossible."

"No it's not." Winston was doing it just fine.

"You know what they teach Sapes in those classes?" Chloe asked.

Ruby shook her head. She didn't even know what was taught in her own classes.

"Mind mapping." Chloe pulled her phone out and opened a search engine. "Sapes' brains are like the internet, but they don't come with Google. So they have to build these complex mental filing systems to organize the information. It's exhausting. Some even think it's a disadvantage because they have to work so hard to categorize everything."

"I'd still fake it," Ruby said.

"Oh, shoot." Chloe bolted upright. "That was the last stop."

Ruby jerked her head up, suddenly noticing that there was no one else in the train car with them. "If that was the last stop, where's the train going?"

"It's just turning around. We'll catch Canal Street when it goes back uptown." Chloe crossed the empty car and pointed at one of the dark windows. "Actually, come check this out."

Ruby came over and looked, her eyes blurring out of focus as she watched the cement walls rush by just inches from the glass.

"Look." Chloe pointed.

The tunnel widened and Ruby saw a gently curved platform appear with striped columns and huge chandeliers hanging from vaulted ceilings. It looked like a church. But it was empty and almost dark except for the patches of afternoon sunlight filtering through some skylights.

"What is this?" Ruby asked. It hadn't been on the subway map.

"It's a ghost station called Old City Hall. It was one of the first stations opened, but they don't use it anymore."

"Why not?"

"See how the track curves into the platform?" Chloe pointed. "The turn was too sharp for the newer, longer trains, so they had to shut it down."

"Wow." There was something sad and beautiful about the hollow place. Ruby stared out the window long after they'd passed the ghost station, sliding the details into her mental map.

They exited at Canal Street into a neighborhood with narrow meandering streets and old brick buildings girded with fire escapes. Store signs were in different languages and the sidewalks were full of young, scruffy-looking people. Chloe led Ruby into a small gray building with a poster that read "Broome Street Theatre."

"Just wait here," Chloe said as she ran up the stairs.

Ruby surveyed the lobby, studying the posters framed on the wall. Suddenly she heard loud voices. Outside on the sidewalk, she saw two policemen yelling at a woman. The woman quivered in the corner while they shouted, and the policemen's hands stabbed the air as their faces leaned menacingly toward her.

Ruby charged out the door. "Hey. What's your problem?"

The anger slid off both men's faces as they looked at Ruby, curious. "Can I help you?" the taller one asked politely. He seemed surprised, but not annoyed, at her interference.

Ruby shifted her weight, uncertain.

The other cop took a lazy sip from a water bottle.

"It's okay," the slouchy woman said. Her voice and demeanor had no trace of the terror Ruby had seen moments ago. "It's not real."

"Huh?"

"She's with me." Chloe came up behind Ruby. "Sorry, I should've explained—"

"They were yelling at her and—" Ruby pointed at the woman.

"This is Rohm and Matt and Hannah." Each of them nodded to Ruby as Chloe introduced them. "They're actors too. They were just rehearsing."

"Outside?"

"It helps me get in character," Hannah said.

"Oh." Ruby stared stupidly at them. Her brain furiously buzzed around an idea. Fake cops that looked like real ones.

"Thanks," Ruby said. "You're good actors. It looked really real." She inhaled sharply as the idea came into focus. "Really real."

20

As soon as she and Chloe reached their building, Ruby pulled out her phone, her thumbs trembling as she texted Winston.

Ruby: *I found our fake fire*

Winston: *What are you talking about?*

Ruby: *Our fire. You know, for the you-know-what*

Winston: *What I-know-what?*

Ruby: *The SOLOMON STONE*

Winston: *Oh. Yeah. The metaphorical fire. What is it?*

Ruby: *I'll tell you IRL tomorrow*

Winston: *K*

Ruby: *I'll come by after school. Will need Charlie's help too*

Winston: *Charlie?*

Ruby: *Your brother. Lives with you...*

There was a long pause and the dots that show someone is writing a text appeared and disappeared several times.

Winston: *Fine. Charlie. Hope you don't mind whiners*

Ruby: *Lucky for you, I don't*

Winston: *Lucky for me*

———

"ALICE?" Ruby called as she stepped into the apartment. "I'm home." Her phone buzzed again as she was kicking her shoes off.

Winston: *Check this out*

Attached was a picture of three boys smiling on a green field. She could tell it was Rex, Miles, and Harlan. Ruby's hand tightened. All three wore red soccer jerseys and Harlan clutched a small trophy.

Winston: *From my dad's yearbook, thought you'd like it*
Ruby: *Thx*

Ruby clenched her jaw against the anger rising in her. So Alice didn't have a problem with *kids* playing soccer, she had a problem with *Ruby* playing soccer. "Alice!" Ruby called louder, her heart accelerating as she threaded through the hallways.

"In here." Alice's voice rose from her bedroom.

Barging in, Ruby waved the phone picture in front of Alice's tired-looking eyes. "You let my dad play soccer. And Miles and Harlan."

Alice didn't even look at the picture. "I know."

"So it was fine for them to play soccer but not me?" Ruby crossed her arms.

Alice nodded so slightly that Ruby wondered if she was even paying attention. Her normally straight shoulders sagged.

"They wanted me on their team. They liked me." The words hurt Ruby's throat as she spat them out. "I thought it was because you were just weirdly paranoid about injuries, but you let your own kids play. Do you think Truncs are too stupid to play without getting injured?"

Alice flinched and pulled her eyes up to meet Ruby's. They were swollen and red. "No! I mean, you're right."

Ruby drew an angry breath, then stopped. "What?"

"I should've let you play. I'm sorry. It's not because you're a Trunc. I was just... I was afraid."

The anger slowly ebbed out of Ruby. "Afraid of what?"

Alice's mouth lifted on one side as she finally looked at the picture. "Every time you walk out the door, I'm terrified that I'll never see you again. I can't help it. It's like a dark abyss hovering inches away."

"Oh." Ruby knew all about abysses. "I—" What should she say? *Sorry?* She couldn't apologize for going to school every day. *You shouldn't worry?* But that wouldn't help Alice any more than it helped Ruby deal with the ocean. Suddenly all of Alice's fretting and fussing made sense. It was still annoying, but—something caught Ruby's eye, a glint of bright orange on the bed. "What's that?" Ruby reached over and pulled an orange plastic bag of candy corns out from behind the pillows. "Candy corns?" Ruby asked. "You hide candy corns under your pillow?"

Alice pulled her lips over her teeth. "Yes."

Ruby poured some out. They were shiny and perfectly triangular in her hand and waxy sweet on her tongue. "Want some?"

Alice's mouth twitched up and she extended her palm. She ate them one at a time, carefully biting off the white tip and then the orange middle.

Ruby flicked one up and caught it neatly in her mouth.

Alice arched an eyebrow, obviously impressed.

"You throw one for me," Ruby said, opening her mouth.

Alice's eyes widened, but then they warmed and she tossed one.

It wasn't a great toss. Ruby had to dive over the bed for it, landing in a heap. But then Ruby stood up and opened her mouth, proudly displaying the caught candy.

A halting, bark-like laugh erupted from Alice. Which made Ruby laugh so hard that she snorted, wincing as the sweetness of the candy stung her nostrils. "You sound like a stranded seal," Ruby choked out.

"Are you alright?" Alice asked between barks.

"Yeah." Ruby wiped her eyes. "Your turn." She found the thin Line running from her hand to Alice's mouth and tossed the candy perfectly. It arced over the bed and straight for Alice's mouth. Which, oddly, Alice hadn't opened. Ruby froze as she watched the candy ricochet off Alice's face and land on the rug. *Oops*.

But Alice laughed, again. This time her shoulders shook and tears streamed down her cheeks. She bent to pick up the errant candy, then just slumped to the floor, her back against the bed.

"Sorry." Ruby flopped down beside Alice. "But you're supposed to open your mouth."

Alice shook her head and smiled. "Don't apologize. It was a perfect toss. You have excellent hand-eye coordination."

Ruby thought about saying that her excellent coordination made her a really good at soccer, but she just looked away instead. "What happened to your closet?" she asked, noticing the clothes strewn all over the floor.

"I'm rotating my wardrobe." There was a hitch in Alice's voice.

"Huh?"

"I'm moving my summer clothes into storage to make room for my fall and winter clothes," Alice said.

Ruby bit into another candy corn. "Sheesh, you really are rich."

Alice laughed, biting another tip off a candy corn and tilting her head back against the bedspread. "I am, actually."

Ruby edged into the closet to get a closer look. It was huge and looked like a little fancy store. One side had a bunch of men's suits and shirts hung in tidy lines like soldiers. "Why do you have men's clothes in here?" She swept her fingers over the row of buttery-soft blazers.

Alice stared at the suits, silent. "They're your grandfather's," she finally said.

"You keep a dead guy's clothes in your closet?"

Alice snorted, her face smiling and wincing at the same time as her eyes re-focused. She joined Ruby in the closet, sitting next to a pile of clothes. "I don't know what to do with them."

"Hasn't he been dead for, like, two years?"

"Two years ago today, actually." Alice's voice broke and her face contorted. Tears glistened in her eyes.

"Oh." Ruby passed her the bag of candy.

Alice took some with shaky hands, then cleared her throat and pressed the palm of her hand against her eyes, as if she were trying to stop a wound from bleeding. "I know I should donate them. But then the closet would be so empty."

Ruby nodded, but she didn't agree. All those immaculate, uninhabited suits made the closet feel extra empty.

Beside her, Alice shuddered and then tears came along with deep choking breaths.

Ruby scooted closer and brushed the nape of Alice's neck, making a soothing clicking noise that always worked with upset dogs. Alice's head lolled onto Ruby's shoulder. Ruby didn't move, surprised by the warmth that was spreading through her chest.

"I just can't," Alice whispered, like it was a confession. "They still smell like him."

"'Can't'?" Ruby asked. "We don't say 'can't.' Callahans don't give up, remember?" Ruby couldn't see Alice's face, but she could tell that she was smiling. "You should give them to Harlan and Miles. Or maybe just Miles."

Alice stared at the clothes for several moments, then slowly bobbed her head. "That's a good idea." She crooked her arm up and patted Ruby's cheek. Ruby laid her hand on top of Alice's, curling her fingers around Alice's long, thin ones and listening as their breathing slowly synchronized.

"Alice?"

"Hmm?" Alice sat up. Her face looked calm and tired.

"I won't disappear again. I promise."

Alice's grip tightened on Ruby's hand. "I know."

21

———

"Wait." Charlie's brown eyes bulged as he studied Ruby's and Winston's faces. He sat, legs folded, across from them on his navy blue-striped bedspread. "You two are trying to break into a jewelry store? You're crazy."

"It's not crazy." Ruby's eyes flickered to Winston's, confirming what they'd discussed, and he nodded. "I'm a Levant," she said.

Charlie blinked.

"It's true," Winston confirmed.

"But your mom wasn't even Sighted," Charlie said. "No offense."

"She was a Levant too."

"Ohhhhhhh," Charlie exhaled. "That actually..." he kept blinking, looking like a computer screen flickering through a complex download. "That actually makes sense. She came out of nowhere. She evidently had the Solomon Stone."

"You can't tell anyone," Ruby said, though she already knew he wouldn't.

"I won't," Charlie said. "So, do you have, like, a secret Levant way to get into the jewelry store?"

"No." Ruby sucked her hair. "But we don't need to break in if we can get Steiner to bring the diamond to us." She started sketching a simple but accurate map of the Diamond District and the Academy in the notebook she was holding. "There are these tunnels underneath the Diamond District—"

"You mean the Rockefeller tunnels?" Charlie's left eyebrow arched. "I thought those were a myth."

"They're real." Winston said. "We've been inside them."

"Really? What are they like?"

"Super dirty," Winston said.

"There's a tunnel that connects the Diamond District to the Academy." Ruby underlined it on the map. "Steiner's already used it to access Pierce's office. But to get to the Academy tunnel, he has to pass near these two intersecting passageways that lead to the street and to Rockefeller Station." Ruby traced the tunnels as both boys leaned in to look. "So, if we take the Academy tunnel to here and wait for him—"

"Why can't we just get there from Rockefeller Station?" Charlie asked.

"I checked those doors," Ruby said, trying to be patient. "They're locked down."

"Makes sense, I guess." Charlie chewed his cheek. "Since the tunnel runs beneath the Diamond District."

"So, if we wait here," Ruby said, making a dot on the page, "then we can take Steiner by surprise, grab the diamond, and escape to the street. Or, if we can't get to the street, we can run into the subway station. Both should be crowded enough to give us cover."

"You want us to attack Steiner?" Winston said, looking doubtfully around at the three admittedly small bodies on Charlie's bed. "Like, physically?"

"He carries the diamond in a black velvet bag," Ruby said. "We just need to grab the bag and run. With a little speed and the element of surprise, it should work."

Winston clicked his teeth, staring at the sketched map.

"How do we get him into the tunnel?" Charlie asked.

Ruby's mouth pulled into a smile. "Fake cops."

"Oh. So, the fake cops are the fake fire?" asked Winston.

"Huh?" asked Charlie.

"We get some actors to dress up like cops," Ruby said. "And they present a fake warrant at Steiner's store and pretend to search it. Steiner knows the diamond is stolen, so he'll panic, grab it from the safe, and head for the Academy tunnel. Only, we'll be here," she said, pointing to the spot on the map where the tunnels converged, "waiting for him."

Winston and Charlie stared at the paper silently.

"They do stuff like this on *True Cops* all the time," Ruby said.

"You know my mom doesn't let us watch that show," Winston said.

"It could work." Charlie carefully considered the map.

"Or it could not work," Winston countered. "It's against the law to impersonate a police officer in the state of New York."

"So?" Ruby said.

"So what actor would agree to do this?"

Charlie snorted. "New York is crawling with desperate actors. We just have to find some that are too stupid to ask questions."

"What if the actors-too-stupid-to-ask-questions get caught and it's traced back to us?" Winston asked.

Ruby sucked her hair. She hadn't thought about that. "We'll use a fake name when we place the ad."

Charlie's head snapped up. "Halloween."

"Halloween?" Ruby asked.

"We'll do it on Halloween. That way, if we *do* get caught, we can say we were just pulling a prank," Charlie said.

"Halloween pranks are very common among over-privileged pre-teens like us," Winston said grudgingly.

"And Alice has some fancy gala dinner thing on Halloween, so it will be easier to sneak out." Ruby swallowed against the guilt tightening in her throat. She was trying hard not to imagine how worried Alice would be if she found out.

"Oooh, and we can dress all in black and say we're being ninjas for Halloween," Charlie broke in.

"Umm, black kind of washes me out," Winston said.

"Robbers always wear black," Charlie said.

"We're not robbers," Ruby said.

Both boys shot Ruby dubious looks.

"We're retrieving a stolen object. That makes us the exact opposite of robbers," she said.

"Whatever. It's basically a smash and grab job," Charlie said casually, sounding like a hardened criminal.

Winston nodded, clicking his teeth as he stared at the sketch. "I guess it's a good plan. Only—"

"What?"

"Halloween is just three days away."

———

HARLAN AND MILES came over the next night for Alice's birthday dinner, and Elena cooked Alice's favorite meal, which was something Ruby couldn't pronounce, let alone eat. She pushed the stuff around her plate, trying to ignore the grating sound of Harlan's voice.

"This is delicious," he said, wiping his mouth dramatically.

Ruby snorted. He lied about *everything*. She stared at the gross brown sauce on her plate and really hoped that Alice's birthday "party" included cake and ice cream. And that her favorite ice cream was chocolate.

"Are you ready for presents?" Miles asked, standing and carrying some plates to the sink.

"Thank you." Alice kissed Miles's cheek as he sat beside her. "This has been lovely. I'm so glad you three are here."

The room stilled, feeling suddenly heavy with absent family members. There were too many empty chairs. And nine empty years gaped like an open wound behind them all.

"This is from all of us," Miles said, breaking the silence as he pulled a slender rectangular box from his pocket and set it in front of Alice.

Alice unwrapped the gift carefully, as if she were undoing an origami animal that she meant to reassemble later. She opened the black velvet box, lifted the pendant and stared at it, tilting it so that the red stone caught the light. "It's... it's a ruby," she choked out, as if she'd never heard of the gem before.

"It was Ruby's idea," Harlan said. "I'm sure Steiner will let you exchange it for a diamond."

Alice wrapped her fingers protectively around the pendant. "No. I love it."

Ruby shot a triumphant look at Harlan. "Now you'll always have a little Ruby with you," she said to Alice.

Alice nodded quietly and drew in an uneven breath as she fastened the necklace around her delicate neck. Her mouth quivered for a moment and she blinked several times. "Thank you," she whispered hoarsely.

For a moment, Ruby's cheeks flushed hot with Halloween-heist guilt. Then she rolled her eyes. New York was making her soft.

22

"Y ou're hogging the mirror!" Charlie elbowed Winston, bumping him into Ruby.

"Watch it." Ruby shoved back. They were all squished into Ruby's bathroom, adjusting their ninja costumes.

"Ruby?" Alice poked her head into the bedroom.

Ruby froze defensively, but reminded herself that they hadn't done anything wrong. Yet. "Yeah?"

"We're leaving." Alice was wearing a navy blue velvet dress that went all the way to the floor. Her hair was swept up, away from her neck, where the ruby pendant hung.

"You're wearing it," Ruby said, touching it gently with two fingers.

"Of course." Alice bent down and kissed Ruby's head and Ruby caught a glimpse of Miles hovering in the hallway. "Harlan is here. He'll watch you until I get back."

Ruby nodded, her chest tightening like it always did when Harlan was around. She listened to the sounds of their departure, waiting until she heard the front door close to turn back to the mirror.

"We still look like ourselves," Charlie said, disappointed.

"Here." Winston fished something out of his backpack and handed it to him.

"What's that?" Charlie asked, turning the thin disk in his hands.

It was smooth, round, and small like the things Ruby'd seen in Alice's vanity. "It looks like makeup."

"It's war paint," Winston said.

"I thought black washed you out," Charlie said.

"It's camouflage," Winston said, popping open the lid to reveal a swirl of green and brown mixed together. "And olive green brings out my eyes."

Ruby side-eyed him as she dipped her fingers into the dark cream and smeared it on her face. It wasn't cape buffalo dung, but it would have to do.

"Not with your fingers!" Winston winced and pulled out a white wedge sponge for each of them.

Ruby and Charlie stared at the sponges, then at Winston.

"What?" Winston dabbed his face. "It's not hygienic to share applicators."

Ruby applied the camouflage, then pulled on a black knit hat and smiled at her reflection. She looked like a shadow. "What time is it?"

"6:17. We have to be in Pierce's office by 6:55," Charlie said, looking at his watch. "To make sure we're in position at 7:30 when the 'cops' show up at Steiner's with the warrant."

Ruby felt the Lines buzzing excitedly around her as she walked to the door. "Time to go."

She found Harlan in the kitchen, perched at the counter eating ice cream straight from the carton, something Alice hated.

"We're going to Winston's to watch a movie. Is that okay?"

"Just be back before Alice gets home at ten."

"No problem."

———

THE ACADEMY'S front entrance was open, thanks to the party in the common room thrown by the upper-grade Sapes. Two girls sat taking tickets at a table just inside the door. Watching the Lines, Ruby waited until the girls were distracted, then  slipped in behind a group of loud boys, pulling Winston and Charlie behind her.

Pierce's office was on the ground level, the same as the common room, so the corridor was sporadically illuminated with bursts of flashing lights as the bass beat thrummed through the floor.

Ruby knelt beside the office doorknob and took out her screwdriver, pocketknife, and flashlight.

"So, if they catch us, we say we were looking for our midterm papers because we wanted to correct a typo." Winston shifted between the balls of his feet.

"Quiet," Ruby said around the flashlight she held in her teeth. She wiped her sweaty hand on her shirt and examined the lock. She took a deep breath, visualizing a Line running through the tumblers within the lock, showing her how to maneuver them. She inserted her screwdriver and pocketknife into the keyhole, listening as the parts inside clinked. With each sound she could feel the invisible space inside the lock as if the clicks were sonar. There was a tinkling thunk when it opened.

"6:53. Exactly on schedule," Charlie announced, blinking against the overhead lights that had turned on automatically when they entered the office.

Ruby nodded. She consulted her Lines, which were taut with attention, but held no hint of alarm. "Perfect." She headed toward the closet, blinking as her eyes re-adjusted to the darkness. She ran her hands along the floor until she found the round edge of the hatch. The office lights that crept through the crack beneath the closet door turned off, leaving them in complete darkness. Ruby grunted, annoyed that she couldn't seem to find what she needed. "Winston, shine your light over here."

"Oh, gutterball," Charlie muttered.

His voice was so grave that Ruby stopped what she was doing to look at him, his face contorted and weirdly illuminated by the bluish light of his phone. "What?" she asked.

"The actors. They... they just texted me that they're finished. But—"

"Finished with what?" Heavy dread crowded in as she heard Charlie swallow and Winston's breath catch.

Charlie's owlish eyes brimmed with alarm. "They've finished fake-searching Steiner's store."

"What!" Ruby stood. "They were supposed to wait until 7:30."

"I know. But—" Charlie turned his phone so that Ruby could read the message herself.

Ruby gasped, prodding the slack Lines that swirled around the broken shards of her plan. "Steiner's in the tunnel right now then. We have to—"

But suddenly the crack beneath the door lit up as the office lights turned on. They heard two sets of footfalls. The darkness crackled with Charlie's and Winston's panic. Ruby gently touched their arms and let them hear her breaths, steady and even, while she consulted the Lines. Rule One of any hunt was "don't panic." Silently, Ruby followed the brightest Line to the far right corner, where Pierce had hung two suits and an overcoat. It wasn't great cover, and they were only three feet away from the trap-door, but it was their only option.

23

"Where's Steiner?" Harlan asked, shutting the office door hard enough that the closet door opened slightly.

Ruby closed her eyes and mouthed a jagged "gutterball" into the darkness. Harlan was here. She could see him and Pierce through the crack in the door.

"He's on his way," Pierce answered.

"Any idea what this is about?"

Pierce shrugged. "You know Steiner. Everything's always a fire drill."

Behind her, Winston and Charlie were standing so close that Ruby could feel their wet breath on her face and neck.

Harlan's phone buzzed. He looked at it and grunted.

"Is that him?" Pierce asked.

"My mother." Harlan pocketed his phone. "She's calling about the brat. I'm supposed to be watching her tonight."

Ruby narrowed her eyes. Had Harlan just called her a *brat*?

"You're the babysitter?" Pierce asked.

"Alice doesn't want outsiders to do it. She's clinically insane when it comes to that kid."

"Sounds a little overprotective." Pierce smiled, but something about his body seemed taut.

"She's trying to save face. Ruby's an embarrassment, so Alice keeps her out of sight as much as possible."

Ruby stared at Harlan, shocked. *An embarrassment?*

"Why? Because she's a Trunc?" Pierce asked.

Harlan shrugged. "Ruby's just not 'Callahan.' Plus, finding her alone on that island made us all look bad. There's no hiding the fact that Rex must've abandoned his own kid. I don't blame him, but still."

Ruby felt suddenly cold as Harlan's words swirled around her, sharp and convincing.

"And Ruby looks exactly like her mother, so she's a constant reminder of how Rex defied our parents to marry some UnSighted nobody from nowhere," Harlan said.

Ruby's throat tightened as she grasped the pocketknife, repeating the mantra *The strength of the wolf is the pack.* But the Callahans weren't a pack. They were a snake pit. Harlan was a thief, Alice was embarrassed by her own granddaughter, and they had all hated Ruby's mother.

"So, Alice and Atticus never suspected that Emmeline was a Levant?" Pierce asked.

Wait. Ruby leaned closer. Pierce and Harlan knew that Emmeline was a Levant?

"My parents were too busy hating her to notice. They still have no idea. I didn't know myself until you called me out of the blue. If you hadn't seen the picture I'd posted and recognized that Emmeline's necklace was the Solomon Stone, I probably wouldn't have figured it out either."

"Ironic. But poor Ruby," said Pierce.

Harlan waved away the sentiment. "She's obnoxious. Always mouthing off and hanging out with these two loser kids in our building."

Beside her, Winston and Charlie made muted sniffles of indignation.

"At least Ruby's reappearance created a pretext to get Miles to finally open the family safe so we could retrieve the Solomon Stone," said Pierce.

"True. But all these years I'd thought that Ruby would be a Levant too. And then we finally find her, and she's just this dumb Truncant. It took her forever to get through that maze in Central Park. She's stone stupid, even for a Trunc."

Ruby gripped the coat in front of her as she swallowed a huff of indignation. Harlan was the stupid one. He hadn't even figured out that his own niece was a Levant.

"That's a shame," Pierce said.

"Yeah. If Ruby were a Levant, this Rendering project would be a lot easier," Harlan said.

"You'd really practice Rendering on Ruby?"

"If she were a Levant, sure. Ruby likes me. It wouldn't be hard to talk her into it."

Ruby choked back the loud bark of disbelief in her throat.

"Even though our other test subject is in a coma?" Pierce asked.

"Pshh," Harlan shrugged. "Levants are made to handle the Solomon Stone. She'd be fine. Probably."

Probably? Repulsion and fear shot down Ruby's spine.

"Emmeline wore the Solomon Stone every day, and it never hurt her," Harlan said.

"True. But I am starting to wonder whether we were

wrong about Emmeline even being a Levant." There was something deliberate about Pierce's words that belied his casual tone. Like he was lying, but Ruby couldn't figure out why. "Maybe Emmeline was just an ordinary person who happened upon the Solomon Stone without knowing what it was. I've never heard of a Levant willingly leaving it behind."

Harlan scoffed. "Don't ask me. I never could figure her out. Did you see her that night, at the party?"

"You mean the night she disappeared? Of course."

"Did you notice how she wouldn't stop touching the Solomon Stone? She kept curling the necklace around her fingers, running the pendant up and down the chain, holding it in her palm."

Pierce squinted as if he was watching a movie from far away, obviously examining his Sape-perfect recollection of that night. "Huh. You're right. She was fiddling with it a lot."

"I don't think she broke contact with it once. It was almost like she knew we were trying to steal it."

Ruby stifled a horrified gasp with her hand. Harlan had tried to rob Emmeline? Ruby felt like the world was liquifying beneath her. Was that why her mother had left?

"But then Emmeline just left it on the dresser and took off, like it was nothing," Harlan continued. "It didn't make sense. I don't know what she was."

Suddenly Ruby heard a scraping noise inside the closet that froze the breath in her lungs. Just a few feet away, the trapdoor moved. Steiner. Ruby held stock-still behind the smelly coat, hoping Steiner wouldn't bother to look around too closely as he emerged. The door lifted and Steiner hauled himself out with an agility that surprised Ruby, especially since his right hand was clutching the black velvet bag. Ruby's Lines tightened and swarmed toward it.

As soon as Steiner's feet hit the ground, he was through the door to the office. "Police," he sputtered to Harlan and Pierce.

"What?" Harlan bounded toward him, snatching the bag and looking inside. "Why? Did you trip the silent alarm?"

"No," Steiner huffed. "Two cops just showed up with a search warrant. They wouldn't even say what they were looking for. Luckily Jonathan was there to deal with them. Do you know how hard it was to smuggle the diamond out without the cops noticing?"

"You assured us that your store was safe." Harlan snarled.

"I didn't know the police would show up!" Steiner wiped his forehead. "Anyway, they'll be gone soon."

"Doesn't matter," Pierce said, his calm voice somehow scarier than all of Harlan's yelling. "The store's been compromised. We don't know who's behind those warrants or what they're looking for."

Ruby silently cursed those shifty, gutterballing, Craigslist actors. She should've known that anyone stupid enough to impersonate cops would be too stupid to follow a schedule. She'd planned to intercept the Solomon Stone when Steiner was alone in the dark, cramped tunnels. Now there were three men with the diamond in a big, well-lit office while Ruby and her friends huddled uselessly in a stuffy closet.

"Where are we going to find another place tonight?" Harlan asked.

Ice cold dread tingled down Ruby's spine. Another place?

"How should I know?" Steiner rolled his eyes. "I have to get back to my 'compromised' store now."

Ruby tensed as Steiner stormed back into the closet, empty-handed. But he was too busy opening the hatch door and letting himself down to look into the corners of the dark space. He lowered his stocky body down the hole, muttering curses the whole time. The trapdoor made a high, scraping noise as he fitted it back into place.

"Now what?" Harlan asked. "We need a secure location with easy access."

"I have a safe in my office." Pierce gestured toward the closet, and every hair on Ruby's neck prickled.

"Seriously?" Harlan's tone was derisive. "I'm not leaving the Solomon Stone with you."

Pierce's jaw clenched, but his voice came out calm. "What then? Are you going to sneak it back into Miles's safe?"

Yes, yes, yes. Ruby was rigid with hope. *Back into Miles's safe.*

"Don't be an idiot. I'll call the Crown Jubilee. Nothing's safer than a casino vault. I own a small stake, so they'll let me use it." He put his phone to his ear and started talking fast and low.

Ruby deflated. A casino vault sounded even worse than Steiner's store.

"That's in Atlantic City," Pierce said.

Harlan nodded, but kept talking into the phone.

Pierce sighed and took out his own phone. "I'll call a car."

"No. We'll take a helicopter. It'll be safer." Harlan shook the bag meaningfully, then poked his phone and put it to his ear again. "Hello? Julius? I need the chopper. Yep. The usual location. Good. We'll meet you there in..." He looked at his watch. "An hour." He ended the call and shoved the phone back into his pocket.

Ruby watched, feeling pinned and helpless as they left, slamming the office door behind them. Moments later the office lights shut off, leaving her, Winston, and Charlie in the dark again.

24

"Whoa," Charlie said, his voice muffled by the coats.

Ruby pulled free of the boys and rushed forward, the office lights flicking on as she left the closet. Wrenching open the second door, she stumbled into the empty hallway. Harlan and Pierce were already gone. "Gutterball," Ruby muttered. But even as she said it, she felt relieved. She wasn't sure what she'd have done if Pierce and Harlan had been standing there in the hallway, discussing how they wished she were a Levant so that they could run Rendering experiments on her too.

Winston's hand nudged her shoulder. "Hey, Ruby?"

Ruby didn't respond. Her chest felt too tight.

"Ruby?" he tried again.

"He knew about my mom—" Ruby couldn't finish the thought. That Harlan's greed had driven Emmeline away. That he'd torn the family apart just to get a diamond. And Alice was embarrassed—

"Ruby, we have to go." Winston shook her shoulder.

Ruby yanked away. "Don't tell me what to do!"

Winston's face clouded with confusion and his eyes slid to Charlie, silently asking for backup.

"She might be transferring some of her anger at Harlan onto us," Charlie said in a clinical voice.

Ruby glared at him. "Shut up, Charlie!"

"See?" Charlie crossed his arms. "Classic transference."

Winston sighed. "They're getting away."

Ruby looked at the corridor. It seemed to stretch for miles.

Winston grunted in frustration. "What's the matter with you?"

His words felt like a slap across her cheek. Ruby looked down at herself, the "embarrassment" who was "just not Callahan," and felt disoriented. "I don't know."

"I think she's trying to process the new information," Charlie said. "Like how no one in her family loves her and stuff."

"Shut up, Charlie!" Winston yelled, then turned back to Ruby. "Forget what Harlan said. He's a liar."

"Harlan and Pierce weren't even supposed to be there." Ruby tried to sort through the tangle of facts, important and unimportant, tumbling through her head. "Those stupid actors!"

"We can still get it back," Winston said. "I mean, you're a Levant. And we'll help you."

Ruby cocked her head and peered into his soft, urgent eyes and felt her heart slowing. Two true things that she could count on. The Lines tightened and strained down the hallway and she pulled in a deep breath, recalibrating until she found the right Line. "Yes," Ruby said, breaking into a run.

———

RUBY BURST through the Academy's main doors and stopped. The Lines led to a yellow cab pulling away from the sidewalk. "That's them!" she shouted. Narrowing her eyes against the pelting rain, she sprinted after the cab. But even Ruby couldn't run faster than a car. She tripped, scraping her hands on the wet concrete.

"Citi bikes!" Winston yelled, yanking her up.

"What's a Citi bike?" she asked as they ran down Fifth Avenue, dodging crowds of costumed people.

Winston was too winded to answer, but, on Fifty-eighth Street, Ruby saw a row of thick blue bicycles lined up on the sidewalk like horses in a stable. Winston pushed some buttons on a nearby machine, then pulled out a bike for Ruby. "Citi bikes," he panted.

Ruby climbed on and smiled. New York never disappointed.

Charlie frowned at Fifth Avenue. The traffic was thick with yellow cabs. "There are, like, a hundred taxis."

"4G97," Winston said, pedaling forward. "License plate."

Ruby nodded. Of course Winston and his super-Sape brain had remembered a license plate that he'd barely seen. The red taillights blurred with the yellow cabs, making Fifth Avenue look like a river of molten lava. Ruby mapped the streets and cabs in front of her, picturing the city as an intricate game board dotted with little plastic cab pieces. She charged straight into the traffic, ignoring the blaring horns, and checking each car's license plate as she passed.

Ruby's Lines twanged with energy as they ran south, and her adrenaline surged as she fell into the familiar rhythm of tracking a predator. Too bad Harlan couldn't see how good she was at tracking, then he would know she wasn't stupid, and then—her heart stammered and Ruby froze mid-pedal—then Harlan would know that she was a Levant.

"What's wrong?" Winston huffed, his hair plastered to his face by the rain.

Ruby swallowed, remembering the few times on Pan'wei when an injured cape buffalo had turned on the hunters. Although Ruby's Lines had kept her safe, the look of deadly fury in the bulls' eyes still chilled her blood. "If we catch up," she said, the words coming slow and jagged, "they might figure out that I'm a Levant, and then they'd—"

Both boys sat stone silent in the rain, their faces becoming pale as her words sunk in. "They'd capture you," Winston whispered.

"Or worse," Charlie added.

Ruby breathed deeply, trying to focus on how it had felt to hold the Solomon Stone, to harness its power and see the world with new eyes. But even that wasn't enough. The Solomon Stone was amazing, but it was just a thing. Harlan's words circled her menacingly. *If she were a Levant—*

"Maybe we should we go back?" Winston finally asked.

Sighing, Ruby turned her handlebars around toward home or, more accurately, toward Alice's apartment, where Ruby was allowed to stay so long as she put up with the thefts and betrayals of the family who barely tolerated her. It wasn't much of a home, but it was better than being in a coma. Probably.

The Lines rushed downtown in protest, urging her to follow the Solomon Stone, but Ruby resisted. They flared brighter, pulling images of her parents from her mind and then racing between pictures of herself, her parents, and the Solomon Stone. She folded her arms, tired and confused. Ruby already knew that the diamond had belonged to her mother and that now it was rightfully hers. But going after it was too dangerous.

The Lines softened until they were shimmering, misty in the rain. They seemed to understand, but still spun a final image for Ruby, one of her parents standing beside her, their arms wrapped tightly around her. And then Ruby understood. The Solomon Stone wasn't just a thing. It was her best shot at finding her mom and dad. Her only shot. She pivoted back. "Let's keep going."

———

It was a full mile before Ruby found 4G97. The cab moved surprisingly fast through the traffic and it took Ruby's full concentration to hold onto the Line running between herself and the car.

A white archway loomed in front of them where Fifth Avenue ended and Harlan's cab swerved left, and then onto Broadway.

Ruby pedaled forward, squinting into the rain. The streets weren't straight anymore. They meandered and twisted and bumped into each other like rivulets of water on a window.

Everything came to a standstill at Canal Street. Blue police barricades stretched across the road, closing it to cars. The cab stopped as it merged into a wall of stationary vehicles. Harlan and Pierce got out and slipped into the throng of people, promptly disappearing.

Unable to pedal through the crowd, Ruby flung her bike onto the sidewalk and strained to find Harlan and Pierce.

Hundreds of people milled around like they were waiting for something. It looked like a street fair without stalls. A heavy rhythmic beat pulsed through unseen speakers, vibrating the sidewalk beneath her feet. Flashing strobe lights blinked sporadically, making everything look like it was moving in slow motion. "What's going on?" she yelled.

"The Halloween parade," Charlie said.

"Where?" Ruby stared as a cop rode by on a huge brown horse, wondering if it was a real cop or just someone with a really good costume.

"A few blocks away."

"But—" Ruby swallowed hard as more people than the entire population of Pan'wei crowded and jostled around her. There were too many people, too many flashing lights, and too much blaring noise. Even though they were outside, everything felt cramped. The air felt wrong, too warm and sweaty for New York in October, and the uneven ground glinted with dark puddles. Even the Lines slackened and tangled as they fought to find order in the swarming chaos around her.

Ruby's heart accelerated as a foreign sense of disorientation crept over her. For the first time, she felt frightened and small in the anonymous crowd. Her fingers found Winston's arm, clinging to it like a lifeline.

A man dressed like a cat, with wire whiskers poking out from his cheeks and a tail that seemed to move on its own, plucked Ruby's hat off. Indignant, she stared in shock as he held it in his teeth the way a cat might, then picked up Ruby's bike and rode through the crowd, meowing at people who were in his way.

"I don't see them anywhere," Charlie said, straining on

his tiptoes.

Ruby tried to look around, but all she saw was the mass of bodies right next to her. A stab of desperation shot through her. How could she track anyone in this chaos?

Suddenly Ruby saw a huge hulking snake, undulating just inches from her face. She screamed and jumped back, splashing in a shallow puddle. She sprang away, slamming into Charlie, who grunted. A man dressed in a flesh-colored nylon bodysuit had the biggest snake she had ever seen wrapped around him like a blanket. The snake's head weaved through the air at his shoulder, probably trying to decide which person in the crowd it was going to eat. "Holy mother of all gutterballs," Ruby whispered.

"It's just the snake guy," Winston said, slipping himself between her and the reptile.

"Just?" Ruby's heart raced. Leaning against Winston, she tried to get her bearings. But for the first time in her life, she was lost, trapped by puddles and surrounded by people who dressed like cats and wore snakes.

"It's okay," Winston said.

"You have to do your Levanty stuff to find them," Charlie said.

Ruby pulled in a deep breath and closed her eyes, trying to calm down and ignore her wet left foot. This wasn't the ocean. There were Lines. She just had to use them. Her heart slowed and her breath came easier. When she opened her eyes, the snake man was gone and she focused on her friends. "Okay. Charlie." She tugged on his shirt. "I need to get on your shoulders."

Charlie looked like he wanted to protest, but Winston was already boosting Ruby up. Using Charlie's pocket as a foothold, she clambered up his narrow back onto his pointy shoulders.

"Easy," Charlie grunted.

"Shhh," Ruby said as she surveyed the crowd. A barrage of strange costumes and wild hair assaulted her eyes. Lights flashed and glowing circlets floated in the darkness. Most of the people were standing still or drifting west, probably toward the parade. But Harlan and Pierce wouldn't go that way. The Lines shifted and blurred around her, but they told her nothing. Ruby thought about the diamond, picturing it, remembering how it had felt in her hand. Nothing. She swallowed and imagined her parents, together, with her. A faint hum buzzed in her left ear and she turned toward it. A bright Line solidified and she saw Harlan's slick blonde hair duck behind someone.

Ruby jumped down and ran after him, weaving and dodging people and puddles as she went. Winston and Charlie followed close behind. It was slow going at first, but the crowd thinned out after two blocks. Then it was easy enough to see the two men making their way through the streets. Ruby hung back, keeping to the edges of the buildings, afraid Pierce or Harlan would turn and see her.

The buildings got taller as they went, looking more like midtown. Ruby could feel the tension of the diamond pulling her closer. It was hard to keep a block between them, especially since she'd figured out where Harlan was going. His office was on the fortieth floor of the Brixton building, which was just five blocks ahead. She and Miles had picked him up there the day they'd gone shopping for Alice's birthday present.

"Does the Brixton building have a helipad?" she whispered to Winston.

He thought for a minute and then nodded, his eyes bulging.

25

_____

The Brixton building towered above the pavement, like every other building around it. Ruby couldn't remember what Harlan's job was, but it was something important because his offices took up seven floors and had their own separate entrance.

Inside the elevator, Ruby's hand froze, hovering next to the number forty. She looked at Winston and Charlie, shivering in their damp clothes, the last remnants of makeup running down their faces. "We need a plan."

"Right," Charlie said authoritatively.

Ruby waited for him to say something else, but he didn't. "Okay," she sighed, rubbing her forehead. "So they're in Harlan's office with the diamond." Ruby ticked off her fingers. "And the helicopter should be here in..." She fished out her phone to check the time. There was a text message from Alice.

How's everything going?

She stared at the words as if they were in French. Harlan's words, _Ruby's an embarrassment_, seemed to be there too, and Ruby couldn't make sense of either sentence.

"Ruby?" Winston said.

"Yeah?" Ruby blinked, trying to remember what they were talking about.

"Maybe we can use the helicopter," Winston said.

"Huh?" Ruby put her phone away and shook her head to clear it.

"Winston thinks we should steal the helicopter, so we obviously need you to come up with a better plan," Charlie grumbled.

Ruby pulled out her phone again. She'd forgotten to check the time. 8:10. The helicopter would be there in ten minutes, unless it was early.

"I didn't say we should steal a helicopter," Winston said. "I meant that we should use it as a distraction."

"How?" Ruby asked.

"If there was a problem with the helipad, they'd have to go onto the roof to deal with it," he said.

"And they wouldn't take the diamond because it's windy and dangerous on the roof." Ruby grasped the first tendrilled Lines of the plan.

"Right. Then maybe we could sneak into the office and grab the diamond," Winston said.

"What kind of problem with the helipad?" Ruby asked.

"Helicopters need special lights to land on buildings at night. If we find the circuit breaker on the roof and cut off the power, then the pilot won't be able to land."

Charlie pointed excitedly at his brother. "Right! This building was built by the Hammerstein Group in 1964, the same year they did a major update on our apartment building, and, at the time, their wiring infrastructure model—"

"Charlie!" Ruby interrupted.

"I know where it is," Charlie said. "I'll shut off the power on the roof while you and Winston wait on the fortieth floor. As soon as Pierce and Harlan leave, you guys can grab the diamond and run."

"Your uncle won't even know we were here. Everything can go back to normal," Winston said.

Ruby's face fell. Normal. "Normal's gone." She kept her voice flat, not wanting to feel the dark things that hovered around the corners of her mind. She needed to focus. She pushed the button for the thirty-ninth floor.

"He's on the fortieth floor," Winston said.

"They'd notice the elevator opening," she said. "We'll get out at thirty-nine and take the stairs." She turned to Charlie. "When you're done on the roof, go straight home. We'll meet you there. Don't wait for Harlan and Pierce to show up. Just flip the breaker and run," she said.

"Right." Charlie heaved a big breath into his small chest.

"Are you up to this?" Ruby asked as the elevator doors opened. "It could be dangerous."

Charlie leveled a serious gaze at her. "This is the most exciting night of my whole life," he said simply.

Ruby smiled, giving Charlie a thumbs-up as she and Winston exited.

The stairwell was easy to find. Ruby crept up soundlessly, impressed that, for once, Winston was walking quietly too.

Ruby nudged open the door and dropped to the ground. The entire fortieth floor was a large open space broken up only by desks and tables. There were no hallways or doors to use for cover. Harlan's office was the only separate room, and his lights were on, shining through the glass walls like a beacon. The Lines highlighted the quickest way to get to his office unseen.

Lying on her stomach, Ruby pulled herself forward

with her elbows, navigating toward Harlan's office. She felt the diamond's hum vibrating the floor beneath her. It slowed her breath and loosened the tension in her shoulders.

Behind her, Winston sputtered as he struggled forward using only his twiggy arms.

"Push with your knees," Ruby whispered.

Winston's movements got jerkier as he tried to coordinate the momentum of his legs and arms.

Moments later they crouched beneath the desk closest to Harlan's office, peeping through the cord holes. Harlan stood, clutching the velvet bag, rain streaking the windows behind him. They were so close they could've been in the same room. A familiar thrill of anticipation surged through Ruby, the same thing she felt whenever she got this close to prey. But it soon fizzled into anxiety. This wasn't a recreational safari, and Harlan definitely wasn't a cape buffalo. He was a lying, stealing jerk-face.

Harlan's phone buzzed. "Yes? What?" he yelled into it. "That's not—I'll be right up." He glared at Pierce. "Helipad's gone dark," he said, his voice thick with suspicion.

"Huh." Pierce shrugged. "Maybe the storm..."

Harlan opened a wall panel, revealing a small safe.

Ruby's stomach tightened. *Gutterball.* She hadn't considered that Harlan might have an office safe.

"Winston, what do we—"

He shushed her, muttering under his breath and pressing his face tight to the hole.

"I'm sure it's nothing," Pierce said. His eyes were fixed on the bag as Harlan spun the combination dial.

Harlan turned to block Pierce's view as he finished and opened the safe. He placed the black bag inside and pulled out a small shiny handgun.

Ruby froze. She had seen a lot of guns before. Held them, cleaned them, even fired them. But there was something terrifying about the way Harlan looked as he pointed this gun at Pierce.

"Is this some kind of trick?" Harlan asked.

Pierce took a small step back, his palms raised. "It's just a blackout," he said slowly, as if talking to a small child. "Probably from the storm. Let's go check it out. Together."

"You first," Harlan said.

"Okay." Pierce stepped in front and out the office door. Harlan followed, unable to see Pierce's expression dissolve into an angry glare. They walked right by the desk that Ruby and Winston were crouched beneath. Moments later, Ruby heard the elevator doors open and sigh shut. Then there was only silence.

Ruby looked at Winston, not sure if he was up for this.

His eyes were big but determined. "C'mon," he said.

Ruby went straight for the safe and tugged on its door. It was locked fast. Her cheeks flushed in frustration. They were so close.

"Here," Winston pushed past her and grabbed the dial. "I watched Harlan put in the combination."

"You could see that?"

"Sort of. I memorized the length and direction of each turn, so I think I can work it out."

"Wow. That's, like, incredi—"

"If you'll let me concentrate," he cut her off.

"Sorry," Ruby mumbled, watching the elevator bank as Winston's fingers whirled around the dial. Just how long did it take to flip a breaker? Then the safe clicked and Ruby turned, shocked at how fast Winston had done it.

He smiled and shrugged.

Her hand shaking, Ruby reached for the bag. Relief

coursed through her as her fingers wrapped around the soft velvet. The Lines pulsed excitedly, swarming the bag. Her eyes gleamed at Winston. They had done it. They had retrieved the Solomon Stone. Despite all the turmoil of the night, she finally felt safe, confident she could face anything.

"Careful," Winston said.

"It's okay. I've held it before," Ruby said.

"Have you really?" a voice said from behind. Ruby froze. It was Pierce.

"Gutterball," whispered Winston.

Ruby turned, her eyes immediately drawn to Pierce's right hand, which held Harlan's shiny black gun. "Double gutterball," she said.

26

———

Pierce stepped closer and Ruby pivoted, trying to keep the diamond behind her back. She looked at Winston, silently urging him to run, but he just huddled closer to her. "It's mine," she said to Pierce.

Pierce smiled. The diamond in his ring glinted as he flexed his hand. "Perhaps. But possession is nine-tenths of the law. And this diamond," he said, flicking his arm so fast that Ruby didn't realize he'd snatched the velvet bag until she saw it in his hand, "is in my possession."

Unconsciously, Ruby's fingers trailed after the bag, as if the single strong Line connecting her to it was a tractor beam. But she willed her arm back to her side, very aware of Pierce's gun.

"Whatever." Ruby schooled her voice to sound casual as she searched for a Line that would help them escape. But there was just the one, and it ran from her to the bag in a thick, bright streak. "You robbed two twelve-year-olds. Good job. C'mon Winston." She grabbed his hand, which was cold and shaking. "Let's get out of here."

Pierce laughed, shifting his weight so that more of his

bulk stood between Ruby and the door. "We both know you're not leaving." He looked at the bag in his hand, then at her. "A Levant could never bear to leave the Solomon Stone."

A quiver of panic flushed through Ruby. "What? I'm not—"

"Only a Levant could've tracked the Solomon Stone here tonight. Besides, you didn't swim at camp. Even Winston swam, and he's afraid of everything, including his own Sapience."

Winston let out a squeaking gasp that made Pierce smirk.

"Neither of you are half so clever as you think," he said. "In fact, I'm a little disappointed. My whole life I've been told how impossible it is to capture a Levant, but then I get the Solomon Stone and you come straight to me. Even your extremely protective family was no match for your own stupidity. So," he said, clenching the bag and smiling, "as long as I have the diamond, I have you."

"Winston has to go home." Ruby twisted to look at Winston, silently begging him to run, certain that Pierce wouldn't leave her to chase Winston. But Winston just stared at Pierce like a bird mesmerized by a cobra. "He has a curfew."

Pierce snorted. "No one leaves." He turned his attention and the gun to Winston.

Winston moved his mouth, but no sound came out.

Ruby turned so she wouldn't have to see his terror. Her mind raced. There had to be a way out of this. She scanned the room for her Lines but there was just one, stubbornly clinging to the velvet bag. "We'll be missed," she said, wondering if it were true in her case. What exactly would Alice do if she got home and found the apartment empty?

Pierce ignored her. "Seems like the Solomon Stone makes more trouble than it solves." He tussled the bag. "I mean, your friend," he gestured at Winston. "He's not much, but he's yours, isn't he? Your first real friend. Loyal and true, if unimpressive, physically speaking. But once you met this," he lifted the bag and tipped it so that the Solomon Stone slid out onto the desk. "Well, poor Winston couldn't compete with this, could he?"

The single Line connecting her to the diamond disappeared into the stone, then hundreds of Lines burst from its center, thin but implacable, connecting Ruby to everything in the room, the building, the city, maybe even the world. Ruby's lungs loosened. Finally. Eyes wide, she studied the Lines and their source, searching for the threads that would help them escape.

Pierce watched her face and smiled, probably misreading her expression for devotion and wonder. "It's not your fault, really," Pierce said.

"Duh." Ruby scowled. "You're the psychopath holding two kids at gunpoint, not me." Ruby wished he would just shut up so that she could work the Lines. She'd isolated the ones she needed, but didn't quite understand or, more accurately, believe, what they were trying to tell her. Rather than showing a plan to disarm Pierce or a secret escape route from the office, as she'd expected, they seemed to be pulling her toward the two diamonds, the large one on the desk and the small one embedded in the ring on Pierce's finger.

Surprisingly, Pierce removed his ring and shoved it into Winston's hand. Then he wrenched Winston's other arm, positioning it directly above the Solomon Stone.

Ruby's heart jerked. Winston looked exactly like Octavius had in Pierce's office before he'd passed out.

Winston shuddered, staring at the ring in his hand like it was poison.

"The Solomon Stone is corrosive," Pierce went on, apparently not caring that no one was listening to him. "It builds empires but cankers everything else. Just look at your family. Your uncle betrayed his own brother just for this. And he didn't even know—"

"Shut up," said Ruby. Her eyes flicked between Winston and the Lines.

Pierce raised an eyebrow at Ruby. Then he tightened the gun's aim on Winston. "Pick up the diamond," he ordered Winston.

"No." Winston's lips were so taut that Ruby was amazed any sound came out.

Pierce cocked the gun. "Yes."

Winston raised his quivering chin. He was trying not to cry.

Ruby took a final breath and hoped desperately that the Lines were right. She stepped between Winston and Pierce's gun, hoping Pierce wouldn't shoot a Levant. She grabbed the ring from Winston's clammy hand. Then Ruby took one deep breath and reached for the Solomon Stone. The diamond jumped into her palm, sending a white-hot flash of pain surging through her arm. She screamed.

"No!" Pierce said.

"Ruby!" Winston shrieked.

Both voices echoed strangely in her head. Ruby braced herself for the pain and darkness that had overcome Octavius. But there was only the sharp sting in her arm, which was subsiding every second into a throbbing, but bearable, ache. None of Pierce's memories poured from the diamond into her brain. But something else, larger, and indistinct, crowded around her mental space.

The office was blurry and Ruby saw everything twice, like she was looking through binoculars with just one eye. A shot of pain split through her head as she tried to merge the images together. She whimpered and the noise somehow echoed. A heavy darkness engulfed her mind. Greed, malice, and fear intermingled with shadowy thoughts and feelings that she didn't have names for. Closing her eyes, she fell to her knees.

But she still saw herself—a tiny white-haired child cowering on the floor. It was like watching security camera footage of a room she was still in. She saw Winston from an incongruent angle and contempt flickered through her. Toward Winston? That wasn't right. She saw Pierce too, but only his hands.

Ruby gasped as she suddenly understood what was happening. She wasn't Rendering memories from Pierce's diamond. She was reading his mind. Everything he saw, heard, and thought right now crowded into her head next to her own thoughts. And Winston was right—other people's feelings were excruciating.

"Ruby," Pierce said.

And Ruby could feel all the fear and alarm that was hidden within that word. She inhaled deeply, trying to think. Mentally, she reached for the Lines that were with her inside Pierce's head. It felt like a room with thousands of little drawers. In front of the drawers she saw an image of herself on the ground with Winston beside her.

She felt Pierce's mind racing round and round the drawers as he stared at Ruby grasping the diamonds. He thought of her like a winning lottery ticket sitting next to a raging fire. If he didn't do something soon, she would end up worthless.

"Ruby," he said in a soft, fatherly voice.

But he wasn't her father. Her mother and father were gone thanks to him and Harlan. A Line quivered and tightened with this last thought. Ruby grasped it. Harlan? How could Harlan help her? "Where's Harlan?" she asked, wincing at the limpness of her words as they pinged around the strange space.

Pierce's mind tightened at the name. "He's seeing to things upstairs," he said.

He was lying. Ruby could see it. A drawer in his mind slid open, and an image of Harlan emerged. Ruby watched as Pierce's memory replayed his attack on Harlan just minutes ago. In just three moves, Pierce had disarmed and knocked Harlan unconscious. Ruby's own muscles twitched as Pierce's mind re-lived the encounter. She could feel the precision of intense training in his muscle memory. How had Pierce learned to fight like that?

"Who are you?" Ruby whispered.

"Drop the diamond," Pierce said, ignoring her question. But a distant corner of his mind answered it automatically. Ruby followed a Line to a drawer sliding open in the back of Pierce's consciousness. An echo of foreign words murmured, accompanying the feel of white-hot sun reflecting off scorched sand. Other men, just like Pierce, were there too, performing the same drills, repeating the same words, sharing the same purpose. The whole memory was infused with one word that Ruby recognized. *Azarians*.

Ruby's eyes flew open, and a new flash of dissonant pain stabbed her. Pierce was an Azarian. She and Winston were being held at gunpoint by an Azarian operative. The air in the room seemed to thicken as cold dread flooded her own mind. There was no way out of this. Even the Lines swirled in circles around the information.

"Put the diamond down and you'll be fine," Pierce said.

Ruby could feel his hands itching to snatch it from her fingers, but he didn't. He was afraid that the carbon from his skin would join the bonds and pull him into the Rendering. Then he'd end up in a pile on the floor like Octavius.

Ruby sensed something, a slight tightening of a Line that she felt but couldn't see. She frantically traced every Line, but whatever it was remained out of reach.

Pierce frowned, regarding her clinically. The girl was fading. Her dirty face was pale and shaking. He stepped toward her, dozens of drawers opening and closing in succession, but he knew that their contents—information he'd collected and stored throughout his life—wouldn't help with this. He needed to break the Rendering. Should he shoot her somewhere non-lethally, or just shoot the boy? But then Pierce hefted the gun, which was just a little lighter than it should be. He frowned. Harlan was a civilian. Sketchy enough to keep a gun in his safe, but not a loaded gun. The bullets were probably somewhere nearby, but finding them would waste time. And the girl could collapse any second. Or she might disappear the moment his eyes left her, like the Levant she was.

Ruby exhaled as the Line she'd been searching for flared brightly, showing her their one narrow shot at escape. Rising slowly, she locked eyes with Pierce. She could feel his surprise at the ferocity on her face and it made her smile. Through his eyes she looked almost feral.

Ruby slowly twisted Pierce's ring so that the diamond didn't touch her skin. The weight and darkness of the drawers disappeared. And she felt only the intense sharpening of her senses that had come the first time she'd held the Solomon Stone.

Ruby grabbed Winston's hand, found the brightest Line, and ran out of the office. The instant their hands touched, Ruby felt something sealing them together. Instinctively she knew that the skin-to-skin contact had pulled Winston into her experience with the Solomon Stone. Winston gasped, but his legs moved faster than Ruby would have thought was possible. Together they ran through the dim open office floor, dodging desks and chairs in unspoken unity. Intense energy was everywhere, almost pulling them forward, making Ruby feel like a train racing down a track.

One of Ruby's Lines tracked Pierce, who she could see in her peripheral vision. He tore through Harlan's office, looking for the bullets. When he found them, he jammed a couple of bullets into the gun's clip and shoved the rest in his pocket. Gun loaded, he ran after Ruby and Winston.

In front of her, Ruby saw the four green letters of the exit sign above the stairwell. Squeezing Winston's hand, she ran faster. Beside her, a small Line registered Winston's smile as he gave a burst of speed to match her pace.

27

_____

Ruby and Winston crashed through the fire exit and rushed down the stairs, so fast and smooth that Ruby felt like water flowing down a cliff. She closed her eyes against the glare of the fluorescent lights but didn't slow down. The Lines were strong enough that she could sense them with her eyes shut. The diamond pulsed and burned in her hand, sending prickly tingles all over her body, whispering all the secrets of the space to her.

Several seconds later the door crashed open and Ruby heard Pierce's clunky footsteps on the landing. Winston gurgled a scream. Pierce blurred past the railings two stories above them. Then a spark of light flashed and the terrible sound of gunfire split through the stairwell. A chunk of cement tore off the wall by Ruby's left shoulder. Anger and panic rushed through her, but were quickly dissolved by the diamond's energy.

Dropping Winston's hand, she jammed her thumb onto Pierce's diamond. Seeing through Pierce's eyes was like watching herself in a horror movie. She and Winston looked like prey, their delicate black limbs moving in shadows and her white shock of hair standing out in the dim fluorescent light. Pierce moved unevenly, favoring his left leg. Some old injury in his left knee sent pain up his leg each time his foot hit concrete.

Coolly professional, Pierce ignored the pain and kept the gun trained on Ruby. Ruby could see the dark calculations jumping through his thoughts. A moving shooter aiming at a moving target couldn't guarantee a clean shot. Pierce trained the gun on her legs anyway, telling himself that, if worse came to worst, Ruby could still be a Levant with only one leg.

Ruby swerved hard, away from the gun barrel. Pierce responded automatically, swinging the gun as she moved. But the quick movement left him off balance and he stumbled, landing hard on his left knee. Ruby yanked her thumb away from Pierce's diamond, but not before she felt the pain explode through his mind.

Before Pierce could get up, Ruby shoved open the fire door and yanked Winston through, leaving the echoes of Pierce's cursing behind them. The thirty-second floor was dark, but the Lines showed her exactly where the elevator bank was and she sprinted toward it. She jammed the call button before she'd even fully stopped.

"Are you sure about this?" Winston panted.

"We can't outrun a gun."

He nodded, still gulping for breath. "Was that... was I, when we—" he stuttered, clasping his hands together.

"When we held hands?" The numbers above the elevator lit up slowly one at a time—twenty-three... a billion unbearable seconds... twenty-four...

Ruby touched the diamond in Pierce's ring again, wincing as she saw him pass the thirty-fourth floor landing.

Winston blushed. "It was like a turbo charge. I could

see everything. The Lines, the space. My legs knew exactly how to move, and fast."

Ruby nodded, her eyes riveted to the elevator door, willing the car up the shaft toward them. Twenty-six... twenty-seven... twenty-eight...

"It was incredible. Is that what you feel—"

"Shh," Ruby said, as if his words were somehow slowing down the elevator. She scanned the area around them, sending her Lines out to find hiding places in case Pierce arrived before the elevator did. Twenty-nine... thirty. Just two more floors. Thirty-one...

She tapped Pierce's ring. *Gutterball.* He was on their landing now. He burst onto the floor and Ruby held perfectly still, hoping he wouldn't see them and would move on to the next floor. But just then the elevator pinged and the doors slid open. Pierce's head whipped around and he raced toward them.

Ruby dove into the car, Winston crashing beside her. She punched the first floor and the "close door" button repeatedly. "C'mon, c'mon, c'mon," she pleaded. It seemed like the doors were going in slow motion. They finally closed just as Pierce skidded to a stop in front of them, his face contorted with rage.

Ruby exhaled and slumped against the wall. They'd made it. Into the elevator, at least.

"Whoa," Winston whispered.

"You okay?"

He blinked several times, then looked down at himself. "Yeah. I guess so. Are you? Did the Rendering hurt you?"

"No. It wasn't..." There was no easy way to explain what had happened. "It wasn't the same for me. Can you text Charlie and see if he got out?" Ruby stroked the diamond on Pierce's ring. There was an aching pain in her forehead as she closed her eyes and dropped into his mind.

Pierce quickly reloaded the gun and then started pacing, glaring at the elevator bank as pain shot through his left knee. Ruby gasped as she felt echoes of the sensation. She dropped the ring into her pocket and dug her palms into her eyes.

"Charlie's headed home," Winston said.

Ruby nodded, relieved. That was something.

"So... Pierce knows you're a Levant."

"Yeah." Ruby wrapped her fingers around the Solomon Stone in her pocket, taking comfort from the strangely familiar feel of it. Her Lines stretched beyond the elevator's narrow walls and reached into the dark city beyond. She would need every single one of them to get out of this.

"That's pretty bad."

"Yeah." The small space felt crowded with her unspoken words.

"Do you think Pierce will tell Harlan that you're a Levant?"

"No." Ruby was much more worried that Pierce would tell the Azarians that she was a Levant, but she didn't say it. Telling Winston that Pierce was an Azarian would only freak him out and put him in more danger. "I think Pierce was just using Harlan to get to the Solomon Stone."

"And to get to you."

"That too." The Lines were constructing a map of the city so detailed that it looked like a live image. Dozens of other Lines careened around it, probing for an escape route. Ruby glared at them, not liking the options they were finding. But she couldn't argue with them either. The brightest Line led to Fulton Street Station, hopped the uptown train that would arrive in exactly eight minutes, rode it to Grand

Central Station, ditched Winston, and boarded the first train out of the city. Alone.

"I think you should tell Alice that you're a Levant, and that Pierce is after you," Winston said. "He's just a teacher. She can protect you from him."

"Mmm." Ruby answered noncommittally. *Alice.* If she left tonight, she'd never see Alice again. Her chest was tight at the thought. But then Harlan's words cut in. *Ruby's not "Callahan."* Ruby dragged her hand across her face. Maybe Alice wouldn't care.

Winston sighed and tilted his head onto her shoulder. "So what do we do now?" he asked.

Tears pricked Ruby's eyes. She'd have to leave Winston too. And he would actually miss her. Maybe as much as she would miss him. More, probably, because his life had been pretty lame before her. She would miss Charlie too, and Miles, and Chloe, and even the nervous little dogs.

Suddenly Ruby felt exhausted. She tapped Pierce's ring and winced at the headache that came. Pierce was in an elevator now too, glaring at the floor indicator as it flicked from eighteen to seventeen. His head swam with images that shimmered and shifted, all focused on Ruby. Over and over he pictured yanking her off the ground by her hair. Ruby grimaced and pulled her finger away. *Psychopath.*

"If we're fast, we can make it to Fulton Street Station." Ruby struggled to keep her voice even. "There's an uptown express every six minutes. If we get on it before Pierce catches up, we're clear."

Winston nodded. "But when you tell Alice that you're a Levant, make her promise not to tell Harlan. I don't think you can trust him."

"Yeah. No kidding." Ruby smiled at the understatement. Then the elevator slowed and she stood, all of her muscles straining taut. She looked at Winston and smiled as if they weren't in mortal peril. "Run fast." She winked.

Winston tried unsuccessfully to wink back. "I will."

The doors opened and they bolted through the lobby, hurtling through the exit into the wet, cold night.

The rain fell in sheets now, as if someone was dumping truckloads of water off the roofs. The pavement glistened with puddles of dark water. Cold black spots edged Ruby's vision and her breath came short. There was no time for this. Pierce was coming and she had to get to the subway, fast. Grasping the diamond, she focused on the brightest Line and ran, zigzagging and weaving around each tiny pool of terrifying water.

Tapping Pierce's diamond, she saw that he was outside too, cold and angry as he followed the speck of white-blonde hair moving through the wet empty streets like a beacon. Ruby grunted. She really hated that cat guy for stealing her hat.

———

 A CROWD of people huddled at the entrance of Fulton Street Station, waiting for the rain to stop. Using her Lines, Ruby fought through them, plunging though the crush and onto the uptown platform. Everything was thick and hot from too many people breathing the same air. Squinting, Ruby found a Line through the shifting masses and tugged Winston's arm, ducking and dodging as they went.

At the edge of the platform, Ruby leaned out and looked down the tunnel. Two round lights shook through the darkness and the ground beneath her rumbled. Hot air lifted her hair from her face as the train approached.

Ruby checked behind her. There was no sign of Pierce. The Lines hummed optimistically around them. If she and Winston could just get onto the train, they would be safe. Seconds oozed slowly by until the train finally screeched up to the platform. Ruby squeezed Winston's hand and smiled. Something had finally gone their way.

The doors opened and Ruby had one foot on the car before everyone had even gotten off. But suddenly an icy hand clamped onto her shoulder and yanked her back. She turned around. Pierce.

He sneered, his eyes slitted and hard, like a snake ready to strike. His hand clenched her shoulder like a vise.

Ruby turned to Winston. He could still get away. But one look at his face told her that he wouldn't leave her. Stupid boy was too loyal for his own good. The train doors were about to close.

"Winston," she said.

"What?" he asked.

"I'm sorry."

"Huh?"

The doors chimed and slid toward each other. Ruby pivoted and kicked Winston hard in the stomach, sending him sprawling onto the dirty floor of the train. Gasping, he lifted his head and looked at Ruby, his face a mess of shock. The doors shut and the train lurched forward.

Ruby winced. That's the last thing Winston would remember about her.

Pierce grunted and jammed her forward, limping as he walked. Ruby wanted to scream and jerk away, but the press of the gun barrel against her rib cage stopped her. She had seen enough of Pierce's mind to know that he would use it, even in a crowd.

Ruby wrapped her fingertips around the Solomon Stone tucked in her pocket, but the Lines buzzed pointlessly around the station in a tangled mess, showing her how clearly trapped she was. Just one Line flickered, but it dove uselessly off the platform. Then something glinted in her peripheral vision. Ruby turned and saw a small ladder hanging off the lip of the platform, leading onto the tracks. Her eyes widened as she realized the Line's meaning.

"You'll only hurt yourself struggling," Pierce hissed in her ear, keeping her close as they jostled through the thinning crowd.

Inhaling slowly, Ruby collected all her anger and fear and forced her shoulders to assume a slumped, defeated posture.

Pierce quickened his pace. "Finally. I knew you'd eventually get tired and give up."

"Except..." Ruby said softly.

"Huh?" Pierce tilted his head closer to hers, unconsciously shifting the gun away from her.

His fingers still pressed into her arm like talons, but Ruby pulled back as far as she could, hoping her submissive posture would buy her a few inches. "Except I'm a Callahan," she said, her chin lifting despite everything she had learned about her family tonight. Her muscles tensed. She would only get one chance. "And Callahans never give up." Igniting her stacked rage, Ruby kicked Pierce's injured knee. There was a satisfying grinding, cracking noise. Pierce cried out and his grip loosened. Ruby twisted and ducked out of his hand. Then she leapt off the edge of the platform, landing in the cool darkness of the subway tunnel.

28

———

The darkness didn't bother Ruby. It never had. Not when she had the Lines. But even so, the ground in the tunnel was uneven and railroad ties kept springing up, tripping her every other step. An ethereal blue light reflected off the metal tracks. The tunnel was narrow, barely wide enough for two trains. Ruby swallowed down the dread in her throat. She was not supposed to be here. It was dangerous. But Pierce and his gun were worse.

She thought about her bedroom at home, cozy and safe. Tears collected in the corners of her eyes. She would never go home again. *Keep running*, she told herself. *Survive now and you can cry later*. The tunnel widened, revealing a squat hut with a metal roof perched between the two tracks.

Something echoed in the dark behind her. Footfalls. Big, irregular, clumping footfalls. Pierce. He had followed her into the tunnel. She could see him, silhouetted in the smoky blue haze, stumbling and limping as he picked his way forward.

Ruby veered to the edge, hugging the darkness near the

wall. Tightening her fingers around the Solomon Stone, she ran, clinging to the shadows like a cockroach. Pierce was injured and she was fast. If she stayed silent and unseen, he wouldn't be able to catch up.

Then the ground shook and Ruby's heart stuttered. Two round white lights materialized in the darkness behind her. A train was coming. Fast. Her ears filled with the roar of the engine and the blaring horn.

Ruby jumped to the empty tracks and ran, stumbling on the uneven railroad ties as she tore through the dark and the noise. Then a terrible rumble shuddered through the trackbed and a second pair of white circles appeared in front of her. Ruby's breath caught. Another train. Death rushed toward her from both sides. The Solomon Stone throbbed against her palm, and Ruby saw a bright white Line running straight toward the little hut.

Against every instinct, Ruby followed the Line, sprinting toward the oncoming train. She narrowed her eyes and sucked in stinging breaths, willing her legs to move faster. To her left, the northbound train passed, an endless wall of screeching metal.

The train in front of her was closing in fast. Its horn screamed and its brakes squealed, showering Ruby's face with sparks. She had five seconds until impact. Four, three... now! Ruby leapt off the track, smashing into the corrugated metal of the shack. Pressing herself flat against the wall, she felt the train roar by, inches away, its terrible noise filling Ruby's senses so completely that nothing else seemed to exist.

The train finally passed, leaving an echo of wind and light in the tunnel. Ruby lifted her head, blinking at the tracks where she had almost died. Metallic air stung her nostrils as she tried to slow her breathing. Rising shakily, she brushed the dust off her hands.

A loud crack filled the tunnel and a searing pang slashed through her right thigh. A sickening burnt smell wafted up through the darkness. Ruby touched her leg and sticky, warm blood coated her palm. Pierce!

"You shot me?" Ruby screamed into the darkness, cursing the hut's dim light. "You idiot!" Stomach turning, she probed the wound with shaky fingers. The bullet had grazed her outer thigh. It wasn't life threatening, but it hurt like a nest of angry wasps.

Ruby jumped onto the tracks and ran, glad that her leg still bore her weight. She had chased enough wounded animals to know that the injury would hamper her soon. The pain interfered with the Lines, making them seem slow and blurry. But she already knew that the next station was less than a mile away. Getting there first was her only chance. She sprinted flat out, every cell in her body dedicated to forward momentum.

Even as the Lines informed her that the distance between them was growing, she knew she couldn't outrun Pierce anymore. In a few minutes, her adrenaline would burn off and she would slow down. Her Lines automatically calculated their separate speeds and the distance between them like a deadly story problem. She had five or six minutes, if he didn't shoot her again.

Tears blurred her vision. She pushed an angry fist across her eyes and kept running. *Callahans don't give up.* They might rob, embarrass, and betray each other, but they didn't give up.

"Ruby!" Pierce yelled in a raspy voice. His injured knee must be taking its toll. That was something at least. "Ruby, come back before you get hit by a train."

Ruby didn't bother answering. She had to keep moving and find a place to hide.

"I won't hurt you," he said.

"You just shot me," she snorted, instantly regretting the wasted breath.

"We can work together. I can teach you how to use the diamond."

The diamond. Ruby reached into her pocket and clenched it tight. The pain lessened as her Lines sharpened and the space around her snapped into order. She ran faster, suddenly part of the concrete, steel, and darkness. There was a way out of this. She just had to find it. And she could find anything.

Ruby's Lines probed the tunnel ahead. There was something there. Something familiar but forgotten. Stroking the diamond, she listened to the space. Then she remembered. That ghost station, Old City Hall, was on this subway line. And it was close. She might be able to make it there before Pierce caught up.

"I know where your parents are," Pierce yelled.

Ruby stumbled. "What?"

"Your parents. They're alive and I can help you find them."

The diamond burned in her hand, filling her body with a single command: *Move*. Pushing away Pierce's words, Ruby squeezed the diamond and ran.

After a few hard minutes, Ruby could feel the adrenaline wearing off. Her feet grew heavier with each step. But it didn't matter. A few yards ahead the track curved and sloped upwards. Then a huge space opened like a cathedral rising out of the darkness. The ceiling soared over graceful brick arches as moonlight filtered through the skylights.

Ruby climbed awkwardly up the ladder, smiling as she glimpsed the exit doors beyond a stairwell. Finally.

But her heart tightened when she stepped onto the platform. A pool of dark water stretched from wall to wall, barring her exit.

29

———

Ruby's leg throbbed as she limped to the edge of the water, looking for a narrow place to cross. There was none. The pool of water was at least fifteen feet wide. She tried to tell herself it was only a big puddle, probably just a few inches deep, but it might as well have been the Pacific Ocean. Even as she held the Solomon Stone, all her Lines stopped abruptly at its edge.

A lone exit sign flickered just a few yards away. Clutching the wall, Ruby closed her eyes and tried to order her fear away. Breathing deep, she nudged her foot in. Nothing happened. Another step and one toe was wet. Dark spots blurred her vision. *Gutterball.* Maybe she could outrun it. Quickly she forced another step and the water sloshed around her ankle, icy and terrible. Panic burned up her throat. Gasping, Ruby opened her eyes and saw nothing but dark, unfathomable water. She tried to run across it, but her injured leg buckled and she splashed down, half-immersed in the frigid blackness. Screaming, she scuttled backwards to the dry ground and cowered against the tile wall.

She needed to get away, to hide, but she couldn't move. Pressing her palms against the cold cement, Ruby tried to convince her brain that they were on dry ground. That they were safe. But she wasn't safe, and her brain knew it. She sat, wounded and trapped, defeated by a few inches of water. Exhausted, she gave in, shuddering as her sobs escaped in barking gasps and tears streamed down her dirty face.

Eventually her breath slowed and the tears stopped. Light-headed, Ruby surveyed herself in the dim light, shivering as her wet clothes sucked the warmth from her. A thin film of blackish-orange dust covered her shirt, and her pants were soaked with blood. She pulled the fabric away from her wound and winced. It was bad. Blood seeped out steadily, and little yellow pearls of fat peeked out. It needed stitches. "Gutterball," she said aloud.

Suddenly her ears pricked at a noise: a shoe landing on cement. Pierce. Ruby struggled to her feet. She had to cross, right now. But her legs wouldn't budge.

Pierce's cold laugh echoed through the empty station.

Ruby slid his ring onto her left hand, clasping the Solomon Stone with her right. The headache crashed back as she stole into his mind.

Pain shot through Pierce's knee with each limping step. He grimaced at Ruby. Stupid feral child. She'd probably broken something when she'd kicked him. He gripped the gun tighter. She'd pay for that.

Ruby shuffled closer to the tunnel.

"I'll shoot if you run," he said. "Levant or no Levant, I'm not going into that rathole again."

Ruby's breath caught. He wasn't lying. She watched Pierce look at her, cringing as she felt him assess her pathetic state. Coldly, he evaluated Ruby's bloody leg, quickly concluding that it was a flesh wound. But the girl still looked pale and drawn. It was time to finish this.

"Do you really know where my parents are?" Ruby asked.

"Of course," Pierce answered. But no memory-drawer slid open to back up his claim. Instead, Ruby felt a dark, shifting haze encircling his words. Her heart fell. He was lying.

Pierce fished a crumpled brown bag from his pocket and held it out with his left hand, keeping the gun steady with his right. "Drop the diamond in here," he said, still not wanting to touch it. "Then I'll take you to your parents." Another lie.

"What are you really going to do with me?" Ruby asked. A wispy image formed in Pierce's mind. For a moment, Ruby saw herself locked in a clean, windowless room. Like an animal in a cage. But the image was shadowy and uncertain, and Ruby realized that, despite all his efforts to capture her, Pierce hadn't decided what to do with her yet.

"I'll take care of you," Pierce said, wanting to calm her down.

Ruby snorted. All his thoughts about her future were cloaked with malice and haze. "You? You and Harlan are the reason my parents left."

"Don't be ridiculous," he said, as the fog of deceit thickened in his mind. But Ruby knew her words would prompt a flurry of drawers to open, and she followed Pierce's memory as he slunk through a hallway in Alice's apartment. Alice and Atticus were hosting a large party and Harlan had invited Pierce. But Pierce had slipped away from the crowds to look for *it*. He assumed a casual posture as he passed the living room, brimming with people. His expert eyes picked out Harlan, deep in conversation with Emmeline. He knew

Harlan was distracting her, waiting for Pierce to show up and deftly switch Emmeline's pendant with the decoy, as they'd planned. But Pierce crept past them. He had bigger plans.

He crept on until finally he followed a dim light to a room. Silently, he peeked through the door crack, his heart racing when he saw that it was the master bedroom. And there she was. Ruby, the Levant child, lying on the bed. Pierce's fingers tightened, ready, but he kept stone still. The Levant child wasn't alone. Alice lay on the bed beside her, legs tucked under her expensive sequined dress, oblivious to her messy hair and smudged makeup. She lay nose to nose with Ruby, giggling and cooing with her.

Shivering in the Old City Hall Station, Ruby studied Alice's face looking at hers through Pierce's recollection. It was glowing with unmistakable happiness and... love. But Pierce's memory took little notice, fixated instead on the thing the Azarians had been searching for for generations. A Levant child.

Ruby gasped, squinting through her headache at Pierce's face. "You wanted more than just the Solomon Stone, didn't you? You were after me the whole time."

Pierce smiled, considering the twelve-year-old girl before him now. Not as malleable as a three-year-old, but she would do. "You were always the primary target. But I knew that if I played with the Solomon Stone long enough that it would eventually draw you out."

Played? He'd put Octavius in a coma. All this time Ruby thought she'd been tracking the Solomon Stone, outwitting Pierce and Harlan. But in reality, she'd just been circling the trap that Pierce had baited for her. "Why didn't you just take me and the diamond nine years ago?"

"Things didn't go to plan," he said simply. In his mind,

entire rows of drawers flew open and Pierce was back in the apartment, this time in Atticus's office at 2 a.m., trying to remain unnoticed as dozens of policemen and federal agents milled around. Pierce's mind was tight with frustration and failure. And his skin crawled at the proximity of so many federal agents. How had Atticus Callahan managed to summon this many FBI agents at 2 a.m.? He itched to leave, but he couldn't afford to miss any of the information that was kicking around this room.

Ruby scoured Pierce's memory of the library until she found Alice, crying by the large desk. A younger Miles stood beside her, an arm around her shoulders, his own face gaunt and his eyes bloodshot.

At the desk, Atticus Callahan looked alert as he showed the Solomon Stone to an FBI agent. "Emmeline never took it off," he said. "But then tonight, after we noticed that they were missing, I found it on my desk."

Ruby's throat tightened at the thought of leaving the Solomon Stone somewhere and walking away. How had Emmeline done it?

"The clasp isn't broken," the agent said. "It looks like she removed it herself."

Pierce's jaw clenched as he strained to hear the conversation. It didn't make sense. No Levant would leave the Solomon Stone behind.

"Do you need to take it for evidence?" Atticus asked.

"No. But we'll dust it for prints."

Pierce's spine stiffened and a string of foreign curse words paraded through his head. The Solomon Stone was his best chance at finding Emmeline and the Levant child. But now there were federal agents everywhere, inspecting it, cataloguing it, and dusting it for prints. He wiped his face with his hand. How could Emmeline be gone if the Solomon Stone was still here?

Ruby laid her cheek against the cold tile wall, trying to anchor herself. Pierce's mind was dragging her through the memories so fast that she felt dizzy.

"I'm sure Harlan could help with that," Atticus's authoritative, tired voice cut in to Pierce's musings. Several people looked at Harlan, who stood a little apart from the rest of his family, his keen eyes tracking the Solomon Stone as the agent studied it.

"Harlan?" Atticus said.

"Huh?" Harlan didn't even glance up.

"The agents need a list of Rex's friends and associates."

"Oh." Harlan rubbed his eyes, which were still fixed on the stone. "Sure."

In his corner, Pierce cringed. So transparent. Harlan might as well write *I want to steal that necklace* on his forehead.

When the agent finished, he handed the Solomon Stone to Atticus, who boxed it up neatly and locked it in his safe. "She'll want it when she comes back," he said quietly.

Alice and Miles nodded passively, but Harlan's eyes burned with something approaching horror as the Solomon Stone slipped behind the biometrically secured walls of the safe.

Pierce watched too, scoffing at Harlan's shortsightedness. The real prize had slipped through his stubby fingers hours ago.

Then suddenly Pierce's brain shifted, and Ruby saw him blaze through dozens of drawers, snatching fragments of the evening and inspecting them. He lingered on an image of Harlan talking to Emmeline, his hungry eyes never leaving her pendant.

Pierce's mind held this fact tight, snapping it together with everything else he knew about Emmeline until understanding sparked. What if Emmeline *had* guessed that Harlan intended to steal her diamond that night? She could have deduced everything from that. Including the fact that an Azarian was using Harlan to get to Ruby. It would explain why Emmeline had done the unthinkable and left the Solomon Stone behind. She'd left it so Harlan wouldn't have a reason to help Pierce. She'd sacrificed the diamond to save Ruby.

Pierce's mind raced ahead, noting how well Emmeline's plan had worked, at first. She'd cleverly hidden Ruby on an island, the one place on earth he would never think to check. And Harlan had indeed been too obsessed with the diamond locked in his father's safe to search for his niece. But then Miles had found Ruby. And Harlan had called Pierce the next day, begging for advice on how to get Miles to open the safe now that Ruby was coming back.

Ruby wrenched her fingers from Pierce's diamond, unable to tolerate the torrent of information any longer. She sagged against the wall, panting as she tried to find her bearings.

But the moonlight glinting off of Pierce's gun brought her brutally back to the present. Azarian, gun, trapped. Right. Things were bad. But the ground beneath her feet somehow felt firmer as she touched the pocketknife through her pants pocket. *The strength of the wolf is the pack.* She had a pack. Harlan was wrong. Emmeline hadn't abandoned her and Alice wasn't embarrassed. Alice missed her and was waiting for her at home. With Chloe and Miles and... she shivered. *Harlan.*

"Put the diamond in the bag," Pierce ordered, "then I'll take you to a doctor."

Ruby studied Pierce, desperately trying to calculate her options. The Lines were bright, refracting around the space, but not one of them could find a way to escape a gun at short range.

"Now!" Pierce barked. "Or I swear I'll shoot your other leg."

Ruby inched the Solomon Stone from her pocket and raised both her hands. "Okay, okay." Pierce hadn't lied when he'd said he would take care of her. Maybe the locked room wouldn't be so bad, so long as he let her keep the diamond.

"In the bag," Pierce said.

"I'll go with you," she said. "but only if you let me keep the diamond." The Solomon Stone flared hot in her hand. *Let go.*

Ruby and Pierce stared at each other, Pierce's head swaying slightly. "This isn't a negotiation." His finger twitched on the trigger.

"I need it," she said softly. The diamond throbbed hot. *Let go.* But Ruby's fingers wouldn't budge. Then suddenly the Solomon Stone went cold and Ruby gasped as its power dissipated. Pain shot through her wounded leg like lightning, and she almost stumbled. But she knew. She had to leave the diamond to save herself. Like Emmeline had. The diamond wanted it. Emmeline wanted it. Everyone who loved her wanted it. The faintest whisper of a word slinked up her arm. *Run.*

Moonlight bounced off the water, pulling Ruby's attention upwards. What had Alice said about celestial navigation? There were no stars, but the lights of the surrounding buildings shone in steady bright rows like gridlines on a map.

Ruby took a deep breath and threw the diamond at

Pierce's face. He fumbled to catch it, dropping the gun, but missed. The Solomon Stone skittered across the platform toward the tracks and he scrambled after it, probably confident that the puddle prevented Ruby's escape.

Eyes fixed on the sky, Ruby charged into the water. She focused on the lights above, pushing through the darkness lapping at her feet. Panic hovered all around her, but she kept moving, following the skylight map. Her muscles strained as if she were running through tar. But her feet splashed on through the swirling abyss until they found dry concrete.

Exhilaration thrummed through her as she stumbled up the stairs and reached for the door, practically tasting her freedom.

But there was splashing behind her. Of course. Pierce wasn't afraid of the puddle.

Ruby lunged for the door, but she wasn't fast enough. Pierce yanked her wrist, sending red pain up her arm that blurred her vision.

He was clutching the Solomon Stone and staring wildly at her. Ruby kicked at his bad knee but missed. Pierce swerved away from her foot but didn't let go. Ruby yanked hard and stumbled, her right leg stiff with pain. Pierce's grip slipped and Ruby wrenched hard until all but her fingers were free. Pierce gripped them tight, crushing the diamond ring into her fingers. Yelping, Ruby tried to pull her finger out of the ring, but she couldn't. Desperate, she twisted her hand and pushed the ring's diamond into Pierce's fleshy palm.

They both screamed.

30

Ruby gasped as a deluge of information flooded her brain. Scenes, words, and pictures from Pierce's past all crashed into her mind, bringing a heavy confusion that made it hard to move. Only one of her own thoughts was discernible—that she needed to break contact with Pierce's diamond or she would end up like Octavius.

She yanked and twisted, frantic to free her fingers, but it was like trying to pry two magnets apart. She wrenched her hand hard until a searing pain shot up her palm and her finger snapped free. Ruby stumbled back, breathing hard as her mind cleared.

Now Pierce held both diamonds, his fists clenched in front of him. "It works!" he panted in amazement. "This is... this is unbelievable. We should've been Rendering our own diamonds all along."

Ruby backed up the steps toward the street exit, limping and cradling her throbbing hand. It was the perfect time to escape, but she couldn't look away from Pierce.

His wide eyes flickered side to side, like he was reading two books at once. He smiled nostalgically into the darkness. "I can see everything that ever happened to me." Then his face suddenly contorted in agonized rage. "You!" He took a shaky step toward Ruby. "You touched my diamond. Now your traces are all over—" His forehead puckered as one eye squinted shut. "You were inside my head, watching me chase you—Don't shoot!" he yelled at whatever he was seeing in his head. Then he yelped and grabbed his right thigh as if he'd been shot instead of Ruby.

Ruby shuddered. If the diamond was showing him everything she'd experienced tonight, he was in trouble. Octavius had collapsed after re-living a few minutes of a birthday party.

Pierce's fists trembled, almost knocking together. He shook his arms like he was trying to drop the diamonds, but his hands remained locked tight. He staggered toward Ruby, his eyes wide with terror. "Take them."

Ruby backed away instinctively, recalling that nothing was deadlier than a wounded predator. Pierce collapsed to his knees. "Take them!" he shouted.

Ruby shook her head. She couldn't. They were bonded to his skin.

Pierce snarled and lunged.

Ruby sprang away, crying out as pain shot up her injured leg.

Pierce slammed to the ground, writhing and moaning as he convulsed on the concrete. He screamed and then his eyes closed and his body lay still.

Ruby stared dumbly at him as the ghosts of his scream echoed around her. His clenched hand opened and the Solomon Stone clinked against the cement floor. Her leg burned as she limped over and pushed her fingers to his neck. He was alive. Ruby didn't know whether to be relieved or disappointed. She picked up the Solomon

Stone, surprised at its warmth. Pulling her jacket tight around her shivering frame, she carefully zipped the diamond into her pocket. She swayed, dizzy from loss of blood. Leaning hard against the wall, she slowly climbed the stairs and pressed open the door, practically falling through it.

Traffic noise enveloped her as she stumbled into the fresh air. She was in some kind of park or garden. Cool, moist autumn air blew against her face. Gasping, she tried to make her legs move. The street was still thick with Halloween crowds. People brushed by Ruby, no one noticing that she was limping and her pants were caked in blood. Her strength ebbed out of her with each step. She needed a hospital. Scanning the streets, she tried to sense where one might be. But the Lines blurred and shifted weakly around her.

Dazed, she reached for her phone, but someone bumped her from behind, knocking Ruby to her knees.

A woman knelt down. "Are you okay?"

"No," Ruby choked.

The woman's eyes widened when she saw Ruby's leg. "I'm calling an ambulance." She pulled out her phone. "What's your name?"

Ruby blinked, disoriented.

"Tell me your name so I can find your parents," the woman said.

"Yes!" Ruby slurred. "Find my parents." Her vision was getting fuzzy. But in her delirium she was delighted that someone was finally going to locate Rex and Emmeline.

"Little girl," the woman gently shook her shoulder. "You need help. Who should I call?"

Ruby swam through the darkness, trying to break the surface where this woman was talking. She nudged her own

phone at the woman. "Alice," she croaked. "Call Alice."
Then everything went black.

———

Ruby could feel warm pressure on
her hand before she opened her eyes.
She blinked and saw Alice.
"Shhh. It's okay. You're okay,"
Alice said, tucking a strand of hair
behind Ruby's ear. "You're in the
hospital, Ruby." Alice's hair was done up, but messy. Something about the disarray was warm and familiar to Ruby.
Like she'd seen it in a movie or something—

Ruby bolted upright as her mind cleared. Pierce, the
diamond, Harlan. She lurched to get out of the bed, but her
leg was too stiff and heavy.

"Easy," Miles said, steadying her shoulders.

"My leg—" Hysteria edged Ruby's voice. Pierce had
shot her. And Harlan—

"It's going to be fine. You just needed stitches."

"Where's Harlan?" Ruby squinted against the pale
morning light coming in through a window.

Alice's mouth tightened as she exchanged a cold glance
with Miles. "He's downstairs, checking on a friend," Miles
said.

"Who?"

"Dr. Pierce," Miles said. "He's in a coma."

"Pierce is here?" Ruby winced at the panic in her voice.
She needed to calm down.

"I'm sorry," Alice said. "I know it's a shock."

"Is he... is he, like, completely unconscious?" Ruby
tensed, knowing her whole future hung on the answer.

"Yes," Miles said.

Ruby blinked and leaned back on the bed, relieved. She reached for the diamond in her jacket pocket, but her fingers grabbed some kind of papery hospital gown instead. "Where are my clothes?"

"In the cupboard," Miles said. Ruby looked where he'd pointed. The cupboard door was closed, but she could sense the diamond's thrumming energy within and her Lines were all straining toward it. She closed her eyes, grateful.

"Except for your pants," Miles said pointedly. "We had to throw them away because they were soaked with blood."

"Blood?" Dread knotted Ruby's stomach. There would be a long list of questions ahead.

"You passed out from blood loss. In the Financial District," Miles said. "How—"

"The Financial District?" Ruby stalled, trying to cobble together some explanation for last night, but her mind was too tangled with everything she couldn't say.

"Do you think she has amnesia?" Alice asked, fretting her lip.

Miles frowned and raised a doubtful eyebrow, but didn't answer.

Ruby rolled her shoulders. Amnesia was a good idea.

"Do you remember how you got there, Ruby?" Alice asked.

"Ummmm." Ruby squinted as if she were probing the depths of her memory. The cover story would have to be good, first time out of the gate. "We went to... Winston's... to watch a movie... and then—"

Harlan walked in, his face swollen with a black eye and a jagged line of black stitches slanted across his forehead. He looked relieved to see her awake, but something unhinged and dangerous flickered underneath his expression.

Ruby gulped. Did he know? Had Pierce somehow told him that she was a Levant? Suddenly there wasn't enough air in the room. Ruby tried to keep her face neutral, but her chest heaved erratically and the machine behind her beeped faster.

Miles wrapped his cool fingers around Ruby's wrist, taking her pulse. Something about this gesture anchored her. Miles. He was exactly what he had always seemed. Competent, reliable, and kind. She curled her fingers around his hand and matched her breath to his.

"Ruby, thank goodness you're awake. Are you alright?" Harlan's voice sounded genuinely concerned as he settled next to her bed.

Ruby looked at her uncle. His eyes were so warm and gentle that she almost wondered if last night was a lie and this was the real Harlan. "What happened to you?" she asked.

"Oh, this?" Harlan tried to smile but Alice's frown wouldn't allow it. "I was mugged."

Ruby nodded at his lie.

"Ruby, I—" Harlan started and stopped. He looked at her injuries and winced as if he were in pain too. The air prickled with Alice's and Miles's anger.

"Where did you go last night?" Ruby sniffled.

"I... I got called in for an emergency," Harlan mumbled. Miles snorted.

"Doctors aren't the only ones who have emergencies," Harlan snapped, glaring at his brother.

"There was a life and death real estate situation?" Miles scoffed. "In the middle of the night?"

Ruby raised an eyebrow, pleased at Harlan's discomfort.

"I came back from Winston's and you were gone," she said softly. "The door was locked and I couldn't get in. I was so scared."

"Scared?" Harlan glanced nervously at Alice and Miles. He looked so pathetic and tired that Ruby felt a sliver of pity poke through her anger and fear. "There was no reason to be scared."

"I thought maybe you went to your office, so I tried to go there, but then I got caught in this crazy Halloween parade, and this weird cat guy stole my hat, and then there was this man with a snake—"

"You went downtown by yourself?" Alice gasped. "At night?"

"I had to find Harlan," Ruby said, trying to keep Alice's anger aimed at the right target.

"Why didn't you just call me?" A hint of desperation tinged Harlan's voice. "Or have the doorman let you in?"

"Ruby, you could've been..." Alice's voice wobbled then broke off. She pulled Ruby into a tight hug. Ruby nestled close, keeping one triumphant eye on Harlan.

"I cannot believe you left her." Miles stood, his eyes blazing at Harlan. "She's just a kid."

Harlan stood too, but he still had to look up to meet Miles's gaze. "It was an emergency," he said between gritted teeth.

"Then you should've called me, or Chloe, or Mom to come back and watch her."

"What do you want me to say?" Harlan snapped. "My night wasn't exactly a picnic either."

"'Sorry.' I want you to say 'sorry,'" Miles said. "For Caesar's sake, Har. Nine years. We spent nine years looking for her. Rex and Emmeline's only child. Our only niece, and you abandon her in the middle of the night to go to your office?"

Harlan pinched the bridge of his nose. "Right." He looked at Ruby with clear blue eyes. "I'm so sorry, Ruby," he said, still lying.

"I forgive you," she lied back.

———

THE HOSPITAL LINOLEUM was cold on Ruby's bare feet as she hobbled to the cupboard. She tugged her robe tighter around her. Alice had brought it from home, and it smelled like her. Ruby sifted through the big Ziploc bag that held her filthy clothes. She found the diamond and smiled as her Lines rushed into it and burst out again.

There was a knock on the door. Ruby dropped the diamond into her pocket and closed the cupboard. She was limping back to bed when Miles stepped in.

"Hey," Ruby said.

"Hi," Miles said. "How's your leg? Any tightness or swelling?" He helped her sit down and then examined the bandage.

"No."

"Any pus or unpleasant smells?"

"Gross. No."

One corner of Miles's mouth lifted. "We have to make sure there's no infection. Are you sure you don't remember what you fell on?"

Ruby nodded, hoping that a gash from a bullet could've been made by almost any sharp object. "So..." She pulled her leg away from Miles as she tried to change the subject. "Are you, like, *into* Chloe?"

Miles sucked on his cheek, smiling softly. "Chloe's an excellent dog walker. Agamemnon is very fond of her."

"You should ask her out."

"Ruby, it's really not—"

"But you like her, right?"

"Yes." Miles flushed. "I mean, she's lovely. But—"

"But what? Is it because she's a Truncant?"

"No." His clear blue eyes looked wounded as he lowered himself into the chair beside her bed. "Of course not."

"Then what?"

"I..." He uncrossed and re-crossed his legs, then tugged on his tie. "I don't think..." He cleared his perfectly clear throat. Then his eyes met Ruby's and he sighed. "I'm not sure she would... want to."

Ruby snorted. "She likes you. I mean, she, like, *like*-likes you."

Miles's ears burned and he readjusted his tie. "Did she... I mean... why do you think that?"

Ruby shrugged. "She told me."

"You asked her?"

"I was actually trying to talk her out of it, because, well, it's a long story. At the time, I thought maybe you were, like, a kleptomaniac—"

"What? I'm not a kleptomaniac."

"Duh. I know that." Ruby shifted. "Now."

Miles's face twisted in confusion. "Wait. You told Chloe that I have a compulsive stealing disorder?"

"Of course not. I just told her that she could do better. Because I thought, at the time, you were... you know. But she was all like, 'Oh no, Miles is amazing, blah blah blah, Miles is so nice, blah blah blah, Miles.'"

"Ruby, you shouldn't—she said that?"

"Yeah." Ruby's mouth curled at the timid smile lighting Miles's face. "Well, not the blah blah blah part."

"Hmmm. You've given me some interesting information to consider." His voice was serious, but his eyes sparkled. "Why did you think I was a kleptomaniac?"

"I thought you'd stolen something from me. But then I found it."

Miles raised an eyebrow. "Something important?"

Ruby studied the blanket and shook her head, remembering how she'd thrown the diamond at Pierce to escape. "Not as important as other things."

"That's funny," Miles said. "Because I actually lost something recently. Something really important to me."

Ruby smiled and blushed, certain he was talking about her. She *was* pretty important.

"You remember that knife I showed you on Pan'wei?" he asked.

Gutterball. "Um, yeah. I think so." Ruby tried not to wince.

"It was your father's knife, so it was very special to me. But I lost it on that trip."

Ruby sucked on a strand of hair, keeping her eyes on the blanket.

"I always thought that when we found you, I would give it to you. So I felt terrible about losing it," Miles said.

"Oh. Um, that's okay," Ruby mumbled.

"But then last night..." Miles pulled the knife from his lab coat. "This fell out of your pants pocket while the nurses were prepping you for stitches."

"Oh." Ruby said. "Um, thank you?"

"You stole it from me on Pan'wei, didn't you?"

"Well, you stole my hair."

Miles pressed his lips together, suppressing a smile. "Fair enough."

Ruby took the knife, running her index finger along the inscription. "The strength of the wolf is the pack," she said aloud.

"I think I understand why you wanted it," Miles said quietly. "But did you know that that's only half of the quote?"

"Really?" Ruby flipped over the knife as if there would suddenly be more words on the other side.

"It's from *The Jungle Book*. The full quote is: 'For the strength of the pack is the wolf, and the strength of the wolf is the pack.'"

"The strength of the pack is the wolf," Ruby repeated, trying out the new arrangement of the familiar words.

"Yeah. Because the pack," he said, looking at her intently, "needs each wolf. So those wolves should be careful not to run around Manhattan alone on Halloween. Especially if any of those wolves ever want to play soccer again."

Ruby straightened. "You can get me back into soccer?"

"Maybe. When your leg heals. If you can stay out of trouble long enough for me to convince your grandmother." He stood. "Now, get some rest. In a few hours we're going home."

Ruby snuggled into the stiff mattress. Home.

———

RUBY LAY in her hospital bed, studying the words on the knife, visible and invisible. *The strength of the pack is the wolf.* But what should the pack do if one of those wolves is a lying, stealing, two-faced jerk like Harlan? She chewed on a stray strand of hair, fidgeting with the knife as the motto spun through her mind. She wasn't a good enough liar to pretend that everything was normal. Her stomach turned just at the thought of sitting next to Harlan for Sunday dinner. And if he ever found out that she was a Levant—

"Hey," Winston said, walking in. The left side of his forehead was bruised, probably from when she'd kicked him into a train last night.

"Hey." Ruby winced. "Sorry about your head."

He shrugged. "It makes me look tough."

It didn't, but she nodded anyway.

"So." He perched next to her. "What happened? Start with your leg."

"Pierce shot me." It felt good to verbalize the words with the indignation they deserved.

Winston's eyes bulged. "Seriously?"

"Yeah. And," Ruby scooted close and lowered her voice, "he's an Azarian."

Winston blinked and Ruby saw several questions cross his face. "He told you that?" he finally asked.

Ruby took a long gulp of water and tried explaining how she'd been sucked into Pierce's mind when she'd touched his diamond. But it was hard to find words for what had happened, and the explanation got tangled with the details of everything that had happened in the tunnels and on the platform.

"Wait," Winston interrupted, shaking his head at the mess of information she was spreading everywhere. "When you touched Pierce's ring-diamond, you, like, read his mind?"

"Yeah."

"How?"

"I... I don't know. I thought all this past information would flood in and screw up my brain, like what happened to Octavius, but I just saw whatever Pierce was seeing, thinking, or feeling right then."

"Huh." Winston's eyes darted back and forth as he digested the information. "Maybe," Winston said slowly, "it's because you're a Levant, so the diamond showed you Pierce's present instead of his past." Winston's hands started fidgeting. "Ruby?"

"Hmm?"

"Last night, I thought... when you grabbed the two diamonds and screamed... I was... it was... I'm glad you're okay."

"I'm glad you're okay too," she said.

"I should've known the Solomon Stone wouldn't hurt a Levant."

Ruby nodded. There was more she needed to tell him about Pierce and the Azarians and what she'd seen, but there was an idea flickering in the back of her head that seemed more important right now.

"All the stories say it clarifies energies, protecting and healing people," Winston said.

"Octavius!" Ruby bolted upright as the idea she'd been chasing crystalized. "We have to go." She slid awkwardly out of bed, almost falling to the floor.

Winston put his arm around her waist to steady her. "Where?" he asked.

"To wake up Octavius."

31

———

Ruby and Winston watched Octavius's chest gently rise and fall in the dark hospital room. The only other sound was a low beeping from the machine behind the bed.

"So, you think if he holds the Solomon Stone by itself, without touching other diamonds, it will 'clarify his energies'?" Winston asked.

"Yeah." Ruby shifted. It'd sounded better inside her head. She stroked one of the diamond's facets with her thumb, reassured by the sharpening of her own senses. She focused on the bright Line connecting the diamond to Octavius's hand.

"And that will wake him up?" Winston clicked his teeth.

"I think so." Neither of them moved.

"What if doesn't work?"

"He can't get much worse," Ruby said.

"He could die."

"He won't die," Ruby said as she grabbed Octavius's hand, her splinted finger making her clumsy. "Probably."

Faint black lines crisscrossed his palm, matching the facets of the diamond she held. Ruby took a deep breath and placed the Solomon Stone in Octavius's hand, folding his fingers around it.

Nothing happened. Ruby's heart pulled in disappointment. Octavius's fingers listlessly circled the diamond as if it was any ordinary rock. Ruby's eyes stung as they met Winston's. She'd really believed it would work. Poor Octavius.

Then the monitor behind him started beeping faster. He stirred and his eyelashes fluttered.

"C'mon!" Winston whisper-shouted, nodding at the door.

Ruby pried the Solomon Stone out of Octavius's palm. His fingers stuck to it and she felt a hint of the velvet darkness around him as they both touched the diamond. Ignoring the pain from her splinted finger, Ruby wrenched the diamond free and ran with Winston to the door.

Behind them Octavius grunted and croaked out a bleary "Hey," just as the door closed.

———

PIERCE'S ROOM was identical to Octavius's, but it felt darker and colder. Ruby pulled her fluffy robe tight around herself, inhaling its aroma of home.

"I don't like this," Winston said. "We should go."

Ruby didn't look at Pierce as she searched through the cupboards for his Ziploc clothing bag. "I have to make sure he didn't tell Harlan about me."

"Oh," Winston said. Then, "Ohhhhhh. But if Pierce told Harlan that you're a Levant, then—"

"Yeah." Ruby rifled through Pierce's clothes bag until she found his phone. It was locked. Biting back repulsion, she placed Pierce's limp right thumb on the screen to unlock it. The phone lit up and Ruby scrolled through the recent texts and calls. There were a few to Harlan early yesterday evening, but then nothing. "Phew."

"Lemme see." Winston took the phone and looked through several apps. "Nothing," he confirmed. "So... Harlan doesn't know you're a Levant. Which is good, but you can't just pretend you don't know what he did. And what if he does figure out one day that you're a Levant?"

"I know."

"So what are you going to do?" He moved to return Pierce's phone to the Ziploc bag.

Ruby sighed and turned away from Winston and his impossible questions. Harlan was too dangerous to have around, but he was still family. She rolled the Solomon Stone's cool, flat facets against her cheek. A pulse of heat emanated from the stone and she looked at it. It shimmered in the darkness as if it were lit from within. The tendrils of an idea flitted through Ruby's mind and she straightened.

"Wait," Ruby said. "Lemme see that." Ruby grabbed the phone, turning off the passcode settings before dropping it in her pocket. She leaned a little on Winston and limped toward the door.

"Are you going to tell me why we're robbing a guy in a coma?" Winston asked.

Ruby clasped the Solomon Stone tighter in her hand. "We're going to send Harlan into exile."

———

RUBY PULLED the paper out of the printer in the Sapient computer lab. She studied the strange intersection of red lines on the heavy white paper. Charlie was right. The printers were better here. The insignia looked crisp and professional. "I still think it's a weird logo," she said, handing the paper to Charlie.

"It's the Azarian seal," Charlie said. "It's over a thousand years old."

"I thought it would have, like, an 'A' and a 'Z' intertwined or something," she said.

"They're ancient Hebrew letters," Winston said.

Ruby carefully placed the Solomon Stone on the paper and Charlie took a picture of it with Pierce's phone.

"So we send Harlan this picture and then... he just runs off to Egypt?" Winston whispered, looking over his shoulder even though they were alone in the lab.

"We need Harlan to know that Pierce was an Azarian. When he sees this, he'll assume that the Azarians double-crossed Pierce, stole the Solomon Stone, and left him unconscious in that abandoned station," Ruby said.

Winston clicked his teeth. "But if the Azarians really had stolen the Solomon Stone from Pierce, why would they send a picture of it to Harlan?"

Charlie shrugged. "He's a bad guy, they're bad guys. Maybe they'd want to summon him so they could do even bigger bad guy things together."

"Or maybe they'd be, like, triple-double-crossing someone else," Ruby said. "The point is, Harlan's obsessed with the Solomon Stone. When he sees it next to this seal, he'll assume that the Azarians have it, and he'll go after it on a wild goose chase. And I won't have to see him at Sunday dinners."

"You're sure Harlan can't trace the email back to us?" Winston asked Charlie.

"Yeah. We took the picture with Pierce's phone and we're sending it from his email account," Charlie said. "Through the Academy's servers."

"Because the imaginary Azarians also stole Pierce's phone?" Winston asked.

"Of course," Ruby said. "So they could contact Harlan without disclosing their location."

"It's scary how easily you think like a criminal," Winston said.

"Don't worry. There's nothing to connect it to us. And Ruby will keep one of Harlan's diamond rings so she can monitor his mind," Charlie said.

Ruby nodded. She'd already slipped into Harlan's room and taken the ring from his dresser. "How long do you think he'll be gone?"

Charlie shrugged. "Maybe two or three months. But we can send him more fake clues to keep him away longer."

Ruby's heart pulled as she picked up Pierce's phone and moved her thumb over the send button. She still didn't believe that every nice word or smile from Harlan had been a lie. But she wasn't about to let a traitor stay in her pack. She touched the screen and the email whooshed off. "Sorry, Harlan. You're just not 'Callahan.'"

32

_____

Ruby's fingers flipped through the cards as fast as they could, but Alice was fast too. The bedspread wrinkled with the impact, further complicating the game. There was a pause while Ruby tried to figure out whether she could play any of her four cards.

"Flip," Alice said.

"How do you know I can't play anything?"

"There are only two threes and one five left."

Ruby rolled her eyes. Playing card games with Sapes was ridiculous. She scowled and flipped a new card, eyeing Alice's fast-diminishing deck and the bag of candy corns in the middle of her bed.

Alice slapped down several cards in a long sequence then threw up her empty hands. "I win," she laughed.

"Cheater," Ruby mumbled. Sapes always counted cards.

"Don't be a bad loser." Alice grabbed the candy corns and counted out ten. She ate them slowly, section by section.

"Play again?" Ruby asked. It had been two hands since she had won any candy.

"Sure." Alice collected the cards.

Ruby snitched from Alice's candy corn pile as she did.

"Hey," Chloe said, walking in with Agamemnon nestled in her arms.

Miles followed, carrying his leather medical bag. "I need to check Ruby's stitches," he said as he bent to kiss Alice's cheek, then pulled a chair up to the bed. Agamemnon jumped into Ruby's lap, basking in the patch of Sunday afternoon sun that came in from the window.

Alice frowned. Ruby knew she didn't like dogs in her house, especially not on the beds, but she didn't say anything as Agamemnon rested his head in the crook of Ruby's elbow.

Ruby stroked the dog's ears until his eyes closed in bliss. She rolled up her pajama pants so Miles could see the black spidery stitches climbing up her leg.

"How does it look?" Alice asked.

Miles pressed a few places along Ruby's leg and nodded. "They're ready to come out."

Ruby watched as Miles carefully pulled up each black thread with a pair of tweezers, snipped it with some little scissors, then tugged it out of her skin.

"Is Chloe staying for dinner?" Ruby asked.

A slight blush tinted Miles's cheek, but it was nothing compared to Chloe's crimson face.

"Ruby, I don't have to—" Chloe stammered, eyes sliding to Alice.

"Harlan's gone, so we have room," Ruby said.

"Where's Harlan?" Chloe asked.

"Cairo," Miles said.

"What's in Cairo?" Chloe asked.

"Nothing," Ruby whispered, her whole body warmed with triumph.

"Speaking of dinner, maybe you should lay off the candy," Miles said.

"My body needs energy to heal," Ruby said. "Any *good* doctor would know that."

"You know what else helps with healing," Miles said as he worked. "Soccer."

Alice stiffened. "Miles." Her voice was half plea, half warning.

"Ruby needs exercise," Miles said. "And fresh air. Like any kid."

"She's not 'any kid.'" Tension thickened as Alice and Miles looked at each other.

"I know." Miles said.

"You should listen to him," Ruby said. Both their gazes softened as they looked at her. "He's a really good doctor."

"But you could get hurt—"

"Then Miles can fix me up," Ruby said.

Alice sat, statue-still.

"Please, Grandma?" Ruby felt herself blush as the new word crossed her mouth.

Alice's eyes glistened and she gave a miniscule nod, apparently unable to even verbalize the "yes."

Ruby hugged her, closing her eyes as Alice's warmth folded around her.

"Thank you," Ruby whispered.

———

"I brought something for you," Winston said shyly, handing Ruby a thin rectangular box. "It's, like, a late get-well present."

Ruby smiled and opened the box. A thin silver chain sparkled on a nest of velvet. "Oh, a necklace. Thanks."

"It's made for holding keys, so it's really strong."

"Oh." Ruby couldn't think why she would want a key around her neck. "Great..."

Winston smiled, lowering his voice even though they were alone in her room. "It's for the Solomon Stone."

"Oh!" Ruby said, finally understanding. "That's perfect." She pulled the diamond from her pocket and threaded the chain through the delicate loop mounted on top of the diamond. The chain was long enough that she could slip it over her head. The diamond hung just a few inches above her belly button.

"Statistically speaking," Winston said quickly, "the safest place to keep jewelry is on your person. That's probably why your mom always wore it."

"Winston?" she asked, rubbing the diamond's ice-hot surface with her thumb. "Do you think Rex and Emmeline are still alive?" The diamond flared hot in her palm and throbbed as if it had a heartbeat. Ruby gaped in surprise.

"I don't know," Winston said pensively.

But Ruby did. The Solomon Stone had answered her question as she'd asked it. She rubbed the diamond, wondering if traces of Octavius or Pierce remained on the surface. Maybe there was a little bit of Solomon or Alexander the Great. Or Emmeline.

Ruby raised her head and blinked at the thought. Solomon was a long shot. But Emmeline was possible. If

Emmeline had left behind a second diamond, a pendant or an earring, would Ruby be able to read her mother's mind?

"I'm going to find them," she said, cupping the stone in both her hands.

"How?"

"I'm a Levant," she said. "I can find anything."

ABOUT THE AUTHOR

Christine Sandgren grew up in the small town of Wenatchee, Washington. Although she spent many years in cities like New York, Palo Alto, and Moscow, she eventually made her way back to the Pacific Northwest, settling in Portland, Oregon, where she now lives with her husband and three children.

The Solomon Stone is Christine's debut novel. When she isn't writing, Christine spends her time skiing, enjoying the theatre, eating out, going to bookstores, shopping, and being the only person in Portland who doesn't like to run.

ARE YOU A CODEBREAKER?
SHARE YOUR ANSWER ON SOCIAL MEDIA WITH
#SOLOMONSTONE

If you enjoyed this book and would like more adventures featuring Ruby, please have an adult help you do one or more of the following:

- Leave a review on your favorite book review site
- Tell a friend about the *The Solomon Stone* and Christine Sandgren
- Ask your local library to put Christine Sandgren's work on the shelf
- Recommend Fawkes Press books to your local bookstore

VISIT US ONLINE

WWW.CHRISTINESANDGREN.COM

WWW.FAWKESPRESS.COM

FAWKES PRESS